Tin Fish

SUDEEP CHAKRAVARTI

HarperCollins *Publishers* India

First published in India in 2005 by Penguin Books India

This edition published in India by
HarperCollins *Publishers* in 2011

Building 10, Tower A, 4th Floor, DLF Cyber City, Phase II,
Gurugram Haryana – 122002, India
www.harpercollins.co.in

2 4 6 8 10 9 7 5 3

Part of the speech on pp. 162–63 is excerpted from Leo Puri's article 'The Floating Island' in Mayoor. Reproduced with permission of Mayo College, Ajmer.

P-ISBN: 978-93-5029-176-4
E-ISBN: 978-93-5029-315-7

Typeset in 11/15 Adobe Jenson Pro
Jojy Philip New Delhi 110 015

Printed and bound at
MicroPrints India, New Delhi

For Subir,

The Keeper of Dreams

So there we were, Fish, Porridge, PT Shoe and I, Brandy. We were brothers without barriers, and friends until death.

They first called me Brownie, instantly shortening it from Barun, but Sajjad, who was Muslim, and for some reason called Moses, saved me, saying it sounded too much like a dog, and no human being deserved a dog's name. So the dorm settled on Brandy.

I liked it. Brandy seemed a bit more grown-up than Brownie, and it would really upset my father when he found out. Papa never drank, didn't like those who did, and thought drinking alcohol was almost as bad as killing someone. The only alcohol we had at home was stocked in Ma's prized showcase—the little bottles from foreign airlines that she collected. She had never been abroad, and greeted the arrival of each bottle like a postcard from some exotic land. Over time, family and friends, and even friends of family and family of friends, everyone who had heard of Ma's passion for miniature booze bottles, would bring over or arrange to send her one, but of course Papa never got her any. If a guest asked for a drink when Papa was not home, Ma would bring out a bottle from her collection of hundreds, and empty it ceremonially into a glass in which she usually served orange juice—it was rounded, dotted with tiny glass pimples and had these ugly flowers etched all round the rim. She would then return the empty bottle to the showcase, and lock it. Sometimes

Suman, my younger sister, and I would steal the key, take out the opened bottles, twist the caps open and take deep breaths. At times, we would get dizzy. Sometimes, we would tip the bottle over our mouths, and a last drop would trickle out, burn our tongues and make our eyes water, but we dared not make a sound because we were sure Ma and Papa would thrash us if they ever caught us.

Fish was Sanjay, and he was a king swimmer. During trials for the school team just after he had joined in our second year in Mayo College for the autumn term in 1975, he had beaten the school champ at butterfly. That was a big deal, because when we tried to do the butterfly, it felt like our backs would break and our arms would come out of the sockets. I had once even managed to knee my chin in panic, almost drowning with shock.

Fish seemed a good name for a guy who swam like a fish but hated eating any, except the sardines in tins that I brought from home because the thick tomato sauce hid the smell, and he always complained about Singapore, which he called 'Sing' and where his parents stayed, saying it had lovely shops, streets and parks and was clean, but always smelled of fish because 'Chinks eat rice and fish broth even for breakfast.'

Yuck, we thought, how could anyone eat anything but toast, eggs, butter and jam in the morning?

Porridge was Michael, and usually ate three bowls of the disgusting grey thing they served us at breakfast. He was renamed for ever after his second breakfast in school. At the time of his first breakfast, he was still being called Mike, Mickey and Mack—a term for a Christian. But the second three-helping of sludge confirmed he was mad. Porridge it was.

PT Shoe was Pratap Singh, son of a Rajput princeling from

near Udaipur, who *had* to polish his white gym shoes every night before brushing, and for a reason nobody could ever fathom, always called a pair of shoes, 'shoe'. We were protective of PT Shoe, because some of the other prince-types used to bug him, saying those who were princes didn't hang around with people who were not prince-types, or at least from the warrior caste. But PT Shoe seemed to take all insults like he was the Buddha. He wasn't a prince, he would tell us—in India there were no princes anymore, only some rich guys with big moustaches who owned forts which people bought tickets to see. He would get a real job when he grew up, PT Shoe said, because he didn't want to marry a woman who only wore chiffon saris and pearl necklaces, always covered her head and kept her eyes down in front of men, like the women in his family and others he had seen in his clan. Nor would he pretend to be a royal, because all they were really doing was selling tickets to tourists.

'I am not going to be a bloody guide,' PT Shoe once whispered fiercely to us. 'I will go to America, make lots of dosh and marry a gora chick.'

We were impressed. The gora chicks we saw in the movies, in Pat's pondies and during the camel fair in Pushkar looked pretty nice, and never seemed to look down, though some of the dirty ones with matted hair in Pushkar smelt awful if we got too close, usually to peer at their pale white boobs through the gap in their short-sleeved blouses or T-shirts. Nobody told us anything, which we thought was fair, because firang tourists would be taking pictures of village women bathing in the holy kund and they would get really crazy with their telephoto lenses and shutters when the women came out from the lake after their holy dip past midnight in that freezing November weather, their breasts sometimes bare or showing against wet blouses, the nipples sticking out like raisins. It was great fun for us when some gora chicks tried to copy the village women, and then it was like eating vanilla and chocolate ice cream together.

None of us bothered much about what had brought us together. We used to hang around with other guys, and then one day we were hanging around with each other. 'Destiny,' Fish had said once, providing a reason. He was always using these big words.

He talked about destiny a lot, Fish did, especially in the days before he killed himself in front of the whole school.

I can't remember the exact reason why I went away to boarding school. Oh, I knew I was fascinated with the idea from the time Joy came back for his first break from boarding school during the Durga Puja holidays. The neighbourhood kids had gathered in the park, and Joy, the oldest among us, was the centre of attraction. He smartly lit a Wills Navy Cut filter-tipped cigarette, which everyone in Calcutta called 'Philtaar Ueelsh' in the Bengali way, took a puff without choking and passed it to me, his sidekick from the old days before he went away to boarding school four months earlier. I took a puff and immediately started to cough. Joy laughed, and all the other kids joined him, even Chicklet and Dopey, whose father had lost his job the week before because he drank too much after losing money at the races. They were going away soon to stay with their grandparents somewhere south of Calcutta, which they described as 'a village, with no clubs and all, shit,' and acted as if we would never see each other again, which we didn't.

Joy had gone away to a school called Doon School, far away in the hills of Uttar Pradesh, and he was full of stories about dorms and football teams and tennis and a huge Mess for meals and how kids would call senior students 'Sir' and how new boys in school were called 'Newboy'. Then he told us about how the kids talked to one another.

'When they say I'm going to hit you they don't say "I'm going to hit you",' Joy pronounced, as we hung on to every word. 'They say "I'm going to fuck you".'

I was nine, and Joy, at eleven, was already a god.

Joy's stories were good enough for me, and South Point School was getting boring anyway. I played football and was goalkeeper and I dived all over the place to save goals and we won most matches so that was all right. There was also this girl called Noyona who sat next to me. We would put our heads down on the desk and look at each other and smile, and sometimes she would write her name on my palm with a felt-tipped pen during the break while we were sharing sandwiches, and she would take some water from her pink water bottle and wash her name off my palm as if it was our special secret, and that was all right too. But I dreamt of a school far away which would become a new home, where you were forbidden to eat with your bare hands and had to wear ties and blazers like some sort of sahib and you could say 'fuck you' to anyone provided you were bigger or were prepared to fight.

I kept quiet, and carried on ignoring my teachers, sharing my cheese and guava-jelly sandwiches with Noyona, and sometimes walking around with her, holding hands, during the break. We would hold hands on the way home in the school bus as well, ignoring those who sniggered and pointed and called us 'boyfriend-girlfriend'. Maybe they were right, because I had given her the small false-leather bag Papa had brought for me from America many years ago, when I was still a child. The bag had 'World's Fair New York 1964-65' written on the sides in big blue and red letters, and on one side had a boy and a girl wearing coats with red stripes and blue pants and they had nice smiles with red dots on their cheeks.

If we were not boyfriend-girlfriend why would I give Noyona the bag that Papa had got for me from this wonderful place he talked about that even had a nickname written on the bag, Big Apple, and its proper name was New York, New York, United States of America?

I think Mayo happened for some other reasons. Papa and Ma had not been happy with the way things were going in Calcutta, and Papa often talked about how Calcutta had no future. The streets were always being dug up to lay all sizes of pipes, it took forever to go from one place to another, there would always be strikes, and fights would break out whenever some procession was taken out, and the police always seemed to be beating up and killing people, especially people who called themselves Naxals.

I had heard Papa call it the 'Naxalite Movement' and asked him and Ma if it was like the 'Freedom Movement' our teachers told us about—the movement that had made India free from England. Then I asked him, now that India was free, was the Naxalite Movement about being free from India? Ma had covered her mouth, her eyes growing even bigger than they already were, her red bindi moving up a little along with the wrinkles on her forehead, while Papa looked sternly at her and said, 'See Leela, see what politics has come to, even little children are not safe from it, not that they ever were.'

Then he looked at me and decided I deserved an answer, but what he said was not straightforward, like he didn't want to spell it out because I was too young, or maybe the facts were too unpleasant: 'When people are unhappy with the king, they will tell him, and if the king doesn't listen, then his subjects will do what they have to do. It has always been this way.'

'Calcutta used to be the capital of India when the British were here,' Papa said then. 'And see it now, it's becoming the capital of hell. Shame-shame.' Ma nodded her head sadly.

According to Papa, things had started to go bad from before 1971, when India and Pakistan fought a war, and India won. Suman and I could understand why India won. All India Radio would play patriotic songs and marching tunes, and every now and then a newsreader would boom 'This is All India Radio bringing you the news' and tell us about how another Indian soldier had 'made the supreme sacrifice for the motherland'.

Fighter planes would sometimes swoop over our house as they roared eastwards, where Papa said East Pakistan was, which these fighters at full speed could reach in less time than it would take us to climb the four floors to the rooftop. The headlights of our car, like every other car, bus and truck in Calcutta, were half covered with black paint, and at night, we would draw curtains to prevent light from escaping, and sometimes even switch off lights that were not required when the air-raid siren went off, so Pakistani planes would not know where to bomb because they wouldn't be able to see. The Howrah Bridge across the Hooghly River, which Papa told us was as well known across India as the Victoria Memorial, had huge guns on both sides with soldiers guarding them, and Papa always showed off by calling them 'ack-ack guns'. How could India lose?

When the air-raid sirens went off, Suman and I used to take turns being a Pakistani fighter plane, screaming and swooping on the bed, and one of us would be on the ground, spinning around like a top with arms raised, going 'ack-ack'. Whoever was the Pakistani fighter plane always got ack-acked, falling on the bed and then rolling onto the floor in slow motion.

After the war got over in 1971, trouble seemed to be everywhere. It had something to do with Naxals, who Papa said were fighting and sometimes killing landlords and moneylenders and trying to take away their money to give it to poor people. Papa said they took their name from a place called Naxalbari, which was quite near the road to Darjeeling. He also said that it wasn't just poor people from villages who became Naxals, but some very good students from colleges in big cities, whom he called 'intellectuals', which he explained as 'people with brains who thought a lot, too much sometimes', were also becoming Naxals to help poor people, even if it meant fighting with the government and going to jail and dying, because to help poor people they had to break the law. Papa said Naxals felt that the government, which ruled India after the shada chamra, white skins, had left, hadn't done much to change things for peasants and poor people.

Suman said it was like the story of Robin Hood, but it seemed very different in real life. There were no merry men wearing green tights and hats we read about in books and no Maid Marian for Robin to fall in love with. The pictures of Naxals we saw in the newspaper were different. They wore shirts and trousers, sometimes had unshaven faces, were either in handcuffs, or were so dead.

It was all called politics, and the chief minister of West Bengal, who looked a little like Papa's father, wearing these big, thick glasses and spotless white dhuti, like a thin bed-sheet wrapped nicely around the waist, and panjabi, a kurta with the arm delicately crinkled, used to call them 'criminals' and 'scoundrels'. But Ma would always look at the pictures and say, 'Oh God, they are so young. It is such a tragedy.'

One Sunday, we were going to visit Papa's distant relatives in this great big house in Shyambazar in north Calcutta where the whole family once lived together, and on the way, on Lansdowne Road, which nobody called by its new name, Sarat Bose Road, there was a traffic jam. Papa got out of the car to see what was going on, and suddenly there were these bottles landing on the street and on buses, cars, and rickshaws, and they broke with a huge crash and glass flew everywhere.

We saw some men throwing bottles with flames and we knew what they were called—Molotov Cocktails—because I had read about it in the newspaper and asked Papa the meaning. A police jeep a little distance away from us started burning, and a sergeant, in his sparkling white shirt, came out shooting his revolver and suddenly fell on his face. As we watched, some more policemen came from somewhere and started chasing a group of boys in jeans and kurtas, shooting at them. Suman and I saw a few of them fall on the street, before Ma reached back and shoved us into the gap between the front and back seats. Suman had started to cry.

We didn't go to Shyambazar that day. When the traffic began to move after a long time, Papa drove instead to the riverside to the left of the Howrah Bridge, near the old man-of-war jetty, bought some popcorn for Suman and me, and sat for what seemed like hours looking at the boats and barges on the Hooghly, which was brown and really very dirty and we had seen dead animals floating in it, but it looked nice if you didn't get too close. He moved only when Ma, still upset, said it was time for lunch, and that maybe we should stop at Peiping on Park Street and get some soup and chowmein. We did, and as Papa wanted to cheer us up, he ordered sweet and sour pork and fried prawns as well.

During the summer of 1972, we went out to eat a lot. There was trouble all around, even right in front of our house.

We lived in Jodhpur Park, and right across from our house was a big complex of buildings, all hostels for students of Jadavpur University, which was just one stop away by bus. We could even walk to the main gates, as we had one day with Manohar-babu, our driver, and seen walls covered with slogans in Bengali and English, mostly written in red paint, talking about ending 'torture', 'oppression' and 'imperialism' of the government. Torture we knew about from books and the stories of the war in Bangladesh. Ma had said oppression is what Papa's family did to her. And imperialism is what the English did to Indians. Ma told us never to go to the university again and really shouted at Manohar-babu for taking us there.

But the signs were everywhere. If Manohar-babu were to listen to Ma and keep us away from the signs, we would have to stay home all the time.

The Jadavpur Police Station stood next to the hostel, at one corner of the crossing; our house was near the other. Nobody from the hostel ever bothered us, and we could look right into the rooms, especially if we climbed onto the rooftop. Suman and I called all students we met 'dada', older brother. Some of them—Ramu-da, Vijay-da and Keishing-da, whom Suman and I called Kissing-da—would sometimes come and play cricket with us in the driveway, always letting me bat until I got out three or four times. Then Ma would ask them to come in and give them tea and sandwiches, and somehow, Moyna-di, the tenant's daughter from the third floor whose name meant mynah in Bengali, would always be there as well because she fancied the boys and they couldn't go upstairs to her flat because her parents would never allow it. She was famous in the hostel because she was the only grown-up girl in the three houses right in front of the hostel and had a really nice smile and wore short skirts. In the evenings, after she came back from school, Moyna-di would stand near the windows on the third floor, and it seemed all the boys in the hostel would be at their windows too, looking at her. But she liked Kissing-da the most; we could tell.

Ramu-da, Vijay-da and Keishing-da would come over during festivals, and touch Ma's feet, and shake Papa's hand, because Papa didn't like people touching his feet even if it was tradition to touch the feet of elders. They called her 'Leela-mashima', or aunty, and called Papa 'Sir'. We would sit around and hear them talk about cricket, Satyajit Ray and politics, while Kissing-da and Moyna-di would disappear to do whatever they did near the guava trees in the backyard. 'Kissing,' Suman and I would whisper, and burst into giggles, till Ma whacked us on our heads. Ma was very protective of Moyna-di. We knew she liked her and treated her like a younger sister, and was like Moyna-di's guide, and would even let her read books that she kept away from us, like *Valley of the Dolls* and many books by Harold Robbins. They had sex scenes, as I would find out when I stole into my parents' almirah during one hols after joining Mayo and took the books down from the top shelf. In these books people drank a lot and did rich-people things like buying each other cars and planes for birthdays and having sex like we breathed, and from these books America seemed like a fun place because that was all people seemed to be doing, so maybe PT Shoe knew what he was talking about.

The street in front of the house was dug up because they were laying these big pipes. It was really a big trench and we children were warned about it because it was known that people fell into these trenches that were all over Calcutta and broke their bones or died.

One night, Suman and I woke up to the sound of trucks and heard Papa and Ma talking loudly and they came into our room to see if we were awake. We were, so we opened the windows to see what was going on outside. By the light of the dim street lights, we could make out what seemed like hundreds of men, and there were many more grouping near our house and across the trench, near the gates of the hostel.

'Soldiers', whispered Papa, 'I knew they would do something, but I never thought they would send soldiers.'

Ma wanted to know whether they were going to 'kill the boys'.

'Chup, Leela,' Papa said, looking at us, 'the children are here.'

After some time, some of the soldiers marched into the hostel, and for some hours we could hear shouts and gunfire and sometimes a long burst from a machine gun, a sound we knew from war movies in which German and Japanese soldiers always lost. Suman and I must have fallen asleep at some point, because I woke in the morning to shouting, to see I was back on my bed. Suman was still asleep. I ran out to the balcony. Papa and Ma were already there, and Papa had a cup of tea in his hand and Ma had the end of her sari stuffed into her mouth and was crying.

'Bastards, bastards,' Papa kept saying. Then, seeing me there, he said, 'I'm sorry. You shouldn't say these bad words.'

I wanted to comfort him, tell him that it was okay, I knew what it meant, and only a few days ago, Indrani from next door, who had a German mother had called me 'bloody bastard' and I had called her 'bloodybitchshit', but it didn't seem like a good time to talk about it.

There was a long line of students being brought out of the hostel gates. They had their hands on their heads, just like the war movies and like the photographs of Pakistani soldiers we saw in newspapers. The soldiers, I could see clearly now, wore green uniforms and helmets covered with nets. They stood away from the students, almost politely, guns pointed down, their job done.

The police took over then, and would sometimes hit and kick the students as they marched into the police station. I saw Vijay-da and Kissing-da in the line. Kissing-da's batik kurta was torn, and that seemed to mark him out to the police. One hit him on the head with a stick. Kissing-da fell, and one more policeman came over and the two started to kick him. I thought Papa would ask us to go inside, but he had forgotten we were there. He still held the delicate cup and saucer in his hand, his mouth was a thin line and his face was red with anger. I thought he would explode and scream but Papa didn't. Only, after a while the cup and saucer started rattling a little, which sounded like castanets, a word we knew because Papa had explained it to us. He loved listening to Spanish music by this chap called Roberto Delgado, and there were a lot of castanets in his music. Moyna had appeared as if by magic, and Ma and she held on to each other, sobbing.

The two policemen picked up Kissing-da and dragged him into the police station, and he, Vijay-da and the others disappeared inside. They never came back.

For days afterwards, there would be more lines of students

going into the police station. We could see some being taken away in trucks. All through the day and the night we could hear shouts and screams from the police station. We had always seen the grills of the prison peeking out over the high walls of the police station, but it had never meant much till we heard screams coming from there. We all slept badly those days.

We never found out what happened to the boys. Suman and I talked about whether Vijay-da, Keishing-da and Ramu-da were killed or if they went away to their parents and homes, because many students didn't come back when the hostel reopened after the Durga Puja holidays. Papa and Ma went once to talk to the inspector at the police station, but he refused to say anything and sent them away. 'He threatened me,' Papa said, shaking with rage.

'He asked me to mind my own business,' he would tell visitors for months afterwards. 'Is there no justice? Is this any place for children to grow up? Is this going to be our future?'

Maybe that's when he decided I would be going away, somewhere far from Calcutta, maybe as far as Joy had gone.

It was more than a year later, around the time I was getting ready to go away to boarding school, that Moyna-di came out to the balcony again.

I hated Papa for it, but he dragged me to say goodbye to everyone at the office. I would be leaving for Mayo in three days, and I told him I saw no reason why I had to say goodbye, because I was going to come back for the hols, but he insisted, saying it was the polite and correct thing to do.

We drove to Brabourne Road, in Burra Bazar, which had lots

of offices and shops and was always crowded, and took the ancient lift up to the third floor. The lift had a handle on a notch on a brass plate, and you had to crank it to get to the floor you wanted. The doors opened, and we had arrived. The brass plate by the side of the huge door said 'Ray & Company' in this curling way. Old Bhola was at the door and did a salaam to my father and affectionately ruffled my hair after calling me 'Barun-babu', which made me sound like I was some grand owner of something, but it didn't feel that way even though Papa insisted I wear trousers that day and not 'those silly half-pants because you're a big boy now.'

We made our way down the office, past desks full of paper, and there were these big steel almirahs by the walls on which were stacked more paper and lots of raw cotton, which Papa explained were samples from which they chose the cotton to make various kinds of cloth. There was Shishir-babu, the office peon, who had got me as many Cokes I wanted when I went with Papa to the factory in Shyamnagar, to the north of Calcutta along the Hooghly, two years before. It was for the annual day of the factory and the workers had done well, Papa said, because they made more cloth than they were supposed to. Also, he wanted to show me the factory and wanted me to watch him play football with the employees, the office team versus the factory team. Papa chose to play for the factory team and even scored a goal, and that made the team play even harder and they beat the office team 3-1. Not bad for a father and all. It didn't matter that Papa had slipped and sprained his back soon after he scored a goal. He had to be carried away, and for days after that he would make my sister and me walk up and down on his back to lessen the pain.

Pulok-kaka, a distant cousin of Papa's who worked as a clerk, came up to me and hugged me. Everyone was smiling, and I kept wondering why going away to boarding school was such a big thing. We skipped going into Papa's office and went instead to the office of The Bastards, as I called Papa's uncles, who were the bosses since my grandfather had died and were always creating trouble for Papa. They sat together in this long room, side by side, at big teakwood desks separated by waist-level partitions to mark territories, the oldest to the left and the youngest to the right, and whenever I was at the office, I would have to begin from the left and move right, oldest to youngest. I hated them because they hardly ever smiled and never seemed to say or do anything kind and they made Papa unhappy.

'How are you, Mejo-dadu?' I asked the first Bastard on the left, in the chronological manner relatives are called in Bengal if there is more than one of a type. Mejo was number two to my grandfather, who would have been called 'Boro-dadu', big dadu, by my cousins. I touched Mejo-dadu's feet, and asked him, because Papa had insisted I do, to please bless me. Mejo-dadu grunted and smiled, and his face looked like the face of the mummy I had seen in the National Museum on Chowringhee Road.

'How are you, Shejo-dadu?' And I went on with the same routine, left to right, down to Naw-dadu and finally to Chhoto-dadu, the youngest. They all blessed me in their own way, Shejo-dadu with a fart and a smile, Naw-dadu with a scowl and a nod, and Chhoto-dadu, the only one among them who seemed civilized, kept the palm of his right hand on my head for a few seconds in blessing. I looked up and he was smiling.

I was turning away to leave when Mejo-dadu said to Papa, 'Tarun, I still don't understand why you're sending the boy away to a school so far away, and in Rajasthan of all places. Rajasthan is a desert, it has camels, there's no water, no culture other than riding into battle, no literature. No boy of *this* family has ever needed to go out of Calcutta for his education. Are you saying what was good for your father and all of us is not good enough for Barun? And what will you do for his college? Will you send him away and not send him to Presidency College? Your grandfather studied at Presidency College, your father studied at Presidency, all of us have studied at Presidency.'

Papa had taken me one day to Presidency College on College Street, saying it was the grandest college in India, but the place had a sad feel to it, like it used to be a grand place once upon a time but now there was nobody to look after it. He had become depressed seeing some of the buildings crumbling, the windows broken, locked gates, and red flags of communists and Naxals painted on the walls and on any inch of space the rows of bookshops on College Street had left. So he took me across the College Square lake to a juice shop where we sat and drank green mango shorbot, which he said he used to drink when he was a college student, and while the taste of the green mango had remained the same everything else had changed. He looked glum and I wished we could go home, away from this depressing place.

This wasn't the first time Papa had been asked the question about my leaving Calcutta, though only Mejo-dadu had brought up college, which was so far away that I didn't understand why he had brought it up, unless he was getting silly like old people sometimes did and said things that seemed to make no sense, certainly not to children. Ever since Papa got a telegram from Mayo in January, saying they had a place for me and could I go 'with all haste', as the spring term had already begun and I would need time to adjust and catch up in class—Papa had shown me the telegram—he had been asked the question by almost everyone in the family and always had a similar answer: 'Times have changed and things are not so good in Calcutta any more, with all this trouble and the strikes. It will be good for Barun. Boarding schools also build character.'

But before he could reply to The Bastards, I turned and said: '*I* want to go.'

Papa quickly came up to me and pushed me out of the door before I could do more damage. I wondered how he could ever work in that office, even if he was a boss.

After the Dadu-scene for some reason Papa seemed to be happy with me. I didn't know why, but maybe it was because I had talked to The Bastards and saved his face. Just as we left, Papa said grandly, 'Son, tonight we'll go to Mocambo for dinner. And you can have beefsteak.'

This was really big. I had never eaten beef before, and Ma wouldn't allow beef to be brought home, warning my father that Suman and I were not to be given beef and that beef would be brought into the house 'over my dead body'. No meat was worth that, so we never said anything, but we knew Papa occasionally ate beef and enjoyed it. He would eat it when he travelled outside Calcutta or went outside India, and the more Ma told us how bad it was, how 'Hindus do not eat beef' and more so Brahmin children, the more I wanted to try it.

We went to Mocambo. Papa was wearing a brown suit with a really thin and shiny brown tie, and those shoes he loved, with white and brown leather strips criss-crossing, and they always made a tick-tock sound like a busy clock when he walked. Ma was wearing her favourite light blue Dhakai sari, and her favourite necklace, made of gold, with a big topaz in the middle, which Papa had given her, Ma said, 'to make up for all the bad things he does', but would never say what those bad things were, only, 'You will understand Barun, when you grow up,' while Papa looked at her with his eyelids drooping and mouth turned down, his angry face. 'When you grow up' seemed like a long time to wait to understand things. Suman was wearing her best frock and I had on my Gazebo jean shorts and a check shirt that Papa had got for me from Madras, and wore my best shoes, pointy black with buckles. Ma had combed my hair so hard my head still hurt when we walked into the restaurant.

Mocambo was on Free School Street, near the crossing with Park Street, though as far as I could tell, there were no free schools on that street, only a few restaurants and offices and lots of prostitutes, whom Joy called 'pross'. I had looked up the word in Papa's big Chambers dictionary where it said a prostitute was 'a person (usu. a woman or homosexual man) who accepts money in return for sexual intercourse'. I had brought the dictionary to the lakeside in Jodhpur Park one day, and my friends and I had gone through it, looking for other words like 'bastard', 'prick', 'cock' and 'cunt', and marvelled at this book that had all these words and yet it was all right to keep in plain sight of everyone, alongside textbooks, but any book or movie that used these words was either 'bad' or for 'adults'.

Mocambo had dim lights and there was a candle at each table. The head waiter knew Papa well, and he guided us to a table near the band. I knew what they would play at some point: 'Besame mucho' for Papa and 'Blue Spanish eyes' for Ma. Edwin, the tall Anglo-Indian singer with a thin moustache and hair that stuck out two inches in front of his head like a bread roll, would lean towards Ma, look into her Bengali eyes as black as coal, and sing 'Blue Spanish eyes', and Ma would look happy and Papa would laugh.

We all ate prawn cocktail. Ma wanted Chicken a la Kiev, and quickly ordered a Hawaiian Ham Steak for Suman, because Suman loved the way it looked, with a slice of pineapple on top of the slab of ham and a cherry on top of the pineapple, and also I guess because Ma wanted to be sure Papa wouldn't spoil both her children with beef as one new sinner in the family was bad enough. She looked away as Papa grandly ordered 'Shatubriaw' for him and me. While reading the menu I had got as far as 'Chat-eyow-bree-and' and both Papa and Ma had grinned when I said that, but yes, 'Shatubriaw' seemed like a good steak for a big boy to have. I couldn't wait.

The food arrived, and Ma, Suman and I watched Papa cut into his steak with short, neat strokes with the special knife the waiter had got. A little blood had oozed out onto his plate and Ma made a big face when she saw that. He put a piece in his mouth as all of us watched and he closed his eyes, chewed contentedly and said, 'Mmmmmm.' Then all of them turned to me. I cut a little piece and forked it in. It was hot and I instantly burnt my tounge, choked, and my eyes started to water. In a hurry, I reached for the glass of fresh lime soda and knocked it over, and most of it dripped on to Suman's dress. She called me a fool and started sniffling, because it was one of her good frocks.

'See,' Ma turned furiously to Papa, with a quick look at the ceiling, which had a big flat lampshade with flowers painted on it. 'God sees everything.'

'Don't be silly, Leela,' Papa said calmly. 'Suman, put the napkin on your lap. Why didn't you put it there in the first place? And stop crying, these things happen. You can have a tutti-frutti ice cream later. Barun, eat.'

Papa helped me cut the steak and I ate the whole thing. It seemed a bit tough and juicy at the same time, very different from goat, chicken and fish, and then I ate all the boiled beans, carrots, peas and potato with cream that were served with the steak. They watched me eat, even Suman, quiet now, bribed with ice cream.

Much to Ma's disappointment, I didn't burn and lightning didn't strike Papa and me, and God didn't scold us in that deep voice in which he spoke to Moses in *The Ten Commandments*, which Ma had told us 'a God's voice should sound like'. Later, I had a slab of chocolate ice cream, which came with a wafer on top, and in trying to act big, jabbed my gums with a toothpick. It hurt, but I didn't care about the pain.

Papa and I had travelled First Class to Agra on the Toofan Mail. He said it was once the fastest train between Calcutta and Delhi, but that must have been a long time ago because we often stopped at stations to let trains pass us, and I thought that if this was the fastest the train could go, the least the railways could do was change the name from Storm Mail. But that would have ruined it for Papa, who wanted to ride the Toofan Mail with me just like he had ridden it with his father when they used to travel together to Agra and from there to Delhi, before spending the summer at the hill station of Shimla, at the Grand Hotel. On my way to boarding school, there was no other way we were going to make the journey. It never entered Papa's mind, even though he kept complaining right through the day and a half it took us to reach Agra, where we would change trains for Ajmer, and Mayo, which Papa said was a school built many years ago for 'the sons of kings'.

Papa never said 'princes' when he said this to me, or to anyone else at home. It was always 'the sons of kings'. It was grander, though I wondered what I, the son of a businessman, was going to do in a school made for the sons of kings. When I asked Papa this on the Toofan Mail, he smiled and said that was all a long time ago, and that the school was now called a public school, where the sons of anybody, provided they had passed the entrance exams and their parents had the money, could go.

'Don't forget that you are your grandfather's grandson,' he added for emphasis. 'Hold your head up high, and make him proud of you.'

I didn't ask him why I was always my grandfather's grandson and never his son, and why I had to make my grandfather proud but not my father, especially as my grandfather was dead and the only memory I had of him was of being bounced on his big stomach. Mostly, he looked at us sternly from the photograph in the drawing room, which Ma would garland everyday with fresh jasmine, and Grandmother, Papa's mother, who hated Ma because she was dark and came from a family where people worked in other people's offices, would complain about the quality of the flowers and go on about how Grandfather was given no respect while he was alive and certainly not when he was dead by his bou-ma, daughter-in-law, who would have known better had her upbringing been right.

Ma would usually retort under her breath, calling her petni, she-ghost, or daini, witch.

I wondered if Papa felt he was something he did not want me

to be, or thought so highly of his father that in comparison, he thought himself to be nothing. But I kept quiet, because things were not going too well for Papa on the Toofan Mail anyway.

There was no dining car, and Papa sighed and talked about how earlier there used to be one where they served 'first-rate chicken roast with better gravy than even your mother makes' and how the railways, along with much of India, was 'going to the dogs'.

Our first-class coach was next to the steam engine and we either had the option of keeping the windows open and getting coal dust in our eyes or closing the windows and suffocating. The coach always seemed to run beyond the platform, and no attendant or vendor ever came to the coach. Instead of dining in style on roast chicken with boiled vegetables, we sat in our coupé with dark green Rexene seats and light green walls, two small noisy ceiling fans and one lamp with a weak light and a blue night light, I by the window and Papa near the door, which he kept locked most of the time. We ate arrowroot biscuits and grapes Ma had packed, and drank water from a huge stainless steel bottle she insisted we carry with us.

The most interesting thing we did was when we changed into our nightsuits, and I jumped on to the upper berth while Papa took the lower berth, and he read the Bradshaw railway timetable and I read *A Tale of Two Cities* in Bengali and played with the small lamp near the ceiling of the coach which switched on and off when I raised or closed the metal flap.

I was excited about going to a new school, but also very bored, tired of spending hours looking at the beautiful forests, fields of vegetables, wheat and mustard, the scenery changing from green in Bengal and slowly turning brown as we travelled west through

Bihar and Uttar Pradesh. Villages that looked so nice from a distance looked like a bad dream whenever the train passed near one—a jumble of thatched roofs on houses made of mud next to ponds full of moss, people wearing torn dresses, naked children, and cows, buffaloes and people all living together. But the Toofan Mail, even though it was slower than many other trains, moved quickly enough so the bad things I saw went past in a flash, and that was better than being in Calcutta because there the traffic moved so slowly that broken buildings and poor people and beggars were always there, like a slow-motion movie that went on and on, till we reached home or wherever we were going. But the movie never changed every Friday; it stayed week after week like some Super Hit, as I read in the papers and magazines successful movies were called, and nobody had to buy tickets for two-and-a-half rupees in dress circle to see it comfortably because it was always there, you know, free, for whoever wanted to see it.

Papa talked about the time when he travelled in trains with his father, and a houseboy came along. He would hop across from his third-class coach in the morning, go to the train's kitchen and supervise breakfast by yelling at the cook. The oatmeal porridge had to be done perfectly, not too runny and not too thick. The milk had to be just right, and god forbid if a layer had formed on top. The toast was always perfect. There would be poached eggs or omelette, and guava jelly and Darjeeling tea. At a station stop around mealtime, the houseboy would lead a procession to the carriage, deposit the breakfast and then come back at the next station to clear the trays. A similar procession would trot out for lunch and dinner.

Papa was desolate the trip wasn't going according to plan. 'Times have changed,' he kept saying. I nodded, not understanding.

Later, as we had a few hours to spare before boarding the metre-gauge train to Ajmer, Papa took me to see the Taj Mahal. We stood for a long time behind the Taj, looking out across the thin stream of the Yamuna River, a chilly February wind pulling at our clothes, as Papa told me about this beautiful monument which an emperor had built to celebrate his love for his overworked wife—as I would read later in class, they had fourteen children and she died while delivering the fifteenth. That was amazing, because it was four more than Didu, my granny, had produced. And all she ever got for her troubles, Papa would tell Ma sometimes when he was angry because Ma said he should act less like a zamindar and more like a man with a family, was a husband who beat her up and was so drunk most of the time that the only time he knew what was going on was when Didu had yet another baby and he would need to bring more of his bureaucrat's salary back home.

And here Papa would smirk, because for Didu's husband—and he was always 'Didu's husband' for us, this man who had died before Suman and I were born—it was unthinkable that he, the high official to whom everyone bowed and scraped, would ever spend any less. The servants would talk, and then the whole world would know that Telephone-babu could not support his family, and that would be the end of everything. Ma usually started crying when this happened, and stomp off to the bedroom and shut the door, and not speak to Papa for days. When they did, they would speak through Suman and me. 'Barun, ask your father if he wants more toast,' or 'Suman, please tell your mother if she hurries up with her make-up we can get to the cinema on time.'

Papa and I held hands in the shadow of this graveyard, what Papa grandly called 'a temple of love'. He pulled me close, hugging me tight, as if he was about to lose his son. Something had changed. Without saying a word, we both realized this was the last time we would do something so intimate. I was going to boarding school, and that was a grown-up thing to do. Grown-up boys didn't hold the hand of their fathers. They didn't hug anyone except friends. And Papa wasn't a friend, he was just my father. I was going away, to be free.

Times had changed. I understood it then.

I was alone in the dorm when the guys walked in.

I had been alone for two hours, I saw on the new HMT Janata watch Papa had given me saying he would get me a better watch if I did well in my exams, because the housemaster, Mr Bhardwaj, had told Papa it was time to go, because it was better for new boys to get used to boarding school quickly and having parents around wouldn't help to do that.

'We are here, Mr Ray, don't worry,' he told Papa as we stood outside his flat in the old wing of Bharatpur House, his wife, a lady with a kind face, like Ma, by his side. She had served Papa tea and asked me if I wanted anything and had smiled and said 'What a good boy', when I said 'No thank you ma'am', which Papa had taught me on the Toofan Mail was the proper response in English if I didn't want something. He had also told me to say 'Yes please, thank you sir (or ma'am)' if I wanted something, but looked a little upset when I had said 'Thank you sir' to the coach attendant when we got off at Agra, and said, 'You don't need to call a train attendant "sir",' which I couldn't understand, because the coach attendant had looked very pleased and gave me a big salaam when I said it.

'We are now his family as much as you are his family, well not exactly heh-heh-heh,' said Mr Bhardwaj. 'Barun will write letters to his parents and sister regularly, won't you Barun?'

I nodded but I could see Papa didn't like the idea of this new family of mine very much, even though Mr Bhardwaj tried to make it seem all right by turning the whole thing into a joke. But it was too late to change anything now. I would be in Mayo for nine months a year and that was a long time, and Papa would have to depend on others to take care of me.

Papa had walked with me to my new home, Dorm 7, next to the common room, which had some chairs, a TT table and three carom boards. We sat on my bed, which was in the far corner, near the window. All beds had maroon bedcovers and white bed sheets and pillow cases, and because I had poked them with my fingers and so had Papa, I knew the pillow and mattress were hard, not at all like the stuff at home, and the bed didn't even have springs. It was what Papa called a charpoy, which had a white cloth tape neatly woven to make the support for the mattress, like the beds made with rope outside restaurants on highways, which truck drivers used. Papa looked a little worried.

'This is not Calcutta, Barun,' he told me, as I looked out of the jaali door, the screen door of the dorm, already feeling uncomfortable in my 'home clothes,' as Mr Bhardwaj called them, but I knew I would have to wear them for another two or three days, till the tailor had got my gray shorts and togs ready. White shirts I already had.

'This is not Calcutta, Barun,' Papa said again, and I had snapped out of my daydream about playing cricket for the school team and nodded. 'I can't look after you here. You have to learn to look after yourself.' Of course I would, I thought to myself, what did he think I was, but I didn't say it aloud because it would have hurt Papa. 'You take care of your things, don't fight with anybody, listen to Mr Bhardwaj and your teachers and write to us. Be strong.'

Speech over, Papa coughed a couple of times, and then stood up, tucking his shirt in once even though it was perfectly tucked, and then buttoned his coat. 'I have to go now Barun.'

I stood, looking down. I thought he would give me a hug or something, but Papa had other ideas. He stretched out his hand and said, 'Good luck, Mr Ray,' and I looked up, shocked and quite pleased because he had treated me like a grown-up. He had this big smile on his face and I wanted to cry very badly but I didn't and just put my hand in his and he shook it four or five times. Then he turned, and quickly walked out of the door.

After Papa left, I sat on the bed and I cried a little, thinking about Ma and Suman and everything in Calcutta, but then the excitement of being in a boarding school got to me and I got up to explore my new home all by myself.

There were eight beds in the dorm, four on one side, where my bed was, and four on the other, with two on either side of the door-like gap in the wall that led to the cupboards and the changing room. There were two benches in the middle between the cupboards. I went to mine, which was nearest the gap, and opened it. I would only realize it later, but it was probably the only time in school when my cupboard was neat and clean, with everything arranged by Papa, everything in its proper place. The green dressing gown was hanging from a hook on the inside of the cupboard door. My home clothes were on three of the twelve hangers, one had two school ties. The twelve sets of vests and undies neatly folded on the top shelf, along with six white hankies and six sets of grey stockings, two sets of navy-blue games stockings, two pairs of navy-blue shorts, three white singlets, and two pairs of garters that Papa had bought from the Tuck Shop to hold the stockings up. In the corner to the left were my Signal toothpaste, my toothbrush, a red comb and three Pears glycerine soap bars that Ma had packed, saying Ajmer is cold in winter and only glycerine soap would work, one small bottle of Charmis cold cream and one tube of Boroline, on the back of which was written a very funny thing—that Boroline was good for chapped lips and cracked nipples. Suman and I had joked about it and wondered how nipples could be cracked and I had even asked Moyna-di once and she had giggled and called me 'Stupid chheley', but I didn't mind if she called me a stupid boy because she was an older girl and had quite a lot of boobs and I really wondered if she had cracked nipples.

On the second shelf below were my six white shirts and four sets of nightsuits, and on the bottom shelf was a pair of white Bata PT Shoes, a pair of pointed black Bata shoes with a small compass under the sole of the right shoe, and a pair of Hawaii chappals, also from Bata. As far as I knew, Bata made all the shoes in India, except for Chinese shoemakers on Bentinck Street in Calcutta, from whom Papa and Ma bought all their shoes, but they were not meant for 'rough use', Papa had said. Behind the shoes, I had hidden one tin of Bournvita, two tins of sardines, and two packs of cheese biscuits, and one packet of bullseyes and barley sugar sticks from D'Gama in New Market, my only symbol of home, because Papa did not leave me with any photographs of the family, saying if I had kept a photograph, I would think about home and feel sad. But I felt a bit sad looking at the tuck, so I knew Papa was wrong, because you didn't need a photograph to feel sad, just to remember.

I knew the empty places in the cupboard would fill up, with togs and my blazer and the Jodhpuri coat, which Mr Bhardwaj had said we had to wear during Prize Giving and other big occasions along with a turban, which he called a safa. Each house had a colour and the Bharatpur House—my first house—colour was red. My books and notebooks, kilos of them, were already at my place in the prep hall, which was at the other end of the house from my dorm, right next to the big toilet and bath and, though the toilets had doors, I was shocked to see the baths had no doors. I was surprised that Papa hadn't said a word when Kapur-ma'am, the house matron, had taken us around on a trip of the house, as if he didn't care that I would have to bathe in front of other boys, maybe because Kapur-ma'am didn't seem to think it was strange.

When Papa finally gathered the courage to bring it up, Kapur-ma'am had laughed and said 'Don't worry Mr Ray, all boys are alike.' Papa looked shocked and avoided looking at Kapur-ma'am after that, but that didn't stop her smiling from time to time.

Mayo seemed like a better place than Ajmer, which was a dusty and dirty town where people rode mopeds and tongas. We had taken a tonga, which everyone outside school called 'tanga', on our way from the station. There was one curving main road from the north to the south, Station Road, which Papa and I were on, and because there were so many tongas it was full of horse shit, which I hadn't seen much of until then because in Calcutta and other towns we visited in Bihar and Orissa, there was cowshit and dogshit and where poor people lived, which seemed to be everywhere, we would see humanbeingshit.

I passed signs I would get to know a lot better over the next few years, like S.L. Artist, the photograph shop where we went to buy black-and-white film and which took all our house photos and class photos. And there was Mr Artist, as we called him, a balding man with curly hair in a fringe, who would make us shout with laughter when he said 'Riddyshtiddyonetwothreeshmiiile', so every photo had to be taken twice or thrice and still there were boys in the photographs who were grinning like mad though there was nothing so funny about going from one class to another. There was the Bata showroom between the railway station and the curving stone bridge over the railway tracks. The Station Road split and turned left at the base of the bridge, and then the bridge carried it over the tracks towards Mayo. The road to the right, which was really the National Highway but became the Station Road when it came down the hills to the north and into the valley of Ajmer, became the Beawar Road just after the bridge, going straight to Beawar and on to Bombay, as a big sign said. Papa, who seemed to know all train timings and road maps by heart, said the highway was 'NH 8'.

That was also the National Highway to Framjee's, a tiny booze shop just after the bridge, where we would go to drink ice cream soda and watch older boys drink cold beer in a small courtyard at the back curtained off from the main shop, and it looked like something from Hindi movies, with Mayo guys and lokus standing and drinking, with not much distance to separate them.

'Lokus' were the locals. But we rarely mixed with them because they were lokus and therefore different from us, but the lokus who joined Mayo were all right because they stopped behaving like lokus and started behaving like Mayoites. It wasn't difficult to tell a loku from a Mayo guy, because of the way we stood, behaved and walked, like we owned the fucking world, even the lokus' world, the whole world, you know, walking around Ajmer in our grey togs or shorts and white shirts and blazers as if the peacock on our blazers had come alive and turned us all into the beautiful creature that held its head up, looked at the rest of the world like it was full of shit, knowing we were a class apart so we could take our time to strut, one royal step at a time, like India's national bird should.

Even at Framjee's the lokus would never dare pick a fight with us because we knew well how to fight and hated to lose, and the lokus usually kept away from Mayo guys when both species were at Framjee's at the same time. But they wouldn't always keep away. Once, this hippie-type loku with a big moustache and batik shirt and jeans with flares as big as skirts—'Maybe a Government College type, hanging around with gora charsis in Pushkar,' Porridge had whispered to me—pointed at us as we drank Golden Eagle beer from the bottle in great big gulps as we always did, in a hurry because if a Master caught us we'd be jacked. The loku had wagged his finger at us and said, without raising his voice, 'Endangered species, endangered species.'

We didn't get angry because we didn't understand what he meant and 'endangered species' wasn't like any curse or bad word we knew, though it sounded like a curse, the way he said it. I mean, fuck it, how could we ever be in danger?

Papa and I took the road to the left and went past Mridang cinema and straight down past the scooter and cycle repair shops before coming to the Mayo campus, a journey we chaps made so many times that I think every boy knew every twist and turn, every stinking storm drain, pothole, garbage heap and signs like

'Smart Shoppee Tailors Best Suitings and Shirtings' and the Luna moped shop and the mithai shop where we bought dusty, fly-blown, hot jalebis, better than he knew his own family. I think we would be able to tell when we had left Ajmer behind and entered the campus even with our eyes closed, because the smell and noise of India would disappear. Mayo was our India, and it had a different smell and sound, you know?

I had just finished eating the two chicken sandwiches Papa had got for me in a box from Honeydew Restaurant, near the station, because I would have missed lunch at the Mess, when some boys opened the jaali door with a bang and walked in. They saw me and stopped.

'Newboy,' said a fat boy, older than I was. 'Stand up newboy.'

I stood, and they walked towards me, seven of them, and sat around on the beds, surrounding me.

'Who asked you to stay in the dorm, newboy?'

'Mr Bhardwaj.'

They sniggered. 'Mr Bhardwaj, the Housemaster, *sir,*' said Fatboy. 'And he is *Birdie,* not Mr Bhoroddaj,' mimicking my way of saying the name in the Bengali way. 'You a Bongo?' which I had heard was slang for Bengali.

'Yes. Yes sir. From Calcutta.'

'Cal, haan? What's your name, newboy?' Fatboy asked. I wanted to kill him.

'Master Barun Ray, roll number 621,' I said, chin up, and they all laughed, looking at each other.

'MasterBorunRayRollNumber621,' Fatboy said, sniggering, mimicking my accent again, and then he turned to an older boy, saying 'Century, what should we bloody call him-ya? MasterBorunRayRollNumber621 is bloody huge-ya.'

'Brownie, Brownie,' said the boy he called Century, who I learnt ten minutes later was in Class 8 and the dorm captain and was called Century because he was the youngest guy to have scored a century in inter-house cricket, when he was only in Class 6.

'No-ya, Century,' a small boy, who looked as old as I did, spoke up. He had a pale face and always seemed to be frowning. 'Brownie is a dog's name-ya, call him something else, a humanbeingname.' This guy I wanted as a friend, I knew. I smiled at him, and he smiled back.

Century thought about it, nodding his head, and said 'Ya-ya, Moses, well done, thanks. So what do we call him?' He looked around.

Everybody started speaking. I heard all sorts of names being thrown around—Bongo, Bong, Blackie, 621, Pointy Shoes—till Fatboy shouted, 'I know, I know, Brainy, Brainy, no how do I know you're brainy...Brandy, Brandy, Brandy-ya.' They all liked that and said 'Ya-ya.'

Suddenly, it was as if I was okay, not some freak who had walked into their home. Century put out his hand, and spoke to me like he was a big brother. 'My name is Ramesh Handoo. You can call me Century. I'm the dorm leader. If you have any problem, you come to me, okay?'

One by one, I shook everyone's hand—Fatboy, whose nickname was Yo-yo because he always played with yo-yos and could do reverse loops like lightning, Bracey because he wore braces on his teeth, Monaco because the only biscuits he ate were salty and round Monaco biscuits, PT Shoe because he loved to polish his PT Shoes, Porridge because he liked porridge, and

Moses because he was Muslim but they hadn't been able to come up with a nickname from his first name, Sajjad.

There was still more than a year to go before I would meet Fish, who replaced Monaco in the dorm after Monaco's dad died in a car crash while driving from Bombay to Poona, the truck that hit him head-on sending his family a message like the stuff trucks had written at the back—OK TATA, no more money for Mayo and all now that we have pushed the steering wheel through Monaco-uncle's chest. Yo-yo was being kind, now that he had had his fun. 'Don't talk in a Bongo accent or people will make fun of you,' he told me, as I nodded and said 'Thank you, sir.'

'You're welcome, Brandy,' he said, like he was an emperor or something. 'No need to call me "sir".'

Century wanted to see my cupboard. I showed him and he nodded, saying 'Bloody neat-ya,' and because I didn't want to take credit for something I hadn't done, I told him my father had settled the cupboard. He looked at me and nodded. 'Okay, keep it neat, or I'll have to give you PD.'

Punishment detail, he explained, when I asked him what it meant. As I would find out soon enough, it involved running, duck-walking, which was a bad scene, and when things got really bad, like fighting or being late for prep, front rolls and back rolls on the road.

He opened his cupboard. It was neater than mine. Then he asked Bracey to open his cupboard, and said with a grin, 'This is a PD cupboard.'

It was a mess, with clothes, undies and everything all mixed up, and a really stinky smell, which Bracey proudly said was 'toe jam in my stockings,' and that's when I realized what the smell in the dorm was—smelly stockings. Bracey was a pig, but one chap's stockings couldn't have made such a stink. On the inside of the cupboard, he had two small posters. One said 'Jackie Stewart' and had a smiling face in a helmet and lovely-looking racing car below it; the second poster was of a woman with lots of curly hair and a nice smile and boobs as big as watermelons, in a dress with leopard spots which looked like it would burst. There was a name at the bottom and I desperately tried to read it as the boobs filled my eyes. Katy Mirza. I had seen her from a distance on the door of a booze shop in Calcutta. As Papa didn't drink, the only time I had seen Katy, as I now knew her to be, was from the car as we passed the booze shop near the crossing of Theatre Road and Camac Street on the way back from the river or an evening at Victoria Memorial.

I guess my eyes had grown really big, because everyone started to laugh, and I think it was Porridge who clapped me on the back, saying over and over, 'Bloodygood-ya, bloodygood-ya,' as if I had been shown and finally understood the greatest secret in the universe.

I was home.

On my first night, I met the ghosts of Mayo. I was in a strange place, and tossing and turning. I don't know how late in the night it was when I woke up from a dream in which I was walking in the snow in Shimla and turned to Papa and said 'I have to do number one' and stopped to piss on the red brick wall of the big post office at the mall. My piss started to smoke the wall and the snow, while Papa looked really upset and said, 'Master Barun Ray, that is *such* an uncivilized thing to do.'

I woke with a start and sat up, freezing despite the thick quilt, my belly swollen with piss and my pyjamas a little wet with some piss that had leaked out. Everyone in the dorm was asleep, and Bracey, whose bed was next to mine, must have been dreaming too, because he said, 'No-no-no,' and giggled, but he was talking to someone in his head. I could hear the wind howling outside. I was scared, but I *had* to take a piss.

So I put my instantly frozen feet into slippers, put on my green cotton dressing gown, got on my toes to carefully open the jaali door, which wasn't easy with numb fingers, and began the walk towards the toilet at the end of the long corridor, past dorm 8, the house matron's room, and dorm 9 and 10. A light was on in the corridor, and another shone dimly in the toilet, which I had learnt earlier in the day was called 'bogs' and it had 'shitpots' and 'pisspots' but the baths were just called 'baths', which had no doors, and I got laughed at because I had bathed wearing my undies, while boys stood outside my bath stall saying, 'Newboy' and 'Why're you hiding your lulla, arsehole?' I had turned my back on them and tried to bathe from a heavy iron bucket of hot water I had to fetch by myself from the boiler behind the bogs and barely managed to not drop on my toes. I had stood shivering while I soaped with Pears and tried not to step on the soap that I kept dropping from my numbed fingers, and got angry with Papa for getting me into some hell with no bathrooms attached to bedrooms and baths without doors, and wondered if the 'sons of kings' ever had to put up with this sort of stuff, like dragging buckets of water in freezing weather and other boys wanting to see their lulla.

There was a light shining to the right, in the lobby of the old wing, where some of the senior boys and Birdie lived, across the lawn ringed with lovely roses, lilies, snapdragons and poppies in so many colours that I thought I must ask The Bastards to come and see Mayo, so full of trees and fields and flowers, right in the middle of the desert, because Ajmer was a fertile valley, Papa had said, and it even rained a lot in the monsoon and the brown hills kept the desert away. I could make out the metal screen that stopped tennis balls being hit out from the two clay courts.

The wind was making a steady noise, and there were shadows being thrown on the wall near me, and I thought that ghosts of Brahmins that lived in trees, in the stories that Grandmother told us sometimes when she would stop complaining about Ma and remember she was a grandmother and grandmothers were supposed to tell stories to their grandchildren, would come and break my neck because I was a stupid boy who dared to walk along a corridor to go to the pisspot alone at night when the whole world was asleep. As even a stupid boy would know, night was the time for ghosts to awake and rule the world till sunrise, and the school building seemed like a perfect place for ghosts, it was so old, built even before India's independence, just imagine. Ghosts would love Mayo, I thought, because there were so many old buildings in one place and they could choose where they wanted to be and never be crowded out.

I closed my eyes, still standing outside the matron's room, hearing a door bang and the wind howl even more, shivering, colder than I had ever been in my life, because in Cal even if there was a warm breeze chaps would quickly pull on woollen monkey caps, and when I opened my eyes after a few seconds I saw a shadow move in the bogs and I was suddenly shaking with terror, a feeling I knew because when I was younger, I think around the time Kissing-da and the others had disappeared, I had tried to open my eyes one morning and couldn't, as hard as I tried, and I had screamed, saying I cannot see, please help me, please help me and I had heard Papa and Ma shouting 'What happened?' Suman was crying and Ma was cradling me and then Papa put a wet towel on my face and wiped the sleep-gum from my eyes. I had opened my eyes and was surprised I could see again and I saw Papa and Ma looking at me, but they didn't scold me even though I had got so scared for nothing.

I was halfway between the bogs and my dorm and felt so alone and scared to go into the bogs because I was convinced the shadow was the ghost of an Old Boy of Bharatpur House who had come back to use his old pisspot, and I was scared to turn back because I just knew there would be ghosts of Old Boys from Dorm 7 and 8 and even the ghosts of Old House matrons just waiting for me to turn my head so they could all grin at me with their skulls and red eyes, and I wondered if the boys would wear red safas. Then I heard a noise, tick-tock, tick-tock, tick-tock, and it was coming closer, not from the corridor but from the side, on the tarred path that went around the lawns and I knew I would die because all the ghosts of Old Boys were coming to meet the newboy and ghosts never said 'How do you do' but screamed 'Hahahahaha', as Grandmother had explained all ghosts, Brahmin and otherwise, did before they broke people's necks. But I so badly wanted to piss, I squeezed my eyes shut and wished the cold and dark and the ghosts of the Old Boys would go away till the newest newboy of Bharatpur House took a piss, and I would even show them my lulla later, if they wanted.

The tick-tock sound stopped near me. 'Idhar kya kar rahe ho?' someone asked me in Hindi, and I opened my eyes because a ghost wouldn't ask me what I was doing there, just break my neck. It was a chowkidar covered in a blanket, carrying a big lathi. I was so relieved I almost pissed in my pajamas right then. 'Piss,' I said then realizing he may not understand English, I said, 'susu.'

He was smiling. 'Go then, and do your susu. There's nothing to be scared of.' So I went on, grateful to the nightwatchman. He knew enough English, though. As I walked on towards the bogs, I heard him chuckle and say, 'Newboy'.

Mayo College
Ajmer
19.10.74

My dearest Papa,

I'm very sorry for the delay. Nowadays we get too much homework, that's why I take some time to reply. How are you? I am fine. Please give my love to Suman and especially to Ma. Please tell Ma that I will write a letter to her tomorrow in Bengali.

I am okay in Dorm 7. Everyone's become friendly with me. Sometimes they tease me, but I don't bother. I tease them back. We had a tuck party and ate Monaco biscuits with sardines and baked beans. Then for pudding we ate Monaco biscuits with my Signal toothpaste and Forhans. Signal is tastier because it has white and red stripes and it looks like strawberry syrup. Don't tell Ma or she will get upset.

A boy said very bad words to me. I gave him a bashing and he fell down on the floor. Tell Ma that I am in the Athletics Inter-House. And I won a race. But our house didn't win the Inter-House, but won the Football Inter-House this term. You had asked me not to buy more than 5 TT balls and one Drinking

Chocolate this term. Till mid-term I had only bought three TT balls but I am sorry I bought two Drinking Chocolates already because one Sunday we had a dorm party and one tin got over. Please don't mind. I am happy that the cook has at last joined her services. Can she cook chicken roast like Ma or does she only make Bengali kind of food? Is she clean?

Please give my love to Moyna-di and tell her Very Good Luck For Her College Exams.

Is it time for me to read James Hadley Chase books? If it is fine, could you please send me some? I am still playing tabla but it is getting boring because the Master makes me play teen-taal all the time, so I am planning to learn sitar. I think I will end now.

So long,
Barun

That afternoon, Indira Gandhi was riding a donkey.

Fish, Porridge, PT Shoe and I were up on the roof of our old dorm in Bharatpur House, which we still felt a little sentimental about even after moving to Jaipur House, which was a senior house. We had climbed up the neem tree and then hopped on to the roof as we always did, to gorge on our stash of wild berries that were plentiful in Mayo. We were chatting excitedly about if we could ever do what Maindak the frog and his gang did every Saturday afternoon.

Maindak, looking possessed, his huge eyes bulging, led the Piglets, twins who would fight with each other if they didn't find anyone else to fight with, and Bumble, the only bully we knew who wore glasses, in shooting pigeons and doves with a catapult. Then they would skin the birds behind the bathhouse and roast them over a fire of twigs and straw, of which there was always plenty because of the farms on the campus. Sometimes, when they couldn't find bigger birds, they would even kill sparrows, and Maindak made a big show of putting the bird whole into his mouth chewing a bit and then taking out the tiny bones, using his mouth as we would use a fork and knife.

The gang would bring the roasted birds to eat during the movie show at the Bikaner Pavilion every Saturday evening. They would wrap the birds in a plastic sheet, and keep them in a khaki canvas school bag on which Maindak had drawn a peace sign with a ballpoint pen. They would tear bits from the blackened birds, Maindak easily spotted because his big ears stuck out like bugles, quickly stuffing the flesh into their mouths and gnawing on the small bones, licking their fingers and wiping their hands on the woven jute rolls that would serve as seats in the open-air Pavilion, made entirely of red sandstone, which made even such a simple thing look like it was part of a grand palace.

We would sit behind them, crazy with the smell of roasted bird, the prized Saturday dinner of tomato soup, bread rolls, mutton cutlets, boiled vegetables and custard all forgotten. Our eyes would rotate from the action on the sixteen-millimetre screen, with its flickering images of men with thin moustaches and women with breasts as big as pumpkins as they sang to each other in parks full of flowers or while rolling down mountainsides covered in snow, to Maindak and his gang's feast. This was almost as exciting as seeing Pat's collection of foreign porno mags full of naked women, all pink, with blonde or brown hair on their heads and even down there.

We stopped our chatter when we heard the shouting. It was coming closer. Fish slithered down the branch, and Porridge,

PT Shoe and I followed, stepping lightly to clamber up another branch that extended over the wall of the school. About a hundred people were marching in a ragged group on the narrow road, leading a donkey in front. Somebody had rigged a support to its saddle and placed a photograph on it.

The chanting became clearer as they came closer.

'Indira Gandhi hai hai,' they shouted, a group of a few dozen men dressed in scruffy white kurta-pajamas, a scattering of women in white and coloured saris, their hair tightly drawn back, sweaty brown faces made fierce with their open shouting mouths, eyes narrowing with each shout. A few of the House servants' children scampered alongside. A lanky boy wearing a torn vest and dirty shorts jumped up and spat on the photograph, and everybody laughed, pausing for a break from all the shouting. By then, the group was almost directly below us.

We sat absolutely still. The lady in the photograph, Indira Gandhi, the prime minister or PM, as we called her when we wanted to show off, was smiling. That day, over her framed photograph, she wore a necklace of old sandals and shoes. The trademark white streak ran from her forehead across her hair, and the spittle seemed to flow from it, dripping down past the beaked nose, over the grinning teeth, to hit the dam of the frame, ooze over and then wet the cloth of the saddle.

'Heavy,' said PT Shoe. 'Heavy. Fawk.'

He had learnt to say fuck for the first time a week ago, and used it whenever he got a chance. We didn't stop him because it made him feel important.

The lanky boy heard him, looked up, and pointed excitedly at us, four boys on a tree, wearing uniform white shirts, grey shorts, long grey stockings stretched up to the knee and white stripe folded over a garter, and black shoes. The crowd went quiet. The lanky boy, much older than we were, maybe sixteen, made a face.

'Kya dekh raha hai?' he shouted. What are you looking at? 'See, here's your rani, I spit on her.'

We said nothing, didn't move a muscle, which only seemed to provoke him.

'Angrez ke aulad!' he shouted. Sons of Englishmen. He scratched his head and added as an afterthought, 'Saaley, bhainchod.' Shits, sisterfuckers.

That stirred the crowd. A man, who seemed like the leader of the pack—he was holding this big green flag—slapped the boy across the back of his head and looked up. They were all looking up. Some were shuffling.

The man filled his chest with air and raised his hand and shouted at us, 'Indira Gandhi hai hai.' Then, as in deference to the shitty, sisterfucking sons of Englishmen, shouted again, replacing his guttural Hindi with English, to make us understand their mission. 'Indira Gandhi down down.'

I slowly raised a hand, made a fist and shook it, the way I had seen people in the crowd do, and shouted, 'Down, down.'

That seemed to be good enough for the crowd, who took it as a token of support for their great march, and they set off, cursing Indira Gandhi over and over again.

The guys looked at me like I was some sort of freak.

'Man, you're mad-ya,' said Fish, eyeing me with respect.

I felt like a king, wondering whether the act would fall into the category that Papa called 'splendid', a word he used whenever he thought comment was necessary but did not know what to say that would not offend anybody. I thought it was quite splendid for a fourteen-year-old to take on a prime minister.

We had all seen her one year back, in 1976, when she visited the school for the Centenary Prize Giving. She was a real prime minister then, and a special one for us, as she was the only person whom we knew was prime minister of India and wasn't dead.

The whole school, nearly eight hundred of us, had all lined up from the massive wrought iron main gate of the school, what we called Alwar Gate, in two restless rows on either side of the road in the blazing sun, right up to the principal's house where she was to rest before giving her speech and the prizes. We stood for what seemed like hours. Then two large helicopters came from behind Madar Hill and landed on Loch Ground near the main gate where inter-school football matches were played, making a huge racket. Dust flew everywhere. The doors opened and she appeared; it must have been she, because suddenly the crowd rushed forward. Then she came towards us. I could see her far away, standing, waving her hand like a queen, in a huge open-top light-brown car, a colour Ma called 'bezsh' but was spelled beige and I had called 'baij' the first time I read the word.

The four of us had talked about it afterwards, about all the pomp and power that this sharp-eyed woman with a big nose and big smile could bring with her. I told them about snatches I remembered from conversations at home, just after the 1971 war. Papa and Ma had called her an 'iron lady', someone responsible for beating Pakistan in a war, 'who would make India a great nation'.

I could believe it. I had even seen Indira's face on the Durga idol during the pujas in a pandal close to my house, her nose even more beaked than the asura's, who was dressed like a Pakistani soldier years after the war, like they were permanent bad chaps or something, and through whose heart she had driven a spear. Ma had bowed low, her hand folded in prayer, and accepted flowers and fruit from the priest as a blessing from the goddess. I had started giggling then, and set off Suman, continuing even as Ma first tried to hush us and then rushed us out of the pandal, furious, calling us 'shaheber bachcha', sons of sahibs, spitting it out in the same way we heard people in some English movies say 'sonofabitch', her way of cursing us for forgetting our manners and laughing in front of the gods and, we thought, she could also get back at Papa's family at the same time.

But Suman and I couldn't stop giggling, because we remembered the other thing Indira Gandhi was known for, what we had heard from our parents and their friends, read about it in the papers and seen on posters. There was talk of how 'Indira's men' would go around trying to stop people from making any more babies so India could be a richer country by cutting off a tube inside the cock. As far as Suman and I were concerned, she was the goddess who cut men's things off. Anyone who could do that had to be really powerful.

But Indira didn't look powerful on the day Fish, Porridge, PT Shoe and I would mark as the day we officially became the Shitty Sons Of Englishmen. Afterwards, as a joke, and a secret that always remained with us, we even wrote the short form after our names on our notebooks, S.S.O.E., in the same way we had seen capital letters placed after names, as if they simply picked chits from a bowl and put down whatever alphabet they liked, O.B.E., K.B.E. and so many others, especially for people in the huge oil paintings that hung inside the Assembly Hall. The longest belonged to a guy on horseback called 'Major General His Highness Maharaja Sir Pratap Singh Bahadur, G.C.S.I., G.C.V.O., K.C.B., L.L.D., A.P.C., Born 1845 – D.C.L. 1922'. We tried to figure out for a long time just what D.C.L. meant.

Nobody knew, and the best we could do was 'Dead C/o Lord'. We immediately shortened the whole name and, after a while, we even memorized the sequence of letters, and it became our little joke. I would sometimes think of adding random letters like O.O.F. and R.E.A.L.L.Y. somewhere in the middle of all those alphabets, certain that nobody would be able to tell the difference and would think Sir Pratap even more impressive.

The goddess had ridden a donkey with gobs of spit running down her face. If a prime minister had come to that and the police were not beating up people for spitting on her, then it had to be a big deal.

We knew many people were angry with Indira Gandhi because of the Emergency. It had taken us a while to understand the full meaning, but I wasn't sure I really knew what had been going on. For two years of the Emergency the newspapers and mags I read in the library had been full of nice things about Indira Gandhi and her son, whose name was Sanjay, the same as that of Fish. Now that the Emergency was over, these same newspapers and magazines were full of lousy things about her and her son, like someone had turned on another tap. It was as if one day these guys were gods and on another they were the pits and others were trying to be gods, taking turns to do whatever they wanted because they ruled India. It seemed pretty much like when the English were ruling us, only now we seemed to be getting fucked by our own people, though we had our own flag and country, and didn't have to lick any gora's arse.

But something 'wasn't quite tick-tock' with India, as Ma said whenever she found something that could be better. 'Tick-tock' was the mean. For Ma, things were either tick-tock or not, and it seemed to make sense, because in Bengali and Hindi there was a common word, theek-thak, but it sounded so much like tick-tock that I never knew if Ma meant tick-tock like the sound of a clock or was she saying something like we so often did, like saying 'tonga' for 'tanga' in the way the goras had done. We all tried to speak a bit like the goras and always used English when we tried to say something important, though to me theek-thak sounded like a real word, and tick-tock sounded like a bomb.

Vivek Mahanta, our history teacher who also taught us civics and was called Mutt though he wasn't stupid until he got drunk (which was every Saturday night after the movie) had explained it to us in class. He had said it was because of censorship, and now that the Emergency was over, there was no censorship, so people could once again say, do and see whatever they wanted.

'Does that mean we can see boobs in movies?' PT Shoe had whispered, setting us off on a wild giggling spree, with Gary and Pundit rocking back on their chairs, making such a noise that Mutt had intervened in a stern voice, 'Gentlemen, what's so funny? Mr Pratap Singh, please tell the world so that we may all be enlightened.'

When PT Shoe did, looking embarrassed and somehow managing to look very pleased at the same time, the entire class had burst out laughing, even Mutt, who called PT Shoe 'Mr One-Track Singh' from then on. Mutt was a sport, and anyway, he would get the joke, because he was in-charge of getting movies for the Saturday show and ensuring the projector worked properly. We just wished he wouldn't drink so much, because every now and then he would freak out in class or at cricket where he was the umpire and not be the cool-breeze Mutt we knew.

This was definitely a different emergency from the ones we had seen, like the emergency rooms in hospitals and the sign on all trains, 'To Stop Train Pull Chain', which happened a lot when we used to travel to school and back from Cal by the Air-Conditioned Express, which people either called 'de Lux' or 'Vestibule' because it was one of the first trains in India in which you could go from one coach to another, and we often did that, going back to the second-class sleeper coaches, then working our way up to the AC Chair Car where we were, then to the first-class coaches and finally to the Holy Grail, AC first class, walking up and down and driving the attendants crazy. There was always a lot of trouble with the emergency chain whenever we passed through Bihar because people stopped the train as their town or village approached and they wanted to get off. It seemed to be getting as bad as Cal, where everybody did what they wanted.

I remember a holiday when Papa had driven us all from Cal for a tour of Bihar, and between Nalanda, which used to be a big university in ancient times and was now in ruins because some invaders had sacked it, and Rajgir, which had tonnes of Buddhist temples and monasteries, the car engine had overheated. Leaving the car in the care of Manohar-babu, Papa had dragged us on to a bus to Rajgir, where we were staying, with these words of wisdom: 'A taste of the real India will do you good.'

There was hardly any place on the rickety bus, and I had to squeeze in and sit behind the driver on a plank of wood that was placed over the battery, while Papa stood clutching the back of a seat, and Suman sat on Ma's lap in the middle of the bus and I couldn't see them. The bus stopped outside a small town, near the police station, and this daroga-type guy had got on. The conductor had asked him for a ticket as he did from everyone.

But it was a mistake because the policeman called the conductor a motherfucker-sisterfucker-son of a donkey and slapped him. Then he had the bus stopped, dragged the conductor down by his ears, and then went around to the driver's side, pulled the driver out and started to beat them both with a big lathi. He stopped when the driver fell at his feet, shouting at the conductor to do the same. The driver was screaming, asking to be forgiven, because the conductor was new, the sisterfucker, and that is why he had made the mistake of asking daroga-sa'ab to buy a ticket. The whole thing had looked like an emergency scene, but nobody had said a word.

Papa had called it a 'real tragedy' when I asked why policemen didn't have to buy tickets, and said, 'India is not the same it once was.'

That made no sense to me because we seemed to be living in a very violent place, with India and Pakistan fighting all the time and people were always fighting in the streets, or they were like this poor conductor and driver, who were bashed up by the policeman and had been so afraid. The fighting had begun much before I was born so this 'India is not the same it once was' that Papa said made zero sense, because, I mean, Ma would still talk about how bad the riots were in Calcutta during the Partition, in 1946 and 1947, when she was just a child, when India and Pakistan became two countries, and Hindus and Muslims would chop and burn each other, even little children, and Muslims would sometimes use huge butcher's knives to kill Hindus, placing their heads on large chopping blocks like the ones in the meat markets, and the Hindus would sometimes take Muslims to some fish market and cut them on botis, these big blades stuck into planks of wood which they used to cut huge rohu and catla fish.

I had begun to understand how Mahatma Gandhi managed to jack the English. Maybe the goras were so shocked that someone wasn't fighting to kill, they got scared and buggered off from India. If this was true, it was a good plan, but nobody seemed to have the balls to do it anymore.

Anyway, this Emergency was suddenly all right to talk about, as Mutt explained, though for the previous two years not a single teacher had breathed the words 'Emergency', 'censorship' and 'that son of hers' in public because they were shit scared of Indira Gandhi, we knew. Mutt said Indira Gandhi had declared a 'State of Emergency' because her enemies had wanted her to stop being PM, and the Emergency was Indira Gandhi's way of fighting back, by taking away the fundamental rights and freedom of expression of the people, stuff we knew from the civics book. We knew things like fundamental rights and the freedom of expression shit were for grown-ups, because no kid I knew ever had any freedom of expression or fundamental rights and got jacked by grown-ups whenever they tried to do what they wanted.

Mayo was a totally cool-breeze place, or maybe breeze, because when things were really cool-breeze it was more hep to just call it 'breeze', and if they were more disco-breeze, like some Travolta-type chap or a place or happening, then it would be 'cat' but we could change things around because their was no grammar to it, just what we felt, you know, not like some bloody big, fat Wren and Martin book saying you cannot use this construction here and all that because the participle is giving you a fucking headache.

The world was outside, and it was as if whatever happened out there, including to our families, was kept outside the gates.

School was a world in itself—Planet Mayo—which had chaps from all over India who spoke English or tried to speak in English as there was no other way to communicate and Hindi was too much like a language that was only in books and movies and spoken by lokus and all that, and we spoke to them in Hindi also. There were rich chaps and poor chaps on scholarship, and black chaps and white chaps, and guys from all religions and even no religion like Bassy's parents, who were Bramho which, Bassy said, was a 'way of living where folks prayed to a god that was not god', whatever the bloody hell that meant.

And Planet Mayo just happened to be ninety-three million miles from the sun, between Venus and Mars, and had twenty-four-hour days, same as Earth. The seasons were different, though. Instead of spring, summer, autumn and winter, there were only two seasons in school—autumn term and spring term. We knew it was similar in other boarding schools as well, all little planets, with only the duration of terms changing, depending on whether the school was in the hills or the plains, so in the hills in the north winter hols would be longer because it was colder there, like for us summer hols were two-and-a-half months long. Because between May and July the desert winds would blow in and burn everything before school opened for autumn term, and even in April there would sometimes be these storms, so huge that even the hills that protected Ajmer wouldn't be able to keep back the massive columns of sand and dust, so tall and determined they would storm through any pass and even over the hills to turn our world into solid brown. If we were caught outside, the only thing to do would be to duck behind the nearest hedge, close our eyes and squat, our heads between our knees, till the world turned a little blue and green again. Then we would clear the sand from our eyes, dig it out from our ears and chew it for hours because no amount of spitting and rinsing the mouth seemed to get rid of the sand. Porridge had even tried to shampoo his mouth once after one of those storms with his yellow egg shampoo, but never tried it again because he choked and swallowed the muck and had bubbles coming out of his nose and he puked his lunch out. It was both funny and disgusting, with globs of rice and rajma in a puddle with bubbles forming and bursting all around it. Just as the whole world was about to go mad from the heat, the monsoon cooled things down again.

We had talked to some Doscoes who had come over to play a football match, in which they got pasted 3-1 and grumbled later, saying, 'Man, let your squash team come to Doon and we'll fuck you.' If we had lost, we'd have said something similar, so it was okay. This is how wars are fought.

Doscoes were what guys from The Doon School were called, a name we guys made fun of because it made Doon sound like didn't know what it was and you had to say *the* Doon School so that people wouldn't think it was just *a* Doon School. And there was a running joke that when a Dosco and Mayoite met in the bathroom, one of them would intentionally drop the soap and bend to pick it up. When a Dosco told the joke, it was the Mayo guy who dropped the soap. When we cracked the joke, the Dosco dropped the soap. It was quite funny, though Ma had looked very upset when she heard me telling the joke to Suman during the hols, though she never said anything. Suman had laughed though I'm not sure she got the joke, because it was a boy joke, and she was also a kid. She didn't know any girl jokes, and nobody I knew seemed to know girls well enough to know some girl jokes, except for the stuff we read in *Rugby Jokes* and limericks that used to float around, like 'There was this young lass from Madras, whose arse was made of grass.'

Anyway, the Doscoes liked Mayo food and were surprised we could eat as much as we wanted even though we got only one small piece of butter and a blob of jam and one pudding when they were not around, which forced us to trade like we were businessmen—butter for jam, and pudding for helping out with homework. They said nice things about the dorms and rooms, and that it was like living in a palace that looked like a palace from the outside but not from the inside because there were no prince-type things any longer. And they didn't act snooty, so they were okay, you know, not being arseholes or anything. I might even have ended up in Doon, because while I had put Mayo in the number one slot during the common entrance tests at La Martiniere school in Cal, I had put Doon next to 'Second Preference' and Scindia School as 'Third Preference'. I had only put Mayo first because Moyna-di had two cousins in Mayo. One was called Tennis Ball, because he always brought tennis balls but never played tennis, and his brother was Squash, because he loved orange squash. So Papa knew more about Mayo than he did about other schools and though it seemed bloody strange thinking about it sitting in Mayo, I might just have been a Dosco. The Doscoes were like us, only they wore a different uniform, which was expected, and from the look of envy they had walking around campus, we knew they thought the Mayo campus was cat.

It *was* pretty cat, even though I hadn't seen any other boarding school except Scindia School in Gwalior, which was on top of this great hill and looked a lot like Mayo though we would never admit it even if we were whipped. We had these lovely Houses named after kingdoms from the old days like Bikaner, Tonk, Jodhpur, Bharatpur and the one I went to later, Jaipur. They were almost like palaces with domes and spires and lovely balconies. There were lots of rooms, and we stayed in them, like we were part of history or something. But, of course, these were different times and we didn't have servants, only farrash, who helped us sort out clothes or took us to hospi, looked after our stores or tied our turbans as we stood in two lines, because each house had two farrash. We had to do almost everything ourselves from making our beds to polishing shoes and once a month, every boy had to wear an apron and serve at the Mess, so we got to know what the waiters went through and didn't act like we were the sons of kings even though we went to a school meant for the sons of kings.

We were hanging around in Pat's room, because Pat had scored a goal and was now trying to be nice and hospitable to the Doscoes, chatting about this and that and showing off his best pondies, even the fat German ones he kept hidden because they had photos that gave us hard-ons we thought would never come down. Pat was so protective of them he would let us masturbate to these pondies only in his loo, so his loo was among the busiest in Jaipur House. The photos would have also got the guys and chicks in the mags into any circus in the world, and if he had got caught Pat would be sent straight home to Ahmedabad, which he told us was pondie capital of India.

The Doscoes and us had talked about all sorts of things, like music and books and how Zeenat Aman, whom we called Zeenie Baby because we had read that in mags, was such a cat actress and how only Parveen Babi, whom we called Parveen Baby, could match her, style for style, look for look, tit for tit. Well, maybe not look for look because Zeenie Baby was really beautiful. And Zeenie Baby was really clever also, we knew, because she even had a column called 'You've Got a Friend' in a mag called *JS*, which was short for *Junior Statesman* and was a very breeze mag, with nice stories and information about interesting things, Modesty Blaise comics, and these guys who wrote in *JS* used very breeze words like 'cool' and 'primo' and it was the most popular mag in the library. *JS* had even written a story on Mayo in the centenary year, calling it 'India's Eton', though it was not as grand as what a viceroy, Lord Lytton, had told the chaps when he came for Prize Giving in 1879—that 'Ajmer is India's Eton and you are India's Eton boys.'

It sounded really grand though none of us had any idea what Eton was except that it was a school in England where the haw-haw types went and they wore bowler hats and coats with long tails like bloody penguins or something. I had also really liked the line in *JS*, which said, 'From caparisoned elephants and royal students to carpentry and metalwork after lunch.' Times had really changed, you know?

We talked about how teachers were, how the syllabus was the pits and everything except games and trekking and chicks was so boring, and how much freedom we had—or not. It was all the same. Teachers were mostly okay but there were some real arseholes, who thought they were born to give schoolboys a hard time. And as far as freedom went, the rules were simple: if you got caught, you got jacked. But you never sneaked on somebody. I knew what that meant because I had come very close to sneaking on Maindak, but kept quiet because of the unwritten rule about sneaking: A sneak was almost as bad as a thief.

Just the year before, I was standing near the Vice Princi's office one day, waiting for classes to start after the break, looking at the huge school bell high on the Main Building—the bell was tied with a rope tied to a pillar near Vice Princi's office—and Maindak had come and pushed me. I had stumbled four feet on to the red gravel, grazed my arms and knees badly and come running up the steps towards Maindak, half-choking on gravel dust. The bastard had then shoved the point of a divider into my stomach before I could do anything, and I stood there, shocked, before recovering and kicking Maindak in the balls. He doubled over with a scream, I saw with satisfaction, surprise on his face that one of the guys he bullied regularly had suddenly fought back.

Vice-Princi had come by and seen us and asked us what was going on, but neither of us would say a word, so he yelled at us to behave like 'human beings' and sent us off to Udaipur House, the hospi, with me leading, down the steps of the Main Building and past the lovely jacaranda trees, the open-air map of India, the drumstick tree, Jhalawar House, where the Musuem was, and the Contemplation Ground, and Maindak following, bent over for much of the way and then slowly trying to straighten, looking like Man in the evolutionary chart that hung in bio class, like he was trying to become fully human. At that point Maindak didn't look like and I didn't feel like we were going to be the future leaders of India, what Princi had told us at Assembly Mayo trained its boys to become.

I told the compounder I accidentally poked myself with a divider so he put some silvery-red mercurochrome ointment on the tiny blue-black hole and on my cuts, and refused to put me on the sick list or anything, but what the fuck did he know because he gave us an aspirin-type white powder for everything from colds to stomach aches and if that didn't work, he would want to give us enemas, just imagine. 'The bloodyfool compunder,' as PT Shoe would say. We sometimes wondered what the man would do if he ever escaped from Mayo and tried to solve all the bad things in India the only way he knew, calling himself His Holiness the Guru of Aspirin and Enemas or something.

The divider-hole didn't pain much, thank god, and no food came out of it during lunch, but both Maindak and I knew our story wasn't over. I was scared of Maindak because he was a mad bastard, but I was tired of being pushed around.

Anyway, as I was saying, Doscoes and Mayo guys were really quite similar. I had also seen some guys from Sherwood College in Nainital, in the hills of Uttar Pradesh, where we had gone on a Class 8 school trip. We were taken on this beautiful lake ringed by hills by Bunter, our Sanskrit teacher, and we called him that because he was short, fat and wore round glasses like Billy Bunter. We sat in boats and were rowed across by the boat owners from one end, which had a playing field of cinder, to the other, where the bus-stand was, while Bunter kept shouting 'Boys, careful, careful, don't fall overboard,' like we all wanted very badly to jump into the cold black lake and drown ourselves.

We had almost reached the bus-stand end, when these two boats, which Mango, who was sitting next to me, told me later were proper rowing boats, came zipping past with this guy sitting on the stern of the boat screaming 'Stroke, pull, stroke, pull' as four rowers in each boat pulled in unison. It was like a dance. Both boats had gone past and then stopped in a splash of oars, and the man sitting on the stern of one of the boats, who looked like a Master, on seeing our uniforms called out to us, 'Which school are you from?' Bunter had pulled himself up, stood, and almost falling over the side of the boat, and said, 'Mayocollegeajmer.'

Mango whispered, 'That chap is going to disgrace us' but Bunter didn't fall off, thank god, and asked in turn, a little confused, 'Which school you are from?'

The master said, 'Sherwood,' and waved. The Sherwood boys had then started to sing 'Womaan, take me in your arms, rock-your-baby', which was this really cat song by George McRae and we had the LP in the common room, and started rocking their boats. We knew they were doing it to show off, but it *was* a very cat thing to do, and if we had rowing boats we might have done something similar.

But we all seemed to be different from the Paulites, the guys who went to St Paul's in Darjeeling, many of them sons of box-wallahs and planters, and they wore ties made in England, walked around town with tightly rolled umbrellas, and called the locals 'barbs', short for barbarians. They called anybody with high cheekbones and slant eyes 'barbs'. I knew it because Joy's cousin Toy went to St Paul's, and told us these stories during hols, and about how they lived in English-style buildings, got to eat really good ham in the Mess, and ate hot scones and drank hot chocolate in town. These buggers still seemed to think the fucking sun hadn't set on the British Empire.

I am not being honest, actually, because we had the ghosts of goras all over Mayo, beginning with the name. Lord Mayo had been a viceroy in the old days. There was a statue of his in front of the Main Building, planted right in the centre of the road from the Main Gates, between Loch Ground and St Andrew's Field, where we played cricket and football. As a statue, Lord Mayo looked a little like Michael Caine, whom we had seen playing

Peachy Carnahan in *The Man Who Would Be King* and the very breeze Jack Carter in *Get Carter* at the Pavilion, and I thought Michael Caine was really king.

It was a big statue, more than life-size; either that or Lord Mayo was a big bugger. He wore skin-tight leggings like long johns, and a big robe that reached his ankles and was parted in the middle, with two tassels hanging down from the knot near his neck, neatly covering his balls. It was like the statue had been given a 'U' Certificate instead of 'A' by the sculptor, because a viceroy of India couldn't show his balls to his subjects. On the pedestal there was a long message, which Porridge and I thought was the longest sentence we had ever read, even longer than the ones I wrote in English essays, which Yogi kept ticking me off for, saying in his usual sarcastic way, 'Brandy, god created the full stop because he wanted to make the world a better place. Why don't you help him a bit, hmm?' Yogi was king, and I liked him because he had a way with comments. During one end-of-term exam in Class 8 we were asked to write an essay on 'Summer', and Yogi had written 'Wow!' next to the para where I wrote, 'The best season for relaxing is the summer. Nearly all the pleasures can be had, except for skiing or perhaps walking hand in hand with your girlfriend during a soft snowfall.' Some other masters like Johnny or Samosa-sir would have buggered me over that, and deducted marks, but Yogi was breeze. But mostly we loved him because he mixed his sarcastic shit with encouragement for anything creative we did, saying creativity would get us into St Stephen's College in Delhi, because he had been there, and kept saying 'College is the best place in India,' as if every other place was shit.

Anyway, this was the sentence:

'This statue is erected in the honour of

Richard Southwell Bourke
Earl of Mayo
K.P – G.S.M.I.
Viceroy of India from 1868 to 1872
Born February 21, 1822, Died February 8, 1872.

The force of mind and body which enabled him to deal wisely and purely with every branch of public business, the justice which uniformly guided his policy; the benevolence which endeared him to all whom he ruled; the admirable candour and openness of mind which enabled him to learn from all who approached him; and the wonderful sweetness of disposition which subdued even his enemies can never be forgotten by those who knew him, and have produced lasting effects on the Indian Empire in the service of which he spent his best years and lost his life, it was his hope that this college of which he first suggested the foundation might promote among the youth of Rajputana the cardinal virtues of fortitude, temperance, justice and benevolence of which his own life gave a splendid example.'

Lord Mayo seemed like god, or he was just made out that way, at least that's the way it seemed to us, because there was a real arse-licking message at the back of the statue in English, Hindi and Urdu, which said, 'This statue was erected from the funds subscribed in Rajputana to mark the esteem and admiration entertained for the noble founder of the Mayo College.'

It sounded grand, and it made the school quite grand to have these old statues around the place, but we really didn't care because it was all from a long time ago, except maybe for Lord Mayo a little, because there was a king story about Lord Mayo getting off the pedestal on full moon nights exactly at midnight, scaring the shit out of students, asking them for their names and roll numbers in a deep voice. It was a fun story but it was obviously all shit, like what pigeons and crows deposited on his head, and every week a farrash would climb up on a ladder and clean the muck off with a dirty wet rag.

I had quickly become the tuck king of Jaipur House. Every term, I would land up with more weight in tuck than clothes, and almost all of it was tinned fish, because Ma thought they starved us in school, but actually we had as much as we could eat, though all of us seemed to have lost weight when we went back home for the hols. It was clear why that happened, because at home in the hols we did fuck all, hanging around getting our stomachs stuffed by parents, while at school we were slogging from 5.40 in the morning till lights out, with just a couple of hours off between lunch and games and between prep and lights out at 10 p.m. Rat, our geog teacher had explained the whole business to us once, and though we thought it was really funny, we knew it would hassle our parents if they ever heard this because it certainly wasn't written in the Mayo brochure. 'We want you to be so tired by lights out,' Rat had said to us one day in class, 'that you shouldn't even have the energy to masturbate.' We all agreed Rat should stick to drawing pretty diagrams of artesian wells with pink, yellow and green chalk on the blackboard, because he obviously had no idea of the real world.

Being friends, Fish, PT Shoe and Porridge got special treatment, but I wasn't stingy with tuck, none of us were, because one of the first lessons we learnt in school was that if you gave, you got. We had some really grand tuck parties after prep on weekdays but never on Sundays because we had better food on

Sundays than on any day of the week, like mutton biryani, which we hogged till our stomachs came close to bursting.

Fish used to get a lot of Sing-type food, like instant noodles, and lots of biscuits. Porridge would get these yum cookies from Poona, called Shrewsbury, and lots of pickles, and the absolute king pickle was some venison pickle he got once, which his father, a captain in the navy, had got from the Andaman Islands. I had good tinned stuff, but Porridge had the best, because he told me in the navy people could buy things 'dutyfree'. So, besides the pickle for which we worshipped Porridge-aunty, as we called his mother, Porridge would also bring these cat Toblerone chocs and tins of Tulip hot dog sausages and luncheon meat, which had these tiny key at the bottom to open the tins, and that was so breeze because it was much easier than opening tins even with the tin opener with a wheel that I had. Porridge was a good chap and let us open his tins, not saying 'It's my tin bugger so I'll open it,' that some people like Toe Jam, which was Bracey's new name after his braces had come off, and who stayed in the next dorm, used to do. If anybody could beat me at being king of tuck, Porridge would.

PT Shoe never got a damn thing, because his father didn't want him to get soft, and insisted he eat whatever there was in the Mess. We didn't mind and, in fact, always gave him a bigger share of our tuck, but without making a big deal of it because he may have otherwise felt ashamed, as if it was charity. Rajputs had a lot of pride and we didn't want to fuck around with that, and besides, PT Shoe was like a brother.

Tinned fish was like an old friend. I had seen it ever since I could remember. About once a month, Papa used to bring home a couple of tins of sardines in oil or tomato sauce from a shop called East West Food Habits in Jodhpur Park. Sometimes, he would also get cans of tuna fish, in case Ma decided to really celebrate. The rest of the time we ate fresh fish bought from the big market in Gariahat, which Grandmother said we should be doing in the first place instead of trying to 'be like sahibs and eating things from tins'. Ma would tell her then, 'You won't understand,' and even Papa would look a little upset and tell Grandmother, 'Ma, what's the use of saying these things?'

Suman and I thought Grandmother was just jealous because she was a widow and couldn't eat non-vegetarian stuff but that couldn't have really been the case because Ma had an old aunt called Bibi who was widow but she ate meat and even smoked cigarettes. Bibi visited once a year and at those times Grandmother would stay in her room and refuse to come out, saying, 'I will not talk to people who do not know how to behave.'

People were so different, Suman would tell me, and I would nod my head like an old man, and say, yes, because Suman was right and I didn't know what else to say. But Grandmother was right about one thing. We did a lot of sahib-type things even though we were not Anglo, so I guess you didn't need sahib blood, the buggers could as easily get inside your head.

The late breakfast on Sunday was a feast, with perfect toasts, curls of butter, cheddar cheese, watery orange or tomato juice, baked beans, and sardines. It was the one time when my sister and I would be allowed to be pigs, using our fingers to soak up bits of toast with the oil or tomato sauce turned dark with Lea & Perrins Worcestershire sauce and flecked with bits of fish and boiled bone. All fish that came in cans was the same for Ma, and she took sardines, tuna, herring and mackerel and crammed all into a common, new species of fish for the table: 'tin fish'.

Then, it was time for toast with guava jelly, and coffee, while Papa played a Bert Kaempfert LP called 'A Swingin' Safari' in which I liked two numbers, 'Market Day' and 'Tootie Flutie', or an LP called 'Caribia', on the big Grundig stereo in the drawing room. Suman and I would be like zombies, bellies full, to notice how much we hated the music.

Papa would burp a little in satisfaction, not forgetting to cover his mouth, and Ma would beam and flutter her eyelids at him. Suman and I knew we could go off to the neighbours for much of the afternoon. Papa and Ma had other things to do, and no time for us. Their bedroom door would stay shut for the longest time, and we would hear the sound of 'The Mantovani Orchestra', or '50 Guitars of Tommy Garrett' playing on a small Grundig turntable music box that had pride of place on a desk in their bedroom. Some day, I decided, even I wanted a music thing in my bedroom.

Tin fish was always a symbol of celebration, and I never understood how fish stuffed in tins, all neat and orderly, sardines and mackerel in perfect rows and tuna in solid chunks that came away in perfect flakes like some one had blown a whistle and all the fish in the world had said 'Yessirverygoodsir' and had their heads and tails chopped off and then jumped neatly into tins and lay down in tomato sauce and vegetable oil after someone boiled the shit out of them, could make Papa and Ma and us so happy.

Maybe it was the whole ceremony of eating. There would be birthdays at home when Ma would open a tin of tuna, fry it in the pan, and then present an elaborate platter with potato chips, boiled carrots, beans and cauliflower, and a large hunk of bread. Of course, there would be Worcestershire sauce, and some Daw Sen's French mustard, HP sauce and Tabasco. For pudding, Ma would bring out some dark pink, strawberry-flavoured gelatine in a large glass bowl. This was jello, and we ate it with fresh cream. The same way all fish in cans was 'tin fish', all gelatine was 'jello', even though the packets said Wakefield or Rex, and Ma's youngest brother, Mamu, who worked for the American government, would lose his temper trying to correct her, telling her jello was really spelt Jell-O and it was a brand of gelatine, and by the way, could she also please stop calling the fridge 'Frigidaire', and gym shoes 'Keds'.

She would slap him playfully on the arm, and we would all laugh.

It amazed me how the English would look at Indians in the old days, rubbishing us mostly, especially the ones that wrote books during colonial times. The worst of the lot was Rudyard Kipling, whom I didn't like too much because he was always running down Indians and talking about how great the goras were, and he wrote so well it made his love for India and Indian chicks and contempt for other Indians very clear. He'd write about manners and try to say Indians didn't have any, except what they were taught by the goras, but I knew a lot of it was bullshit lobs because when this guy called General Dwyer had ordered Indian soldiers to fire on Indians in Jallianwalla Bagh in 1919 because they were holding a meeting to protest against a gora Act, all peaceful, just making speeches, he didn't ask them to go away or even clear his throat as a warning. He just shot hundreds of men, women and kids, many of whom had tried to escape by jumping into a well, but they had died there too. Rabindranath Tagore had returned his knighthood over it, but Mutt had told us in class 'nobody else had the balls to do anything.'

Mutt spoke that way whenever he was angry, which was often these days. He would drink and then fight with his wife a lot, the guys in Colvin House would tell us. One evening after dinner, Lucky, who was from our class, had come running and called us over to hear them fight, and we heard a lot of shouting, mostly Mutt yelling 'bitch' and there were glasses being smashed, and sounds of crying from inside from Mrs Mutt and their two children, who always slunk around school, as if afraid someone would point a finger at them and say, 'Ah, you're Mutt's kids, aren't you? Poor buggers.'

I think I didn't like Kipling more because he also wrote about how Indians pulled other Indians down. I couldn't deny it, because the stories we read in Hindi class by this really cat chap called Premchand were mostly about poor people who were jacked all the time by zamindars and other rich people, who never seemed to help them even when there was a famine and they were starving. There was also a lot about the trouble over marrying into different castes and religions like it was still the medieval times, and everybody, irrespective of how rich or poor, got trapped in this. The Hindi test papers would be full of questions like 'What is the purpose of the story, "Parda"?' which meant curtain, and I would dutifully write in my Sanskritized Hindi, 'The purpose of the story "Parda" is to illustrate the life of lower-middle-class people.' Sometimes, the poor and honest would win, and so I would describe the purpose of the story, 'Namak ka Daroga', the closest translation of which I could come up for Porridge, whose Hindi was worse than my Eskimo, was The Upright Policeman, and the purpose was, honesty and duty wins over bribery and corruption.

Premchand should have been on that bloody bus in Nalanda

with us, or at our home when the police beat the guys from Jadavpur University, I sometimes thought, and he would surely have written another story for us to learn and be tested.

The shit touched us too, in different ways. There was the way Bwana, the name we had given Fish's father because he had lived in Kenya for a long time and because Fish told us it meant 'boss' in 'ki-Swahili, not Swahili', reacted to Fish's friendship with Masuma, his girlfriend in Bombay. And even at home, Papa's family would always be running down Ma because Ma had a sister who had married a Muslim and that was some sort of huge sin. It was really difficult to figure out what was right and wrong, even with Hindus, forget about Hindus and Muslims. They were always very upset with Ma because Ma didn't come from a Brahmin family and that was supposed to be terrible because Papa's family were all Brahmins of a very high sub-caste—so there were higher Brahmins and lower Brahmins even among Brahmins. The Brahmins were also supposed to be fair, and the lowest in the order, the Shudras, were supposed to be dark, and I was Brahmin and dark, so what the bloody hell was going on?

I asked Papa once some years ago and he had looked serious and told me not to get upset about these things because they didn't make sense. Papa was right. It was all very fucked, and something had to happen soon to make it all right.

There was no getting away from Kipling & Co. The bugger's father, Lockwood Kipling, had been principal of the School of Art in Lahore, which was now in Pakistan, a country I knew nothing about except that India and Pakistan would keep fighting, and Mohenjo-Daro and Harappa, which were great Indus Valley Civilization sites, and Taxila, a great place of Buddhist learning, were all in Pakistan. It was like when the English had divided

India into India and Pakistan, they had deliberately kept what Indians wanted badly—their past—in Pakistan, and it hurt more because it was as if Pakistan didn't seem to give a shit about that history because they always acted, as we read in mags and papers, as if history began in 1947, when their country was born. I had even asked Mutt once if it was possible to go to see Mohenjo-Daro and the other places, and he had laughed and said 'Not in your lifetime'.

Anyway, old Lockwood had even provided the design for the Mayo Coat of Arms, which looked quite grand, with this Bhil tribal warrior and Rajput warrior standing on either side of a shield, which had the five colours of Rajputana, as Rajasthan was called in the olden days—red, gold, blue, white and green—which were also on the Mayo flag that flew on the Main Building and formed the right to left diagonal stripes on our navy-blue ties. On top of the shield was a peacock standing on a double-edged sword, which was called khanda, I read in the school mag, and below, on this grand scroll, was the school's motto: Let There Be Light, as if the goras were in the lighthouse business so we natives wouldn't trip in the dark and fall on our arses.

I had read all of Kipling's books, and so had Porridge, another big Kipling love-hate fan, the same as we were love-hate fans of P.G. Wodehouse and H. Rider Haggard, because they told stories so well, but acted as if they lived on the Planet of the Apes. The one that struck us most was a Kipling story, 'Beyond the Pale', from a book called *Plain Tales from the Hills*. I had copied some pages from the book and I would get very angry and sad reading it. The story opened with the lines, '*Love needs not caste nor sleep a broken bed. I went in search of love and lost myself*—Hindu proverb.'

Porridge and I thought Kipling was full of shit because nobody could tell us if there was really a 'Hindu' proverb like that, so Kipling may have been bullshitting, because who the hell was going to check? It wasn't like we could write him a letter and ask, 'Dear Mr Kipling, How are you? We are fine. Could you please tell us where you get your bloody ideas?' because Rudy, as we called him, had been dead for decades though his books still had the power to capture us and get us all freaked out.

Porridge had even suggested we try planchette, as we had read in a book by a guy called Count Cheiro, which I had picked up from Ma's collection of books and brought to school to show the guys. We wanted to call Kipling and really jack him with some tough questions. Fish thought it was a stupid idea, though PT Shoe said he would help us if after Kipling we agreed to call the ghost of his hero, Pratap Singh of Mewar, who had been among a few Rajput chiefs who stood up to the Mughal emperors when most other Rajput kings were arse-licking them so they could keep their kingdoms. He was a real big shot in history and was known as Maharana Pratap.

We had tried it once after lights out, shutting the door to the dorm, and used PT Shoe's chessboard, some coins Fish had from Sing and two pairs of small scissors, one mine and the other borrowed from Horsey. We must have done something wrong because even though Porridge kept intoning in a cracked voice, 'Mr Pratap Singh, can you hear us? Sir? Maharana?' and 'Mr Kipling, are you with us? Please, sir, give us a sign,' nothing happened. We tried it again, when PT Shoe raised a valid objection, saying that maybe we should invite Maharana Pratap in Hindi, because it was unlikely Indians knew English in the sixteenth century. Still nothing happened. The only sound we heard was our own tense breathing, and after five minutes of it Fish said, 'I have to go piss' and that was the end of that.

I would get really angry when I thought of the opening sentence of 'Beyond the Pale'—'A man should, whatever happens, keep to his own caste, race and creed'—because that is exactly what Papa's family would say, I told Porridge, and that was so wrong. Porridge understood what I meant because his dad was Catholic and had married a Protestant and his mom's people created trouble, and all because they went to different churches. They thought Catholics were 'primitive', Porridge said, because they worshipped the blood of Christ and also because—and this we knew from our history books—Protestants came about because Catholic popes were being nasty and converting people and torturing them, and they didn't like it. It seemed the old Protestants were a bit like the Naxals, and I decided to ask Papa about it next when we got a chance to talk. But it was all a long time ago, and we couldn't understand why this shit should be going on now because in the civics book it said the Indian Constitution guaranteed equality to everyone. People just didn't seem to care about the Constitution, which Mutt had told us once was the 'greatest rule book in the country'.

Porridge had underlined a section of the Kipling story with a pencil, which we knew was a wrong thing to do because it was a library book, but said he had done it so whoever read it next would know how idiotic the whole caste and religion thing was and also because he wanted to show it to PT Shoe, because PT Shoe was always going on about gora chicks and we were concerned for him.

I had copied the underlined sections at the back of my rough-use notebook. 'A week later, Bisesa taxed Trejago with the flirtation. She understood no gradations and spoke openly. Trejago laughed and Bisesa stamped her little feet—little feet, light as marigold flowers, that could lie in the palm of a man's one hand.

'Much that is written about Oriental passion and impulsiveness is exaggerated and compiled at second-hand, but a little of it is true; and when an Englishman finds that little, it is quite as startling as any passion in his own proper life. Bisesa raged and stormed, and finally threatened to kill herself if Trejago did not at once drop the alien *Memsahib* who had come between them. Trejago tried to explain, and show her that she did not understand these things from a Western standpoint. Bisesa drew herself up, and said simply—"I do not. I know only—it is not good that I should have made you dearer than my own heart to me, *Sahib*. You are an Englishman. I am only a black girl"—she was fairer than bar-gold in the Mint—"and the widow of a black man."'

I really hated that part, I mean, how dare Bisesa call herself 'only a black girl', and got really angry with Kipling and thought only a shit like him could have written this and 'Gunga Din', but I couldn't stop reading, like I hadn't been able to stop reading any book written by Kipling, they were so interesting.

The story got really sad after that. There was a beautiful part when Trejago and Bisesa's love went for a toss, because Bisesa's folks wouldn't stand for it. 'There was a young moon,' Kipling wrote, 'and one stream of light fell down into Amir Nath's Gully, and struck the grating which was drawn away as he knocked. From the black dark, Bisesa held out her arms into the moonlight. Both hands had been cut off at the wrists, and stumps were nearly healed.'

Bisesa reminded me of Ma. I sometimes wondered if Grandmother wanted to cut Ma's hands off, or at least wash her in bleach so she would become as white as bed sheets, because Ma was dark and not a Brahmin and, as Grandmother told her when she was angry with Ma, which was often, that she had 'brought shame to the family' and she must have 'done something' to Papa to make Papa fall in love with her and marry her when there were so many fair-skinned Brahmin girls ready to marry Papa because he came from a very good family and had lots of money.

Ma wouldn't cry, and kept quiet because she wanted to be strong for us, but I knew she was very angry and hated Grandmother. But for some reason Grandmother seemed to like me even though I was dark, but maybe it must have been because I was a boy and only boys could carry on the bongsho, as she had told me once many years ago, because lineage matters. That's when I thought Suman was lucky because she was fair like Papa, because being a girl *and* dark may have made Grandmother treat her the same way she treated Ma.

But I liked Ma because she never told us anything bad about Grandmother, which seemed like very good manners, and I wished Grandmother had such manners.

Pat finally let us in on the secret he and his roomie, Vicky, had been keeping to themselves. When PT Shoe had gone to borrow one of Pat's new porno mags, Pat, who was a year senior to us, had grandly said, 'This is nothing, man, just fucking pictures. I *know* what it's like. I laid a pross during the hols. You buggers land up after prep and I'll tell you about it.'

Prep was a daze once PT Shoe had whispered this to us. As soon as prep ended at 9 p.m., we ran to Pat's room. Pat, whom we called 'pondie king' had obviously planned the show-and-tell lesson. We knew it would be good because when Pat did something it was always interesting. The bugger had a good eye for these things, and if it wasn't for Pat, we'd have never seen our first gora boobs, *real* gora boobs, not the pondie stuff.

Some guys—four guys and four girls—from the United World College in Wales, had come to the school. They were much older than we were, almost like college people, and they were going around Indian schools as part of some programme or the other. The guys seemed nice enough and talked easily to us, but all of us were really leching at the chicks, because they were quite good-looking, and moved like real grown-up women. They were staying in Jaipur House and four rooms of the senior wing, beginning with Pat and Vicky's room and ending with Dango and Podgy's room, had been cleared for a week, and the guys had moved in wherever there was space. Bastard Pat had taken my bed, forcing me to crash on the floor on a spare mattress the farrash had brought.

But it had been a price worth paying, because of what happened at night after the show these UWC chaps had put up for us at the Pavilion, acting out and pretend-singing songs from a movie called *Grease* that none of us had seen because it had just been released abroad, but they had a tape of the songs and were playing it over the Pavilion sound system. Barry, one of the guys, had worn a really breeze leather jacket and danced to the music, screaming 'Grease lightnin' every now and then and did something like we had seen limbo dancers do in movies to this song which had a cat part where it kept going 'How low can you go?'

Pat had come charging in to the dorm where we were hanging around in our nightsuits, talking about the show and arguing over which chick was the best-looking, Lucy or Sally, and getting ready to crash.

'Buggers, come on,' Pat whispered, 'jaldi, jaldi, buggers, come *on*, the chicks' room windows are open!' We ran silently down the stairs and crept past the hedgerows behind the senior rooms. We got to the spot outside Pat's room where Vicky was crouching. Pat put a finger to his lips and got into a crouch cum duck-walk, towards a window. We followed, and then, poking up our heads slowly, we had seen Lucy and Sally in the small changing room where the cupboards were, sitting on a small bench and talking. Lucy was in her jeans, and wasn't wearing anything on top, and her boobs were not big but small, but really tight and nice, with pointed nipples.

'Fuck, they're pink,' Porridge had whispered, like he was Archimedes or something.

'Of *course* they're pink,' Pat had said, in a whisper that seemed like a kick on the arse. 'What do you think they would be, orange? Gora chicks have pink nipples, Indian chicks have brown to dark brown nipples and African chicks have dark brown to black nipples. You've seen it in my pondies already, bloody *idiot*.' That we had, so we also knew another fact: Chink chicks could have brown *and* pink nipples. Porridge was obviously not thinking any more.

We carried on looking. Then Sally took off her top, and we got a look at much bigger boobs, with pink nipples, as expected, before Pat and I moved left, to the loo window, leaving Porridge, Fish, Vicky and PT Shoe to look at Sally. We saw Lucy shut the door and start to take her clothes off. Frozen with hard-ons, we watched her bathe under the shower, soaping herself, the other guys suddenly crowding behind us, but she was turned a little away from us, so we couldn't see her pussy, only her back and arse, and a little bit of her boobs when she turned a little or raised her arms to soap herself.

'She's beautiful-ya,' Vicky hissed. Nobody disagreed.

Then, as soon as the show had begun, it ended, when Lucy turned the tap off and towelled herself, still turned away, wrapped the towel around her and walked back to the dressing room. By then we thought we had seen the best of the show and even though Pat whispered, 'Bugger, wait, let's see them through the bedroom window, maybe they're lesbians, maybe they'll screw each other.' But we were a bit scared and didn't want to take the risk of getting caught by the chowkidar or Chalu-Charlie, the House Master, who got that name because he was a king hockey player, pretending to fumble with the ball like he didn't know what he was doing only to totally fool the opposition with magic stick work and make complete arses of them. Housemaster, maths teacher *and* hockey wizard, we had a lot of respect for the bugger's tricks.

We went back to our dorms, our heads filled with Lucy and Sally, and boobs and nipples. Pat had stayed back, and when we asked him later at night if the chicks had really done something to each other, he wouldn't tell us, saying, 'You guys fucked off, why should I tell you?' and Vicky and he had grinned like mad. Pat was a real shit.

Pat's lesson began with mercury. Pat had filched some from the chemistry lab and was showing it to us, trying to create the proper mood by twisting the neck of a desktop lamp and focusing the light on his hands. The mercury quivered in his palm, and he raised it up, putting it just below his eyes. We edged closer.

'Guys, this is what pussy feels like,' declared Pat.

We dared not breathe. Pat's jaw had gone slack, his eyes had shut. He continued sliding the blob of mercury from one palm to another. 'It felt so good, maaaan. I'm going back to her next hols. That chick was fab.'

Pat had gone to Bombay with a cousin, and the cousin, who worked in a company that made commodes and basins, had taken him to get laid. As far as we could tell, none of us had cousins or even friends who would do that for us.

'But she was a pross, man,' said Fish. 'How will you find her? Bombay is a big place, like.'

'Up yours-ya. I *know*, okay?'

'Okay,' said Fish.

'Fawk,' said PT Shoe.

Pat's eyes opened, and he smiled at us. 'Want to feel it, huh? Want to feel some pussy? Try it no, bugger!'

I stretched out one hand and Pat gently transferred the mercury on to my palm. My mouth was dry and my head was throbbing. I just sat, frozen, feeling the slightly moist, slightly metallic and totally soft silvery blob sit quietly in my palm. I closed my eyes in worship.

That's when Porridge lunged. 'Show, show, bastard.'

The mercury was knocked out of my hand; it splattered against the wall and dropped to the floor in dozens of small blobs.

Pat snarled, 'Arsehole! I'll never give you guys my pondies fuck off,' and grabbed a notebook, and started to gather up the mercury with the cover. Vicky, who was laughing so hard he had rolled off his bed, shut up when Pat fixed him a murderous glare, and started to help. We left them like that, scrabbling around on their hand and knees, with Pat muttering, 'Bastards.'

'Pat's sick, man, a mad fucker,' Porridge said as we headed back to the dorm. 'I hope he gets his mercury back. Bugger's upset because he can't fuck his mercury.'

Fish was more philosophical, as always. 'I hope his prick gets mercury poisoning and falls off.'

PT Shoe had other things on his mind. 'How did it feel-ya, Brandy, what was it like? Did it feel like pussy?'

'Ya man, it really did,' I spoke like a pundit. 'Very silky.'

All night, I tossed and turned, wondering what it would really feel like. It *had* to be silky.

None of us had much of an idea about what we wanted to do or what we wanted to be, thinking in a way that, because we went to boarding school things would work out and we would manage to do something, get a job and all and be cats at what we did, you know? Except maybe Fish who, it seemed to us, had known what he wanted to do from the minute he popped out from Mrs Bwana, which is what we called his mother.

I mean, Fish just had to have come out kicking and screaming, then calming down and saying in this injured way, 'But I don't recall being invited.'

We had joked about it once when we had nothing better to do and were bored, and saying stupid things. We knew Fish was morbid anyway; he had even quoted Jean-Paul Sartre to us. He could pronounce Jean-Paul Sartre properly in the French way, which seemed to be a language that could only be spoken while standing on tiptoe and blowing through the mouth like a goldfish that had sucked on too much lemon. We called Jean-Paul Sartre 'Dr Jitendra Pal Sharma' to make him sound like one of the poets in Hindi we read in class, who only seemed to know two moods: depressing or patriotic.

Fish's favourite Sartre saying was, 'I hate my childhood and everything about it.' We weren't surprised.

Porridge, I decided, would have immediately asked his mother for a dash of milk for his porridge. 'Aye seh, Mother dear,' I said, 'may aye please hev a desh of milk?' imitating Vimal Sharma, an old boy who went to Oxford and had taught us English for a term and always acted like he had a cricket stump up his arse. We were laughing so hard, PT Shoe dropped the guavas he had collected the day before from the orchard near where old Jack Gibson, whom people called the greatest princi Mayo ever had, maybe the greatest princi in India, lived in retirement.

We had parked our cycles under a banyan tree behind the squash courts where we came to hang around once in a while, when we wanted to drop out of the world for a few minutes between games and dinner, or on Sunday mornings before breaker.

I was into the role. 'And PT Shoe, bugger,' I carried on between guffaws, 'bugger would have come out riding a stallion like Rana Pratap, waving a sword, screaming "Mughal dogs, I vow not to return to the womb till I have conquered you and driven you away from fair Rajputana."'

Porridge took it on from there. 'And Brandy, arsehole, would have popped out with a rose in his hand and told the nurse, "Won't you be mine, darling?"' Fish and PT Shoe hooted with laughter as Porridge had acted it out, using a bougainvillea stem for a rose.

Fish said, as we all doubled over, clutching our sides, that I had probably popped out with a frown and a red flag and said 'Cholbey na, hobey na'—won't do, can't do—like the protest marchers in Calcutta who were always stopping traffic and work.

I remember riding in the car to Dum Dum Airport with Papa one time. It was during the summer hols and I had come to see Papa off for his flight south to Madras and then to Coimbatore, where Ray & Company had started a new yarn factory because trade unions were making things difficult in the two factories our family had near Calcutta. I had heard Papa say businesses were shutting down or moving away from Calcutta because of labour trouble, and also because there never seemed to be enough electricity. Papa loved going to Coimbatore because he said the people in south India were really nice and the place was so clean, 'I wish we could bring some of those people over to Calcutta to teach the animals here some civic sense.'

This was high praise because Papa thought Bengalis were better than everybody else in just about everything, including destroying things, and called Bengalis the Holy Trinity of Hinduism—Brahma, Vishnu and Shiva—creator, protector and the destroyer, all in one, making the Hindu gods sound like the three-in-one that Jimmy, who was from Oman and was called Pele because he danced with the football, had in his room.

Just before the turning into Kazi Nazrul Islam Avenue, which everyone called VIP Road, and which went straight to the airport, the car had been stopped by a procession of people with what looked like thousands of red flags. The head of the procession was much in front and the leaders of the procession were usually the one who first said a line cursing someone before others down the line took up the chorus. But we saw people pass us by just shouting 'Cholbey na, cholbey na'. It made no sense, because that's all they said, as if they knew something won't do, but not exactly *what* won't do.

'Aja,' Papa had snarled, using the Sanskrit word for goat,

looking at his old Omega Seamaster watch with a snakeskin strap that my grandfather had gifted him when Papa went abroad for the first time, to England and Europe, in 1953. Papa always used Sanskrit words when he wanted to say something really rude in Bengali and didn't want others to understand, but sometimes he got into trouble because it wasn't like he was the only guy who understood Sanskrit, which some people called a dead language. Even I studied Sanskrit in school, and maxed the papers, which made Papa forget for a while that I had scored 8 on 50 in my first Chem test. Papa had reached the airport just in time that day, because Manohar-babu had driven the Ambassador Mark II like 'Stirling Moss', Papa said, and before he got off the car he had given Manohar-babu ten rupees as thanks.

We had retrieved the guavas after a while, and after dusting them with our hankies, finished them off. We were feeling good, four buddies just hanging around, the laughter making us feel like we were here with a purpose and everything was okay in the world. We felt like cats, and that was breeze.

After lining up to pee in the wheat fields, we had got talking about what we were going to do. Porridge wanted to join the World Bank, which only he seemed to know about, and said it was in DC; at least we knew what that meant. Some months ago I had slipped up and asked what DC meant, because the only DC that came to my mind at that point of time was the current, and AC/DC, which played really deadly rock. AC/DC, I also knew, were guys who laid chicks *and* guys, the greedy bastards.

'*Washington* DC,' PT Shoe had said, rolling his eyes, like he was a talking to a really dumb bugger. 'The capital of the United States of *America*, arsehole.'

Papa wanted me to join the Indian Foreign Service and

become a diplomat; I think because he had wanted to join the IFS, as everyone called it, and his father had forced him to join the business, he wanted to live his dreams through me. I had even tried it once, and wrote a letter to Tuby's dad who was posted in Tokyo, saying, 'Dear Sir, I want to join the Indian Foreign Service. Could you please tell me how?' I got a reply, but it didn't impress me too much because it told me to do what the whole bloody world was telling me to do: 'Study hard.'

Bugger the IFS, I really wanted to be a pilot, because I loved planes and knew the names of most fighter and civilian planes from the encyclopaedia Papa had gifted me for my birthday the year I left for boarding school; it was meant as a special gift to make me feel less sad as Grandmother had died while I was at school, and I had looked after it better than any other book I had because I thought it was my passport to another world. I knew I loved planes, but I was a little scared that I wouldn't make it because to become a pilot you needed maths, and I was not that good at maths, even though Chalu-Charlie always took time to help me. Chalu-Charlie was a really good guy. Once for a class test, I had forgotten how to measure the area of a trapezium, but I remembered how to measure the area of a triangle. So I had drawn two dotted lines, from the sides and extended them to form a peak, measured the length of the extended lines, and solved the problem in half a page, beginning with the line, 'Assume this is a triangle.' Chalu-Charlie had given me a duck, but had written on the test sheet, 'A for effort.'

Fish didn't need to say anything about what he wanted to do. We knew it well: Masuma, trekking, a hut in the Himalaya, teaching village children, and lots of babies. We were certain he would find a way to do it, as we were certain Fish would be the school captain from our batch because he was very cat about everything. What Fish wanted, Fish got. Just like that.

PT Shoe was clear he was going to America, and didn't 'give a bloody damn' about studies. He was totally taken up with stories about modern-day cowboys, we suspected, after seeing these stud-looking guys in the ads for Marlboro fags we saw in magazines like *Time* and *Sports Illustrated*, and dreamt of spending the rest of his life wearing a denim jacket, jeans and a Stetson hat, driving around in a small truck with a blond babe on his arm. 'I'm having blue blood,' he told us, 'those firang chicks are going to get damn freaked out when I tell them I'm a prince.'

We were dismissive of this blue-blood business, because when I had bashed Danny Singh during the inter-house boxing match in October, he had bright-red blood pouring out from his nose and from a cut under his left eye—and he had claimed to be a blue-blood though he didn't come from any of the princely states after which most of the houses in Mayo were named.

We knew PT Shoe had a crazy experience during the Dussehra hols the previous year which had confused the hell out of him. While Porridge, Fish, and I had gone off for a trek to a place near Manali, a town far away from Shimla where a lot of hippies went, PT Shoe had gone home instead, because his father's younger brother, whom he called Kakosa in the Rajasthani way, was back from his European holiday, which he took every year after harvesting eucalyptus trees. This Kakosa was a king mad bugger, because he was like the Rajput version of 'Dr Hyde and Mr Jekyll', PT Shoe had said, before we corrected him. When he didn't drink, Kakosa was like any other landlord or princeling-type Rajput who didn't sin any more than the average guy—he lorded over his tenants, and usually acted as if his family still ruled bits of India and Indira Gandhi hadn't fucked them by stopping huge amounts of pocket money they got from the government for what reason nobody knew, maybe because they had chosen to be with India and not Pakistan.

Sober, Kakosa would also be like most Rajputs, dignified and very polite, and would say the formal 'aap' for 'you' even to children, because that's the way manners were in Rajasthan, which was wonderful. Papa had once said that you could recognize well-mannered people because they would be polite even if they were very angry, and they treated servants well. If they had an Olympics for politeness, folks from Rajasthan, Rajputs included, would win the gold medal, I was sure. Kakosa was a handsome guy—PT Shoe had shown us some colour photographs, and we then really understood where he got his idea about jeans, jackets and Stetsons, because Kakosa always wore them, and the jeans were real Levi's, PT Shoe said, not number two stuff with a Levi's label, and the jeans were straight, like the cowboys in Marlboro ads, not bell-bots like the one I bought from Jean Junction in Cal, and Papa had been so upset because the flares were thirty-four inches and they would sweep the street as I walked, and he called me a clown. But Papa knew nothing about fashion. Kakosa even had a Land Rover, which we had all decided was the best car in the world, except maybe the Lamborghini Miura, a cutting of which Moses had pasted in his scrapbook.

But when he began to drink, Kakosa would become 'nutty', PT Shoe said. Sometimes he would begin drinking Old Monk rum well before lunch and carry on drinking till he had finished the bottle, which could take the whole day. One day, when PT Shoe had gone visiting Kakosa at his farm, a half-hour drive by jeep from PT Shoe's own place, Kakosa had been through half a bottle and he hadn't even started lunch. He was seated on a murha on the porch, below a stuffed leopard's head, the bottle of rum and glass on a small table by his side and the earthen matka of water on a stand next to that, his double-barelled twelve-bore gun across his knees. 'I toh shat, bugger,' PT Shoe said.

After asking if all was well in Mayo and if he had broken some legs playing hockey, to which PT Shoe had said he played cricket and Kakosa called it a 'pansy game', Kakosa had stopped talking and looked intensely at a goat that had strayed into the compound through a gap in the stone wall of the farm. Now, this was a sin, PT Shoe explained, as on no account should anything belonging to the tenant enter the master's house without permission. He had stopped talking as the goat, which clearly didn't realize it needed to ask Kakosa's permission, went this way and that, nibbling on the grass, probably quite happy that he was eating blue-blood grass.

After a while, Kakosa had uttered one word: 'Oyebloodybehnchod.' Then he had turned to PT Shoe and asked very politely in Rajasthani, 'Do you want non-veg for dinner?' And as PT Shoe had nodded, trying to please his uncle, Kakosa had picked up the gun and shot one barrel into the goat's head. They ate the goat for dinner, which Kakosa's bawarchi had turned into lal maas, this really king spicy goat meat curry. 'Fawk man, I couldn't eat that goat and I was almost puking but I thought Kakosa would kill me if I didn't eat.' We understood the last part, because hospitality is a big thing, we knew from our childhood.

PT Shoe then told us another story about Kakosa, which seemed like it was like a movie, a bit like *Sholay*, which we had all seen. It had this really cat daku, a bandit, called Gabbar Singh, who had this freaked out line where he said, 'Tera kya hoga, Kaliya?'—What will happen to you now, Blackie?—when some of his gang guys had failed to raid a village. Gabbar had shot Kaliya and two others after laughing like a hyena, and Gabbar always did what he wanted. What got us really worried about PT Shoe was when he told us how Kakosa loved gora chicks, and we had looked at each other without saying a word, because we could tell that while PT Shoe was totally pissed off with some things about Kakosa, he had a grudging admiration for his style.

Anyway, the story was that, one day, Kakosa, quite drunk, had roared into the village in his Land Rover and picked up three girls and brought them back home. He had then made these girls put on lipstick and make-up and some Western style dresses he had brought from London, and made them dance to some English pop songs on his tape recorder.

'Did he screw them?' Porridge wanted to know.

'He must have-ya,' PT Shoe had replied. 'He doesn't have a wife and all, so who's going to stop him?'

And there was a story about his wife too. PT Shoe had told us his aunt had died some years back, and the family gossip was that she had killed herself. But at least that was better than Kakosa's old driver, whose body was found, PT Shoe had told us, in a dry canal with twelve-bore pellets in his chest, but the doctor had written in the post-mortem reports, which we grandly called po-mo, that the cause of death was by drowning.

Kakosa seemed like a king arsehole. I was really happy this kind of guys didn't rule India any more—having a prime minister who got people beaten up, or one that drank his own piss like medicine like Morarji Desai, this really old man who had become PM after Indira Gandhi, was bad enough. These Kakosa-types and political-types also went around saying how great our culture and civilization were, which seemed like a waste of time because we knew it anyway from the books we studied, and all they talked about was the past, caste and religion, as if there was nothing else in India, as if they had no imagination and India had no future.

Man, if these guys thought like this and went around with guns in their hands *and* ruled the country, all of us would be fucked in no time.

Something was wrong, I knew it the minute I had stepped off the train onto the platform, and saw Papa's youngest sister, Jolly-pishi, waiting for me. Her husband and her daughter Roma were there, too. No Papa or Ma. This was unusual, because one or the other would always be there to see me off or receive me; Suman never came to see me off after the first time, sometimes because she had school, but mostly because she would start crying just before I boarded the train and it would make us all feel terrible—not just me, but all the kids going away from home. We could all do without the extra pressure. It was bad enough that we had to act big in front of each other and in front of our parents. Tears would make it a really bad scene. But Suman was usually there when I came back; now there was no Suman, and no explanations. Something was wrong.

I played it cool-breeze, as if my parents and sister not being there was all right, commonplace. Roma waved shyly, Jolly-pishi walked up to me and gave me a big hug, while her husband, whom I called Jolly-pishemoshai, which was much easier than trying to remember his name, got busy haggling with the coolie to take my luggage to the car. We all crammed into the old Ambassador, the light gray car I had seen from the time we used to visit the big bicycle factory near Asansol where Jolly-pishemoshai was some hotshot manager and had this sprawling house.

Pishemoshai was driving, and it was a colourful experience as always. Between the time he drove out of the drive-in parking at Howrah Station to time we had crossed the Howrah Bridge over the Hooghly River into Calcutta, he had said 'gadha', ass, and 'shuor', pig, numerous times, to a range of offenders including two bus drivers, one taxi driver, two pedestrians, and one cow, which decided to cross the street when we drove up, and then decided to stop and turn its head towards us. 'Ass,' growled Jolly-pishemoshai to the cow, which looked at him with total disinterest, contentedly chewing cud, while the stalled traffic behind us went crazy, honking loudly. Just as I thought Jolly-pishemoshai would have a fit, the cow decided to move on, heading towards the flyover that cut through Burrabazar.

'Pig,' he spat. Pishi, sitting by his side, jabbed him in the ribs, so he shut up and drove.

'When are you going back?' Pishi asked me.

'Fourteenth January, Pishi,' I said, 'School is opening a little late for spring term, on the sixteenth.' I didn't mind 1978 beginning a few days later in school. It would give me more time to pig out on Ma's cooking and stock up, like camels stocked up on water.

'Good, you'll be here for Christmas,' Pishi said. 'We must all go for a picnic, maybe to Barrackpore, by the river.'

'Yes Pishi, that'll be nice.' She made super sandwiches and lemonade, and I was sure Ma would bring along some tin-fish miracle. Pishi was nice. She always gifted me Time-Life books ever since she caught me leafing through some at her house many years ago, and seemed to be the only elderly female relative who didn't grab my chin and say 'See how big he has become, he was just a boy the other day' every time she saw me. Pishi was among a few of my father's relatives I didn't feel like strangling instantly.

The drive to Jodhpur Park took almost two hours. The only time the traffic moved at any speed above a crawl was on Red Road, near the maidan, which Papa had told me had been used as an emergency runway for fighter planes during World War II, when Calcutta was within range of Japanese bombers. Throughout the drive, in the back seat Roma held tightly on to my hand. I liked Roma. The previous summer, she had lent me a Bengali literary magazine with some really hot stories, and never told anyone about it. It was our secret. I knew she must have read the magazine, surely taken from Jolly-pishemoshai's collection, and she knew I knew, but we gave each other the respect of privacy. We were friends. She would hold my hands and it was all nice and proper and didn't get me all breathless like I got when I held Neelu's hands—Neelu, the daughter of my mother's youngest sister Milly, who lived in London, and it was always interesting when she visited. But... I shook my head, no thoughts of Neelu now, not while holding Roma's hand.

Jolly-pishi talked non-stop. Pinku was now a proud father of a baby boy, Amy-di had gone to Kedarnath for a pilgrimage, 'just like your trek, Barun'. Smiling, I thought to myself that it couldn't possibly have been anything like the trek I had been on only a couple of months back during the Dussehra break in the middle of autumn term, with Porridge, PT Shoe and Vicky; no Fish, because Fish was busy practising for swimming nationals.

Our parents had given us permission to travel without supervision. All we had to do was get our equipment checked by Rat, who was a great trekker and was taking along a bunch of Class 8 kids, and meet Rat in Kedarnath. Ma had been really happy to hear I was going to Kedarnath, where there was a temple to Shiva, thinking I had finally become civilized because I was going to one of the holiest places in India. It hadn't mattered at all to us because as far as we were concerned it would be the first time we would be allowed out alone, big boy stuff, taking the Jayanti Janata Express to Delhi and then taking a bus from there north to Haridwar and then the hill bus from Rishikesh to Sonprayag, with people puking all over the place while others, including us, sucked madly on bits of lemon we had taken from a roadside chai-wallah. From there we would trek the nineteen kilometers to Kedarnath, 3583 metres high, right in the middle of the Himalaya. Cat.

Feeling like kings, 250 rupees each in our pockets, we hadn't even felt the journey until we reached the holy city of Haridwar, where the Ganga enters the plains, and where fucking bed bugs kept me up through the night in a dharamshala, like pilgrims, and PT Shoe and I had smoked Cool Menthol sticks through the night because he also had a bed bug crawling all over, while Porridge and Vicky slept like dogs. We had finally taken off our clothes and located the bugs when they started their bloody crawl—thank god they hadn't bitten our prick and balls—and flushed five of them, two from me and three from PT Shoe, down the adjacent stinking, shit-streaked Indian-style toilet yelling 'Bugger off' and 'Fuck off'.

That had woken the other two, and they had looked worried for a while before bursting into laughter at the circus PT Shoe and I were putting up. Just so that our trip wouldn't be cursed, Porridge had suggested we donate generously to the dharamshala, so we had put twenty rupees in the donation box for staying one night, which I thought was a lot of money to bribe god with because it was almost *two month's* pocket money. Porridge had also suggested we take a dip in the Ganga to wash off our sins, and maybe the dip in the holy river that looked much cleaner in Haridwar than when its distributary became the Hooghly in Cal had worked, because none of us got a single blister on our feet even though we wore new Hunter boots and even though we ate luncheon meat for a snack at Gandhi Sarovar, a beautiful blue lake named after Mahatma Gandhi high above the holy spot of Kedarnath, before a short trek to Mandakini Glacier. We had later gone to the temple, and Shiva had not rained lightning onto our heads or poked us in the bum with his trishul, thank god, and there was something to the place that made us all stay quiet and walk dutifully around the ancient stone temple with the fantastic Kedar Peak in the background. It was the same feeling I got when Ma would take Suman and me to the huge St Paul's Cathedral in Calcutta and we would sit quietly in the back pews and look at stained glass windows and the statue of Christ at the far end.

At the end of the trek we had spent the night in Gaurikund, from where we would begin our descent into the plains, soaking our feet in the sulphur spring there, smoking Cool sticks like we were kings. We even had some money left over with us to buy hot dogs and Big Boy burgers at Nirula's in Connaught Place before taking the train from Delhi back to Ajmer.

I didn't think old Amy-di, a distant relative of Papa's, would have a similar trek, because she was over sixty and would have been carried on a pony. And she was going for a pilgrimage before she died and faced god, while we had gone because it was our rite of passage. In these books by Leon Uris, which were only about how Jewish people got fucked by everybody, I had read about how Jewish boys celebrated 'Bar Mitzvah' when they turned thirteen. Kedarnath was like our Bar Mitzvah, our trip from 'U' to 'A', you know?

Jolly-pishi was going on about Karna, my cousin, going away to London to study maths in college, and other family bits. 'You missed Ranjan's wedding, it was really grand,' she said, talking about a distant relative who was some sort of star in Bengali films, but nobody in the family seemed to have seen any of his movies. 'There was a grand dinner at the skating rink, and there were ice skaters who danced to Elvis Presley and these modern Hindi movie songs.' Yuck, I thought.

But I kept quiet, and the more I didn't respond, the more Pishi would talk in a high-pitched voice, while Roma's grip grew firmer the closer we got to home. If PT Shoe were here, I thought with a smile, even as my stomach knotted with fear and sadness, though I didn't exactly know why, he would have asked the perfect question for the situation: 'What the fawk?'

We turned into the driveway. Papa, Suman and Moyna-di stood at the top of the stairs. Papa had his hand on Suman's shoulder, and she was hugging Moyna. Gentle Parbati-di the cook was standing a little to the side, her widow's sari in white wrapped around her tiny body. She always reminded of an insect wrapped in a cocoon, but she made a king prawn curry with coconut milk and mustard, and potatoes with khus khus, two of my favourite dishes.

I knew it then: Ma had died.

I smiled at Roma, and got out of the car, and walked up the steps to Papa, Suman and Moyna-di, and we all went in. The drawing room was the same, with low sofas and a Japanese table in the middle, the Grundig system still had Ma's bonsai on top, and the weird-looking black lamp stand which had beautifully carved figurines like in the temples, stacked one on top of the other, ending in a pagoda-type lampshade, and the heavy brass ashtray that Papa told me was actually a Tibetan demon, and it had blue and red beads stuck into little holes in its body and eyes, and its belly was the ashtray. But I didn't see Ma's showcase with all the small bottles and wondered where it had gone. We went down the hallway, past the dining room, and into Grandmother's old room, which Ma used as her workroom after Grandmother died. I saw Ma's showcase there, kept by the side of the door, across from the bed. Ma would sit on that bed, the bed of her former tormentor, and knit, or read books and magazines like *Reader's Digest* and *Woman and Home*.

Papa made me sit on the bed. Suman and Moyna-di came and sat next to me, and both were crying. I looked up, and saw Ma smiling inside a white frame on the wall, with her pointed 1960s glasses and hair done like an actress, below the framed photographs of my grandparents, forming a triangle of dead people with garlands on them. In less than six months since we last met during summer hols, Ma had become a photograph.

Papa kept standing, and in a gentle voice told me about how Ma had been diagnosed with stomach cancer three months earlier, and it was really painful and she would cry at night, sometimes calling my name. The doctors had said there was nothing they could do, so they just gave her strong injections to reduce the pain. Moyna-di had looked after Suman, telling her stories and helping with homework. Just before Ma died in November, she used to ask for me a lot and made Papa promise her he wouldn't stop Suman or me from becoming anything we wanted to be.

'Why didn't you tell me?' I screamed at Papa, really angry with him.

'Your mother said not to tell you because you were far away and would get very upset. She also asked her brothers and sisters not to come. She said there was no point, she wanted you all to remember her as you last saw her.'

Mothers are so stupid, I thought. So stupid to think they could make it all right for everyone, even if they couldn't make it all right for themselves. Stupid, *stupid* Ma. How *dare* she?

They were all waiting for me to start crying, but I was very angry with Ma, and didn't feel like crying. I just got up and went out of the house. Nobody tried to stop me. I went to the lakeside, found an empty bench and sat there, looking at nothing. Roma had followed me there, I realized after some time, and sat silently at the other end of the bench. I don't know how long we were there, but it was getting dark, and she took my hand and walked me back home.

I woke up in the middle of the night. Moyna-di and Suman were asleep on the other bed. Through the open door, I could hear Papa snoring. The light in the hallway was on, and I got out of bed and went to the room that now resembled a morgue, a room full of dead people. Ma's showcase was still full of bottles. I knew where she kept the key, in Grandmother's cupboard, on the shelf next to the locker.

I opened the case, and started taking out the bottles one by one. I counted them; there were 216, ten more than I had seen during the last summer hols. I peered at the bottles and saw quite a few were empty and wondered if Ma had drunk some herself to lessen the pain of her cancer. I had no idea how painful it could be. The most pain I felt was when I had cut my arm on the broken glass on top of the wall at the back of the house, when I had slipped from a branch of a guava tree, where I was sitting and smoking a stick of Chinar. My arm had slit from the elbow almost to my wrist and I had gone running, screaming, into the house. Grandmother was the only one at home, Papa, Ma and Suman had gone out somewhere, I can't remember where, and she had come out of her room, eyes widening at all the blood pouring out. She stopped when she smelt the cigarette on my breath and slapped me once, before wrapping the end of her sari around my arm, and taking me into her bathroom. There, while I stood crying with her spotless white widow-sari turning red with my blood, she grabbed a bottle of Dettol, took my arm out and poured the antiseptic on it. I had screamed loud enough for a policeman from the station across the street to come and ask what was going on. He had helped us get on to a rickshaw and Grandmother had taken me to a doctor down the road. That doctor had put stitches on me, just like that, no anaesthetic, and I had screamed again, almost fainting with the pain. But I had lived, and Ma was dead, so her pain must have been more than mine.

I looked up and saw her in the photograph, looking better than I had ever seen her look. All her life, she and Grandmother had tried to stay away from each other just like two people who really hated each other would try to do, and now that both were dead, they were just a few inches from one another and they couldn't get away unless someone moved them. I could imagine them fighting with Narayan, the god they both loved so much, begging him to start an earthquake or something, so they wouldn't have to stay on the same wall. I thought it was quite possible they would destroy the house if it meant they could get away from one another. Even if they didn't manage to do it while alive, I wasn't so sure they wouldn't do it now that they were dead.

The huge iron almirah was in the same place. Grandmother's parents had given it to her for her marriage in the 1920s, so it was really old. Ma had put her personal things in there after Grandmother died. Papa had never said anything, as if it was okay for the new lady boss to take over things that belonged to the old lady boss. The key was in the lock, and I opened the door handle with a clang, but the door did not creak even after all these years. Ma's best saris were all there, and the photo albums, but I didn't want to look at them.

I was about to shut the door when I saw a notebook lying on the shelf next to the locker. It was the same tattered, moth-eaten one that Ma wouldn't let any of us touch, saying we would ruin it because handling brittle paper was difficult. I was always fascinated by it, as if it came from another time, which it did. It had a black cover and on it was written Universal Exercise Book, and, below that, A.C. Paul, Paper Dealer and Stationers, Calcutta. Inside, pasted on yellowing pages were these neat clippings of recipes and tips from what seemed like ancient newspapers.

The first one that caught my eye was 'Alsatian Hors D'oeuvre', because the only Alsatians I knew were these fierce dogs. Jollypishi used to have one called Rudolf, who was so big that Roma and I used to respectfully call him Rudolf-da. So I wanted to know what an Alsatian Horse Doovery was, without understanding what an apostrophe was doing in the beginning of a word, even though I knew it was in French so it must make sense. Alsatian Horse Doovery, it turned out, was a list of fancy snacks:

Sliced tomatoes, peas and mayonnaise, decorated with sliced, stuffed olives.

Small pieces of smoked salmon, cut wedged shape and placed on a piece of bread the same size. Sardines, laid on each side, garnished with bits of lemon.

Thin pieces of paté on lettuces with bits of smoked salmon.

Mussels in white sauce.

Salmon decorated with slices of gherkins and olives.

Sliced, hard-boiled eggs garnished with bits of tomato and caviar.

My eyes had started to mist as I turned the pages. You know the feeling. First, the chest goes tight and starts to act like a pump and slowly pulls in the all the water from every part of the body and it collects in the stomach like in a reservoir. And then all this water slowly travels up as more water is pumped in, and the head, hands and feet feel like they are empty and on some other planet, and the water slowly rises, filling the lungs and choking the throat, and it feels like drowning and it feels strange to drown on dry land. And still the water rises up through the nose and keeps climbing till the eyes begin to wet, and then a stubborn drop of water goes knock-knock who's there and breaks out of the eyes and brings other drops with it like they're bloody holding hands and going on a picnic and makes the drowning water run like water from a dam, not caring that there is nobody there to open the fucking gates. And it keeps going over the lip of the dam because the water has too much energy to stop, momentum equals mass into speed, too full of the water it has taken from body parts that by then are definitely somewhere beyond the Asteroid Belt.

I came to something called TO REMOVE BLACKHEADS:

'...after five or ten minutes of steaming the blackheads may easily be pressed out, and then a little eau de Cologne should be rubbed over the places to close the pores again. To prevent blackheads (often due to excessive tea-drinking), use the following lotion: 1 oz. tincture of witch hazel, 30g boraic acid, and 6 oz. rose water.'

I started to cry.

Papa came in. He must have woken up when I opened the almirah, and must have been standing there all along, watching me. He came towards me and put out his arms, and I clung to him as I sobbed my heart out, because I had lost Ma, who had always been strong and been a friend in her own way, but I took care to first close the notebook so my tears wouldn't muck it up, and gently place it on the bed. Papa's chin was digging into the top of my head, and after some time, I found my hair getting wet because Papa was crying too.

Things weren't going too well for me. I didn't feel like writing home at all, because I didn't know what the bloody hell to write, and I stopped trying after the day I tore up maybe five of those twenty-paise inland letter cards before deciding it was a waste of money, thinking that writing on pages torn from my notebooks and then putting a letter in a twenty-five-paise envelope would be a better thing to do, because I just couldn't get beyond 'Dear Papa and Suman, how are you? I am fine.' I knew I wasn't fine, and I was so tired of pretending to be fine, something that a 'future leader of India' was supposed to do without any problem, keeping your chin up when you thought the world was shitting all over you. Part of that training was to not be a pansy and cry over every little thing, but I wasn't sure about anything any more.

I wondered what boys in Eton would do at a time like this, I mean, would they cry like bloody fools or would they still act all haw-haw, even if their mother had died and they lived in a country where people were poor and fighting all the time. But I didn't know, and could only wonder if we were really like Eton boys, because we didn't, as Yogi said, go around saying 'I seh old chap' and 'spot of bother' when things went wrong for us.

Fish and I had talked about it one day, debating about this guy Macaulay, who said in the nineteenth century that to hold on to the Empire the goras needed to 'create a class of people—Indian in Blood and Colour but English in opinion, in morals and in intellect', as we had read in a book. As usual I tried to debate the point, which Fish said was 'such a bloody Bongo thing to do' and closed the discussion with 'I don't know about *you*, Brandy bugger, but *I* am a bloody Indian, okay? *Fuck* bloody Macaulay.'

Papa seemed to be having some trouble writing to me as well, as if he were a bit lost. His letters began with 'My dear Barun' and then went on to idiotic things like 'I hope your studies are going well and you are still in the First Court of tennis' and 'Suman is fine, we are both fine', and I knew he was lying because how could anyone be fine when he took care not to mention a word about Ma in any letter he wrote? I knew he was trying to be, you know, nice to me, but it was unnatural to not have any word of Ma, his *wife*, bugger it, and *my mother* and friend, and Suman's too, I knew, because two summer hols earlier Suman had her first periods and she was so afraid that she had come out of the loo and gone running to Ma, and Ma had taken her to her room and shut the door but that didn't stop me from standing outside, trying to listen. I heard Ma talk to her as Suman cried, saying, 'Don't cry you silly girl, this happens, don't worry, it happens to girls', in this soothing voice she had last used when we were a lot younger and would go to her if we had nightmares or there was a big storm or we had covered ourselves with bed sheets and pretended to be ghosts in a darkened room but were too scared to sleep because our own ghosts would come back to haunt us.

Suman had changed after that, became more sure of herself and didn't always ask me about things like she used to, like a younger sister would a big brother, but acted like she was almost my equal even though I was two years older. That was breeze with me because I felt I could talk to her about things like studies and games and even war and politics because now she was becoming a woman from a little girl, the same as we had learnt would happen in bio class, but it was so different seeing it in front of your eyes even though we knew how the machine worked.

Actually, I thought she was quite lucky because something had actually happened to mark her growing up, periods and breasts and all, but guys seemed to have nothing to mark their growing up besides tons of hard-ons and some sad-looking bits of hair on the face, like a baby Fu-Manchu or something. Papa or Ma had never explained anything about growing up to me. Birds flew about just like always and bees usually stung the shit out of me, like when I got attacked by wild bees on a hike to the tiny valley behind Taragarh Hill and saved myself from being hurt more by jumping into a shallow pool where there were more frogs and moss than water. But I still had got stung quite badly, maybe twelve or so all over the body and head but not my face, thank god. I had stripped to my undies on the roof of the small hut the caretaker of the farm in the valley had and felt around my body, taking out these big, ugly purple stings with hooks at the end, which tore out some flesh and skin when I pulled them out.

Some of the luckier guys who had gone on ahead had laughed at my undies, the bastards, which had the British Union Jack on it, and I also had one with the American flag, which my cousin Neelu's mom would buy at Marks & Spencer in London and send to me to school in a parcel with lots of stamps on it, and I always gave Moses the stamps. But the guys stopped laughing when Maindak was carried to the roof, screaming with pain and almost fainting, and we could see why, because while we had run ahead or jumped into the pool, bloody Maindak had squatted and pulled his PT singlet over his head in protection. When Bunter yanked his shirt over his head, we could see Maindak's back covered with stings. It looked like a garden in spring with pretty little white flowers. We all had to help carry him back to the tonga stand on the other side of Taragarh, near the dargah to this famous Muslim saint, Moinuddin Chishti, and Maindak was in hospi for a week with drips sticking out his hand at all times. It was the only time ever that I felt even a little bad for Maindak.

For birds and bees we made do with whatever we could from books and Pat's pondies and generally acting like despos, like we did when Mary's folks drove down to school in this breeze yellow Merc and his sister stepped out of it near the Mess just before lunch and I think everybody in Jaipur, Colvin, Bharatpur and Kashmir Houses dropped their books in shock and instantly fell in love with her, and some despo guys like Funda and Cutlet from Colvin House who had never even spoken to Mary went up to him and said, 'Hello Amar, we're so glad your parents are finally here, it's a pleasure to meet them, and perhaps this is your sister, how nice,' the bastards. At lunch, it was like the whole Mess, fifteen rows of guys had their eyes on Mary's sis, forgetting the rice and minced-mutton curry and bread pudding.

I knew that I shouldn't write anything about Ma to Papa and Suman for a while, until all of us had got used to her not being around, but it was getting really difficult to pretend she wasn't in my head. She would knock politely but insistently, exactly like when she was alive, and would want to come into my head a lot, and then I didn't feel like studying or playing or hanging around with the guys. So I stopped writing letters home, and wouldn't reply to any of Papa's letters until one day he wrote to Chalu-Charlie and Chalu-Charlie asked me to see him.

I thought he would yell at me, because he had already told me I was not paying attention to my appearance, and I knew that was happening because even the guys had pointed it out to me. PT Shoe said one day, 'Brandy, man, your shoes are fawking really dirty-ya' and I thought PT Shoe was being crazy as usual about clean shoes, till old Croc, the bastard Housemaster of Jodhpur House who was also the Squash Master and Princi's younger brother as well, had smashed the handle of my Dunlop racquet on the back of my thighs as punishment for wearing dirty PT shoes at games. He hit me so hard the wooden shaft broke near the head and had burst a big fat boil full of puss on my bum. It had hurt like mad and the purple bruise had stayed for a month. I hadn't made a noise, just got really angry, borrowed Maggu's racquet and pasted Moses 9-0, 9-4 while grumbling to him, 'Does the bastard want me to learn squash or bloody wear clean bloody shoes?' and Moses grinned and looked nervous at the same time and maybe he was nervous because all the puss and red-brown blood was running down my leg. But PT Shoe had a point, because my black shoes were scuffed these days as well, which had got me some football kicks on my arse after Assembly from school monitors, and one was so hard that I had gone flying from Stow's painting all the way to the marble fireplace halfway down the Assembly Hall. But I didn't care. I didn't care at all.

I got angry a lot after Ma died, and the guys were really worried, and Fish even told me to do something to 'cool the anger' in his Buddha way, saying I should do something like he did his swimming, so I took to running, and boxing, which Ma had made me promise I would never do, but it was better than punching the wall in the dorm, like I had done one day after lunch, the day when the story by Pearl S. Buck, *The Good Earth*, which I could practically recite, had disappeared from my head when Yogi asked me to verbally precis the moral of the story. I had stood looking down, my ears burning while Groovy and Jam, with whom I had fought for top marks in English since ages, sniggered. I wanted to hit them. Instead, I had taken it out on the wall of the dorm near the foot of my bed, and Fish and Porridge had pulled me away and forced me to sit down, asking the chaps from other dorms to bugger off for a few minutes, while PT Shoe went and got his bottle of Dettol and poured the disinfectant over my bleeding knuckles. I had welcomed the screaming sting of the liquid, and taken it without flinching. Like, fuck the whole world.

The guys were worried, I could see, especially as I hadn't been going for the Saturday movie for four weeks or so, which was unusual for a movie nut like me, but they didn't bring anything up because it was a private thing, and they knew if I wanted to talk I would, the same way we didn't bring up Bwana, or Porridge's Catholic versus Protestant World War I, II and III and the pretty nuclear mushroom cloud at home between his dad's people and his mom's, or PT Shoe's folks thinking he was a pansy because he wouldn't hang around with BB-types, our code name for blue bloods.

'Come in Barun,' Chalu-Charlie said. 'Please take a seat.'

I sat on the brown Rexine sofa with white lace covers, and looked around as Chalu-Charlie sat across me on the single sofa and looked at some papers. There was a Pan Am calendar on the wall near me, with a smiling stewardess, who reminded me of the face of the chick on the book I had fished out from Papa's cupboard a couple of hols ago called *Coffee, Tea or Me,* a breeze book about these stewardesses screwing all over the place, and even up in the sky. Below the calendar was a framed, signed photograph of the Duke of Edinburgh, who looked like a boiled egg with a long nose. Chalu-Charlie had met him once in London on a trip sponsored by the Duke of Edinburgh Award Scheme, of which Chalu-Charlie was administrator. Next to that, on a dark wood cupboard was a framed print of Mary and baby Jesus, like they were equal to Old Boiled Egg.

On the wall on the opposite side was this hideous clock that reminded me of a black widow spider I had seen in books, only that it had twelve gold and black legs, one for each arm of the hour, with a fat, round body in the middle. In the corner near the kitchen was a Leonard fridge painted green, with a cut-glass vase on it which had fresh roses from the House garden in them, like the fridge was part of the furniture and very breeze décor instead of being a machine that kept food from going bad. The small table between us had a big photograph of the family in a metal frame with lots of flowers, with Charlie-ma'am and their daughter Christine, all smiling, looking very hep in colourful sweaters and woollen caps, posing on ponies in front of a church. It said in a black scrawl at the bottom of the photograph. *A Happy Family, the Mall, Shimla, 22.5.76.*

I wanted to ask if they stayed at the Grand Hotel, but didn't, thinking he might get embarrassed in case they stayed somewhere not as nice as that. Chalu-Charlie, wearing his tweed jacket with a leather elbow patch, looking quite cat in a handlebar moustache like Dennis Lillee, the king pace bowler from Australia, saw me looking at that and snapped his fingers to get my attention. He was waving some of my test papers. He had my attention.

'You're slipping up, Mr Ray, you need to really buck up now, pull your socks up, keep your chin up.' He had a habit of saying 'up' a lot when he gave lectures.

I didn't say anything.

'Your father has a lot of hopes for you, Barun. I'm sure your mother had too. You can't let them down.'

I still didn't say anything.

'Getting angry won't help. Your Yogi-sir and some others have been telling me about your behaviour in class. What's the problem, young man?'

'Nothing sir,' I finally managed. Christine went into the kitchen, with a quick look at us.

'Well, something is the problem, chap. See this.'

It was green, a mid-term report. Shit. I read it. All comments had me going down, so I could see why Chalu-Charlie was going on about me needing to go 'up'. The 'good' and 'satisfactory progress' remarks had almost all turned 'average' and 'can do better' and 'inexplicable slip', except for Work Experience, which for me was music, and I had been playing the sitar like it was a friend. The world would disappear as soon as I slipped the mizraab on my forefinger, rested my elbow on the dried pumpkin shell of the base and placed the tip of my left forefinger, calloused from the cuts from pulling and sliding down the string, and sometimes I would play without the tabla accompaniment, because I would keep rhythm with the beat in my head, loud and alive. That escape got me 'A'.

Chalu-Charlie then handed me two notes. One was a handwritten one from Princi to him, in Princi's neat handwriting, which was less ornamental than Papa's. 'Mr D'Costa, I have recently been receiving adverse comments about Barun Ray's performance and conduct. I have seen some of his tests and talked to his teachers and it appears Barun has not shown any progress though he does seem quite capable. Not working hard enough probably. Will you please look into it and have a word with the boy?'

The other was a letter from Papa to Chalu-Charlie. It began with a crib about how I wasn't writing and asked if all was well, and could Mr D'Costa please look into it, because Barun 'is my only son'. Damnbuggershit. 'Barun's conduct had always been good and he has always tried hard to prove himself. But I fear something is troubling him greatly, and I am not, despite being his father, able to do anything from this great distance. I will be very grateful if you could look into the matter. Mr D'Costa, Barun is my only son.'

Chalu-Charlie must have seen the anger on my face, and I was really angry, thinking I will bloody well never write at all to Papa, but maybe to Suman after some time. Chalu-Charlie asked me to drink the apple juice Christine had left for me on the table between us, which I did, and he told me a story.

'When I was much younger, even younger than you are now, I would hate it when people called me maka or half-breed'. This was deep, I knew, because it was slang we used for Christians and Anglos. 'Some kids would call me fifty-fifty, even some grown-ups. I hated them, and wanted to hit everyone. I would get into fights all the time. We were in Kanpur and my parents even thought of sending me away to a seminary to become a novice priest when my behaviour got from bad to worse.'

I was listening with total attention. This was better than any movie.

'Then a Jesuit priest who was a teacher in our school talked to me like we are talking now. He told me to forget what people said and pick something to do so it gives my mind a holiday for a while. "You can't let anger get the better of you," he told me, and I will tell you the same thing today Mr Barun Ray.'

'What did you do?' I asked him.

'I took up boxing,' he said, smiling. 'Serious boxing. I was even in the nationals.' We never knew, because Chalu-Charlie was such a docile chap, only making fools of people in the hockey field. 'It's better than hitting walls, young man.' Fuck, I thought, this guy knows everything about us.

'Barun, I know it must be very difficult for you without your mother, but please promise me that you will try hard and get your report card back in shape. Buck up, okay?'

I had nodded my thanks, and I had taken to boxing like my life depended on it, and maybe it did, and picked bigger, heavier boys to fight with, like I had something to prove. So when I bashed Danny Singh in the inter-house, Danny who was going for School Colours, punching him with a series of left-rights in the first fifteen seconds of the first round before he could even get his guard up properly, because the bastard had been overconfident and I had put my life into it like I had nothing more to lose, Chalu-Charlie would have to share part of the responsibility for showing me a way to direct my anger.

I had practised practised practised, badgering Lolly, the boxing captain, that I wanted to fight with boys in a heavier weight category, and hadn't cared when some of them beat the shit out of me. I would pick myself up from the floor and charge back into them—like, fuck you guys, you can't put me down—and after a few days they would see me like that, wild, and forget to keep their guard up and back away sometimes.

It felt viciously good, especially when Moses and PT Shoe, my seconds, hugged me and carried me off from the ring with guys screaming my name, like I was a condemned man who had suddenly come back from the dead, as Maindak had announced just before the bout, coming into the room inside the Pavilion like a snake and trying to make me feel more funked than I already was, because Danny was one of the best boxers in school.

'Danny will R.I.P. you bastard behnchod,' Maindak had said, as I stood there in my vest and shorts, blue belt tied around my waist—because Danny's lucky colour was red—gloves laced, mind blank, and something had snapped in my head. The next thing I knew, I had pushed Maindak against the wall, my elbow on his throat, and I was pressing, pressing, pressing and Maindak's eyes were growing even bigger. Then I heard myself quietly telling Maindak something I never said before, 'I hate you.' It must have shown on my face because after I took my arm away Maindak ran from the room clutching his throat.

The hatred must have carried over to the ring because I hadn't cared, hadn't cared at all, so instead of waiting for Danny to come to me I went to him and just kept hitting him. The fight was over before I knew it, and I had barely felt the punches Danny had landed on me, on my face and on my shoulders because I had ducked about, and my face and shoulders were grazed and raw from the grit Danny's gloves had picked up from the canvas cover of the ring, grit that even wiping his gloves on his shorts hadn't fully removed.

It had felt really good then, like I had fucked the world along with Danny Singh, paying them all back for the anger I felt but seemed to be able to do nothing about. But it hadn't felt so good afterwards, when some chaps started avoiding me, looking at me like I was a dangerous guy, you know, and I would explode, tick-tock, and jack them at any time. I could even see PT Shoe looking at me sometimes, as if I had become, to use his phrase, like 'Dr Hyde and Mr Jekyll'.

They weren't me, and yet, I knew I had become a bit like them.

It was an epic Sunday. We saw three movies, ate goat-brain curry for lunch, drank beer, and sometime between movies two and three my life changed.

Fish had stayed behind to write a letter to his sister and father, with whom, he used to say with a smirk, he had a love-hate relationship. 'I love my sister and hate my father.' He would dutifully write to them on alternate Sundays, one Sunday for his sister and the next for his father. His routine never varied. We used to rib him about it, and he would always take it good-naturedly, even Porridge's jibe: 'Just cyclostyle it, bugger, and fill in the dates on top.'

This Sunday, we knew, would be a special letter. Fish's dad had written another of those 'My dearest son, Sanjay' letters to Fish. This is how one went, 'How much I wish for you to uphold the family tradition and become a doctor like me, and my father before me. I know you are swimming captain, and I am sure you will—you must—become school captain, but you must pay particular attention in your science classes if you are to have a future we can all be proud of.' This was typically heavy Bwana bullshit. Fish would fume whenever something like this happened, and take off for a swim, do a mile or so, and come back; as the king of the pool, he could go whenever he wanted, even beyond games timings, and nobody ever told him anything.

He could be many things, but we were convinced Fish would never become a doctor, a rich and famous heart surgeon like Bwana, at least not until he could stop throwing up in bio class every time we had to dissect a frog. He recently made it as far as slitting the soft skin of the tiny frog's underbelly with the scalpel, but puked when the bio teacher, Girish Gupta, whom we called Grundy, came, pulled the flap of the skin open with tweezers, and said, 'Ah Sanjay, having trouble again with your fellow swimmer?' and neatly plucked the tiny heart and placed it on the plastic board. Grundy was a sick piece of shit, but he had style.

What Fish really wanted to do was be in India's Olympic swimming team, especially, as he told us, as no Indian swimmer had been good enough to make it to the last eight in the Olympics. 'I don't want gold, man, just to be in the team would be cool-breeze,' he would say dreamily. And if that didn't work, he would lead treks after he graduated from college, and marry Masuma, his Muslim penfriend-turned-real sweetheart, to whom he would write every week, and whom he would visit on his way to Sing and back from Mayo, because Bwana always booked Fish on flights to Sing via Hong Kong and those flights left from Bombay. 'I will settle in the Himalaya and Masuma and I will have some babies, and you guys will all be, like, godparents, okay?'

In this, his sister was an ally, because Fish had told everyone back home about Masuma, which we thought was a mistake because Bwana, whom he always referred to as 'Mr Verma', would never understand how Fish could like a Muslim girl, Fish said, because Bwana had to come away from Pakistan as a child, because his family had to leave all their land and money behind to save themselves from Muslim mobs killing Hindus. Bwana hated Muslims, Fish said, and thought India would be poor and jacked as long as Muslims lived in the country and thank god he didn't have too many Muslim patients in Kenya or Sing or Bwana would get totally fucked over the Hippocratic oath and his hatred for Muslims. After Bwana had said, 'How can you disgrace me and your ancestors like this,' meaning how could Fish run after a Muslim chick, Fish had stopped saying anything to Bwana and confided in his sister instead, because while his mother understood, she could do nothing because she always said yes to everything Bwana said.

Fish never wrote to his mother, saying Bwana always read her letters, so there was no point, but somehow, Bwana would leave his sister alone, an odd thing, but thank god, Fish said. He always thought of his mother though, this lady the rest of us had come to think of as Mrs Bwana. He would call out for his mother whenever he cried, usually at night after lights out. Sometimes, we would cry too, because his sobs and wails would make us miss home desperately, and then we would feel that we were maybe not as grown-up as we thought because we were crying, but we never had the guts to cry out loud like Fish did.

After a hurried breakfast, we had gone to town to first see *Enter the Dragon* at New Majestic, a special 9:30 show that the school had organized for all the kids. It was this great kung-fu flick in which Bruce Lee seemed to kill everyone on one island before he saved the world from drugs and he said no to all the girls this king bad man called Han gave him to screw the night before a martial arts competition, but this big black guy called Jim Kelly who was very cool-breeze in karate took all of them in. Wow. The hall went wild every time there was a fight sequence, with all of us screaming 'eeeeah' and 'waaeeeee'.

For days afterwards, Porridge and PT Shoe would play out this sequence from the movie whenever they got the chance—

'Kih me,' Bruce would order the student at a martial arts school, and wait for the kick.

The student kicked, and missed.

'Wa is dat, an exbishun? Wooe need emoshnal conten.'

The student would miss again.

'I said emoshnal conten, naw anguh.'

Successful kick.

'Ow di it fwee to you?'

'Leh me tink,' the student would reply, scratching his head, and promptly get swatted on the back of his head by Bruce.

'Don' tink,' Bruce would admonish, wagging a finger, and sounding like Confucius, 'fweeeee.'

After *Enter the Dragon*, we ran to Ajanta, just down the road, to see *Satyam Shivam Sundaram*, which everyone called SSS, and which was all about a gorgeous village woman played by Zeenie Baby. So of course she had huge boobs, and in the movie she had half of her face scarred by an accident in her childhood, but that definitely didn't bother us, and it didn't seem to matter to the hero, a guy called Shashi Kapoor, who played a city man who didn't see the burnt half of Zeenie Baby's face till almost the end of the movie because she always covered it with her hair, which was breeze with us, because then her hair wouldn't cover her boobs. The director was a smart bugger, because all of us would lean forward whenever Zeenie Baby came on the screen, which was often. We thought it was a great movie, because her nipples would show when she had a bath in a sari and nothing else, and once, when she bent down to pick up a pot of water, her breasts almost fell out of the sari and the whole hall, which was full of men, must have got a hard-on because all of us certainly had, as we found when we discussed the plot after the show. The movie was certified 'A', but we got in because Porridge had bribed the gatekeeper with ten rupees the three of us had pooled.

The day was a blur. We hurried after *SSS* to lunch at Khalsa restaurant, pigged out on plates of brain curry and naan bread and Rosy Pelican beer that we were served in tiny rooms on the roof of the restaurant. And then, as we hurried on to Mridang cinema for the 3 o'clock show of a horror flick called *Jadu Tona*, a remake of *The Exorcist*, which only Fish had seen and pronounced 'so bad, you must see it', my heart stopped.

She was standing in line to get in, and she was facing us. She was wearing a floral-patterned kurta and blue jeans with big flares, had these big eyes and curly hair and her light-brown skin was like, like *something* dammit, I thought to myself, searching for a description. She was talking to a bunch of other girls with her, and I heard PT Shoe say, 'Must be Sophia chicks.' She laughed then at something one of her friends had said, arching her back, her breasts pushed up against the fabric of the kurta. My knees turn to jelly and head went numb. Maybe I had Zeenie Baby in my head, but fuck, I could have fainted with the feeling.

'Let's go, bugger,' Porridge said. 'We're getting late. I don't want to miss the ads.'

I hardly looked at the screen, but at the girls who were all seated four rows in front of us in the upper stall and that's where my eyes always ended up. When the movie got over, I dragged Porridge and PT Shoe out to the entrance to wait for the girls. The four came out, talking about how 'gross' the movie was, and went towards a tonga and hopped on. That's when something snapped. I ran to another tonga, jumped on next to the driver and told him, 'Uska peechha karo,' in the best tradition of chase sequences in Bollywood movies. Follow them. Porridge and PT Shoe ran and jumped on at the back.

'What the bloody damn are you doing?' PT Shoe asked in panic. Whenever he panicked, PT Shoe's lingo went for a toss.

'Shut up, bastard,' I said. 'Just shut up. I'm thinking.'

'Didn't know you could think, arsehole,' Porridge said charitably. 'Are we running after those chicks?'

'Ya,' I said. 'I want to meet the one sitting at the back, can you see, the one on the right, wearing jeans?'

They turned around and peered.

'But they are *older* chicks,' Porridge warned, 'they won't even *look* at you. You don't even have a girlfriend and now you're running after a chick who's intro you don't even have, you fucking *mad* or what?' Then he changed his mind, looking at Sophia babes or my face, I don't know. 'You got good taste, bugger,' he said approvingly. 'I could fall in love with her.'

'Fuck off,' I said.

The tonga with the girls had set off at a fast trot, and it turned out PT Shoe was right. They were taking the winding road to Sophia College at the edge of town, just where the highway to Jaipur started to wind down through the hills into Ajmer, and our tonga driver followed like a good sport, grinning, happy to be part of the adventure. Occasionally, the horse would lift its tail and fart, making us gag, and the tonga-wallah would laugh. PT Shoe and Porridge were too excited and for the first time since the morning had given up on their 'Don tink, fweeee' routine.

In about fifteen minutes, the tonga with the girls stopped outside Sophia, which they used to call 'Sofaya', in the same way in American movies they called vitamins 'vytamin'. The girls got off and started to go towards the big gate. I *had* to find out her name, and didn't give a damn about the consequences. I got off the tonga, and ran towards them, shouting, 'Ma'am, excuse me please, ma'am.' They turned around, the smiles disappearing.

I stopped just near them, still panting. Then I gathered my breath and what little remained of my senses, looked up at her face, which I suddenly discovered was about two inches higher than mine and blurted, 'Excuse me, ma'am, I am so sorry to bother you but my name is Barun Ray and my friends call me Brandy but please don't think it rude but please may I know your name?'

The girls burst out laughing, but not she. And she looked more beautiful every second. She was just two feet away and a slightly sweet perfume that Ma would have called 'cheap' came from her, but I was inhaling huge amounts of it, mingled with the smell of sweat and horse shit that was everywhere in Ajmer, as if it was the best perfume on earth.

'You're from Mayo?'

'Yes, ma'am.'

'Which class?'

'Class 10, ma'am.'

'Okay,' she paused, looked around at her friends. I sensed Porridge and PT Shoe behind me.

'My name is Samira Khanna,' she said. 'I'm in first year.'

'Thank you ma'am,' I stammered, the blood pounding in my ears. 'Samira please don't mind but you are the most beautiful girl I have ever seen. Ma'am.'

There, I had said it. I would die now, when she hit me, or when all four of the girls attacked me, and maybe even the Gurkha guard at the gate with his khukuri, his big curved knife would join in. I had been told Gurkha warriors scream 'Ayo Gorkhali' before cutting off heads with one swipe, like they did to Japanese soldiers during the Second World War and like they did during the Dussehra festival with goats. My head would soon be rolling around in front of Samira and I would die happy. The pounding in my ears became deafening and my eyes had begun to go dark.

She didn't hit me. 'That's very sweet, Brandy,' she said instead, looking straight into my eyes. 'Go now, it's getting dark. See you, bye.'

With that, she turned, walked back through the gates with her friends, and it clanged shut.

'Bye ma'am…Samira,' I said to the gate, 'See you.' I was glued to the spot, surprised to find myself still alive.

PT Shoe and Porridge gently pulled me towards the tonga, and we sat silently for almost half an hour on the slow ride back to school on the curving road that went through the cantonment area. Even the horse didn't fart. The tonga-wallah took fifteen instead of twenty rupees saying, 'Ishpecial dishcount sa'ab', apparently impressed by our mad show, and gave us a wavy salute.

I skipped dinner. I had no appetite. I was in love.

Fish and I were eating sardines in the changing room, sitting on the bench near Fish's cupboard, which was open. He was fixing new cleats on his Adidas football boots. Except maybe Bull and Pele, Fish had the best sports stuff, wearing Speedo trunks for swimming and all. When I had asked Papa for Speedo, he looked at me blankly, because he didn't even know what Speedo was. These buggers who lived abroad had a good time, you know?

There was a big black-and-white photograph of Masuma that Fish had stuck on the inside of his cupboard door, and he would sometimes kiss Masuma's lips in the snap, the same as Dipi, who stayed in the neighbouring dorm, would kiss his poster of Farah Fawcett Major and Porridge kissed his poster of Zeenie Baby. Despo chaps.

It was a common changing room for three dorms, but it was empty except for Fish and me, not too strange for an afternoon between lunch and games because most guys would try to crash for a while to get their breath back after a whole day's school or disappear for a quick frig in the bogs.

It was my tuck, sardines in tomato sauce. I had cut my finger on the tin when I tried to yank out the little bit of lid that still remained, and sucked in tomato sauce together with blood before Fish called me an arsehole and put a waterproof Band-aid he got from Sing on my right forefinger. 'Why the fuck don't you open the tin fully?' he asked.

It made sense, but every time I opened three-fourths of the tin or so I'd get into a kind of frenzy to pile on. Of course, I loved the taste, but tin fish also reminded me of happy times, and when I had told the guys about tin fish being a new species of fish that was created to make human beings happy, they had found it quite funny and PT Shoe had clapped me on my back and said

'Bloodyfool Brandy, good joke-ya.' We took turns to scoop the small headless and tailless fish with forefinger and thumb and bite into it, slurping the juice and tomato sauce and then licking our fingertips clean. We took our time though there were only six small fish, savouring the experience. We finished that tin and as I was feeling really breeze, I brought out another tin, my last.

'You really like this chick, haan?' Fish asked. I knew what he meant.

'She's not a chick-ya,' I said. 'Her name's Samira.'

'Ya-ya,' Fish was grinning wickedly. 'Love birds and all.'

'Fuck off,' I said. I was smiling too.

'It'll be nice if Masuma and I can meet you and Samira.'

'Ya.'

'You think you'll see her again? You just met her once, bugger, and it wasn't really a meeting, you know.'

'Ya, of course she'll meet me again. She could have asked me to bugger off, couldn't she?'

'Ya, I suppose.'

Dipi came in then, grinning, carrying a copy of the new issue of *Mayoor*, the school paper. He was always grinning, even in his sleep. 'Buggers, finished already? Bloody hogs. You guys want some Tang?'

We looked at him like he was a creep, I mean, who didn't want Tang? I gave him the last two sardines but not before drinking some tomato sauce from the tin, careful not to cut my lips. Dipi opened the big jar of Tang for us, and we scooped the powder into our mouths with the orange-coloured plastic spoon that came with the jar, letting the little granules burst on our tongues, and chewed contentedly, saliva melting the Tang powder and taking it down our gullets.

'What's the editorial about?' Fish asked. The editorials in *Mayoor* were nearly always fun, raising tough issues about student life and Mayo policies, and even, about how farrash and other staff should be treated better. Sometimes Old Boys would write letters, saying guys shouldn't be allowed to write articles that weakened the institution of Mayo and if they didn't like Mayo they could go to some other school, but I was ashamed to think these buggers had ever been to Mayo because they acted like arseholes who didn't believe in freedom of expression. Ranvir Ahuja had written the editorial this time, and it was about how Mayoites need to stop thinking that they lived in their own world and get ready to move out and adapt to the world outside. It was a standard autumn term editorial, aimed at shaking up the senior class so the buggers wouldn't think they were too cat, because when they went to college they would get jacked. They had to begin showing off from zero, because in college nobody gave a fuck about what school you were from, we had heard from some new Old Boys during last Prize Giving.

There were the usual stories and poems, and Dipi showed us a short story he had written about a guy and a chick going to see the Durga Puja on his mobike, saying, 'How's the story? Breeze, no?' I could tell the bugger was dreaming about Tanya, this chick in Cal he wrote letters to.

There was also an article titled 'The *KKK* Affair' that Cutlet's older brother Omelette had written. It was another of those Emergency things. Dipi read it to us. Some politician who didn't like the Congress-wallahs had made a movie called *Kissa Kursi Ka*, which meant The Affair of the Chair, but it sounded so much nicer in Hindi. The movie had been made in 1975, but a sidekick of Indira Gandhi who was in-charge of censorship, and her son

Sanjay had destroyed prints of the movie when it was submitted to the censors because the movie was a satire on politics and some characters were too much like the rulers of India. The thing was in the courts, and Sanjay was in jail, now that the Emergency was over and the Janata Party buggers were in power, so the new rulers were jacking the old rulers.

Then Dipi said 'Oofuck, oofuck' and pushed the *Mayoor* in our face. 'Oofuck, see, see, Katy Mirza.' We jumped up thinking how could there be Katy Mirza's photograph in the *Mayoor* because Katy's boobs were so big Porridge had once said if she was on a plane and if it ever crashed in the sea, there was no way the plane would sink. But it wasn't about Katy's boobs, but just a mention that she had played a 'femme fatale' in *KKK*. Even that was breeze, because we didn't know she acted.

'These Congress guys are buggered,' Dipi said.

'Don't be silly,' Fish butted in, 'you think these Janata jokers are going to last? We have a PM who drinks piss, other guys are just putting Congress guys in jail and screwing up our scene, getting Coke to leave India and all. They fight all the time and have you seen that guy Raj Narain, he looks like a monkey wearing a scarf.' Raj Narain was one of the new guys and always grinning like mad in photographs. 'Indira will come back, you watch. She's got balls. These Janata guys are pisspots.'

That was Fish's new curse, pisspots, and it sounded breeze but I didn't agree totally with what Fish was saying. I told them about a brother–sister argument between Papa and Jolly-pishi just before the elections, in which Papa said the Janata Party would win because Indira had jacked India and her son had jacked India in many more ways, and the people of the country wanted change. He also said that the Janata Party chaps now had the support of 'lower-caste people and farmers' and that would ensure the Janata Party win because such people made up most of India.

Jolly-pishi, who never disagreed with Papa, had patiently listened to her brother but lost her temper when Papa talked about lower-caste people. 'How can you talk like that, Dada?' she had knocked over her glass of lemonade in anger, forgetting to blush like she usually would if something like this happened at any other time. 'We are Brahmins. Congress is a party for Brahmins and I will always vote for the Congress. I'm not going to vote for jamadars. *Never*.' Ma, Jolly-pishemoshai and us kids had all been shocked by Jolly-pishi's outburst as much as Papa had been shocked by what she said.

'Times are changing, Jolly,' Papa had said, getting up and dragging us out of their house on Chowringhee, before things got worse. On the way home, Papa had fumed about Pishi saying the word 'jamadar', which was used for low-caste people who cleaned toilets. There were a few in Mayo as well, and they were of the lowest caste and we avoided going near them, even I, because they would clean shitpots, though I knew it was crazy because I was a Brahmin but I had to clean my own arse, no jamadar did it for me or anyone else, so I didn't fully understand this caste business. I wasn't sure if anyone did, it was so confusing. 'My own sister talks like this,' Papa had said with a sad face. 'Leela, how will India *ever* progress if people think like this in the twentieth century?'

The guys listened to me, and I felt bad for bringing it up, because it had totally jacked our happy tin-fish-and-Tang mood. But some things needed to be said and I wanted to tell Fish the story to tell him that this other lot of people the Janata guys represented wouldn't run away any more, not when they knew they had the power to jack even Indira Gandhi, no fighting and stuff, just by voting—just imagine.

'Ya, okay, maybe,' Fish said, sulking because he had lost the argument. We sat quietly for a minute, before Dipi rescued us.

'Guess what I've got, guys!' And he went to his cupboard and pulled out a pondie from under his vests. It was called *Color Climax* and on the cover it had this guy who was doing things to this chick with a hammer that we were never taught in carpentry class.

When it was over, we still couldn't get over how it had begun. Squash had as good an explanation as any: 'Mutt's not getting enough sex.'

He was right. It was the booze, and the fighting with Mrs Mutt, and, though we didn't know it for sure, it was rumoured that Mutt wanted to be Vice Princi and Princi very quickly but that was 'tough', as Fish said, because it was as not as if Vice Princi and Princi were about to bugger off into the sunset like Clint Eastwood did in the Westerns, where even the horse, like Clint, seemed to inhale and exhale with pursed lips twitching, totally breeze. Mutt was getting frustrated and, maybe because he drank and fought so much, maybe he wasn't getting laid either.

Instead, Porridge said, he was getting like Indian politicians, who seemed to be ready to lay anything, especially stones. Wherever we went, we always saw signs on buildings, in airports, near bridges and stations, where there was a marble or stone slab saying such and such politicians had Graciously Laid the foundation stone on such and such date. I remember even seeing a similar getting-laid stone, as we called it, at an electric crematorium in Calcutta, where I had gone with the mourners during one hols, when the husband of Moyna-di's older sister had suddenly died of a heart attack. These politician-types were fucking vultures, you know?

Mutt seemed to have nowhere to go, and as he was just a master in a school he wasn't about to lay any foundation stones either, and from what little we knew he wasn't getting laid. So that's why, maybe, he was turning cranky in class. We could see the change, one term to another.

Later, all we could think was that both Mutt and Fish had felt jacked, and just happened to be at the wrong place at the wrong time and said the wrong things. Mostly, Mutt was not a bad history teacher. He would often ask us to close our books, and simply talk to us and tell us the same stuff that was in the books, but told it like a story. So it was as if for a few minutes we were at the court of Emperor Ashoka after the great battle of Kalinga, when he gave up violence after killing thousands and became a great Buddhist and helped to spread the religion outside India. Then, one time, he told us how Humayun, the son of Babur, the first Mughal emperor, slipped and fell down the steps of his library, making Emperor Akbar, the granddad of Shahjahan, one of the youngest emperors ever.

We travelled a lot in Mutt's time machine; it was so much better than mugging stuff at prep, and I wondered why other teachers couldn't make molecules and shit come alive and make parallax experiments seem like Einstein was in the room with us. Mutt had a way of telling stories, using his powerful voice and big eyes, and he would walk up and down the rows of desks and chairs, talking to us, waving his arms, now stopping, then resuming his walk, as we tracked him, turning our bodies this way and that to keep up with him, spellbound. During my first year in Mayo, Mutt had played Muhammad bin Tughlak in a play called *Tughlak,* and we were mesmerized with this guy who played the role of the mad-genius sultan from medieval India so convincingly. Mutt hadn't done any plays recently, and seemed to use his talent in class instead, acting out history, and that was fine with us because he made history fun. Even Chacha, who thought molecules and isotopes were the cool-breezeest things in the world found Mutt interesting.

We were talking about 1857, the year that seemed to be the most important one after 1947. In 1947, we all knew, the English had gone away because they couldn't handle Indians any more. The books would tell us it was because of Mahatma Gandhi and how he got together Indians, even Pakistanis, because those days India and Pakistan were one country. There were also some revolutionaries who killed English soldiers and judges. I knew about them from years ago, because Papa had brought me a book in Bengali called *Binoy, Badal, Dinesh*. It was about these guys in their teens called Binoy, Badal and Dinesh, from Calcutta in the olden days. They weren't that much older than we were and wanted to kill a British police officer because he was being a complete bastard and also because, as the boss of prisons he really hurt political prisoners.

They bought shoes from Cuthbertson & Harper, a shop at Esplanade, which still had the faded sign outside, but these days sold plastic suitcases. They had their tailors make new suits, and some revolutionaries had given them guns. They ate well that morning in 1930—I think it was Binoy's mother who cooked choice curries and desserts for them—then they prayed to goddess Kali and went to complete their job. They hurt the police officer, but were trapped because of some misunderstanding. Binoy died, Badal killed himself so they couldn't capture him, and Dinesh was hanged later. They weren't even twenty, and they must have been really angry at the goras to do what they did. The boys were heroes in Bengal, and the chief minister of Bengal had renamed Dalhousie Square 'BBD Bag' in honour of these boys but many still called the place 'Dalhousie'.

That always surprised me. We were powerful enough to get the English out but we still called places by their old English names and used British spellings. Even Mutt, who yelled at me once because I called the Ganga 'Ganges' and sneeringly said I should get a new name, Jack Brown, instead of Brandy Ray, would himself say 'Cawnpore' and 'Jeypore', and 'Chakkadapore', where his wife was from, instead of Kanpur, Jaipur and Chakradharpur. Maybe there was still some of the English in us, but anyway, sometimes we used to get quite worked up when we studied about the English. I mean, who the hell were they to write 'Dogs and Indians not Allowed' on notice boards?

'You gentlemen know about the first war of Independence in 1857,' Mutt began in his Tughlak voice. Yes we did, and also that after 1857 the English decided to build Mayo following Macaulay's dictation. 'But do you really *know* about it? Do you know about what must have been going through the *mind* of Mangal Pandey, this sepoy chap, when his English officers said he must bite the bullet that was greased with beef tallow? Can you imagine his anger at being humiliated, a Hindu being forced to touch beef because the company bahadur, the East India Company, said he must?' I didn't twitch, because I loved the meat.

Mutt paused, took a deep breath, like he was on a stage, and went on. 'Mangal Pandey wasn't the only one who was angry. There were others who were angry because the English had come and taken over the land and livelihood—and they were *raping* India. Why, Chacha, never heard the word before? Hindus, Muslims, peasants and even some kings, everybody had enough of the East India Company. Word spread, on horseback, on carrier pigeons, through runners called dakia, and the anger began to build. There was no Hindu versus Muslim, just Indians versus the English, but not quite cricket, eh, ha ha ha.'

Mutt stopped and guffawed, pleased with his joke. We laughed, and went along with him. It was quite a show.

That's when Fish piped up. 'But sir, isn't it also called the Indian Mutiny? I mean, there was no India then, really, it was just a map that the British called India. You said so yourself sir, last term.' Ouch, that Fish. But he was right.

Mutt decided to humour Fish, which we all knew was a bad move. With Fish, a question never brought an answer; an answer brought another question. Always. 'The British call it the Indian Mutiny and we call it the First War of Independence, Sanjay, you know that.'

'But what's correct, sir? Nobody answers that question.'

'Correct? Correct? What I am saying is correct,' Mutt was beginning to crack. 'We're Indians, and we shall call it the First War of Independence.'

'But sir…' Fish began, but Mutt cut him off.

'But but but, what is this but but?'

'But sir, this is an interpretation. Don't we have a right to know what is correct?'

'My *dear* Sanjay,' Mutt said through clenched teeth. 'Why do I get the feeling you are deliberately creating trouble? History *can* be about interpretation, *you* know that. What is the problem?

For the British, it was a mutiny; for Indians, it was a war of independence. Both are correct.'

'So sir, if I write Mutiny in the exams, will it be marked incorrect?'

'Shut up.'

'Sir please...'

'Come here.'

'Why sir?'

'Come *here* you idiot!'

'I'm not an idiot, sir.'

This was going downhill, fast. But there was no space to intervene. We sat tense and silent, shocked at what was going on. As I looked around to see what the guys were doing I saw many open mouths and realized my jaw was hanging as well and I shut it quickly. The only guy who was totally uninterested, as always, was Caramel Custard, also known as CC, and CC was doing what he always did in class when a teacher was too caught up in the lesson to pay attention to what the chaps were doing. CC, to my right, was using the point of his compass to carve the desk, writing 'cool' in other languages. I saw Coolati, El Coolo, and Coolabishi, and then CC took his eraser, which was white and had a green strip on top that smelled of sweet menthol, gently blew the wood dust away and then rubbed the eraser on the carvings, and the bits of eraser turned black with the muck from the desk filling the carved letters, ageing them, so if he wasn't caught a bit in flagrente delicto, which Dipi loved to say, then nobody would be able to prove CC had jacked the desk. CC was an artist. He left his mark wherever he went, and his classic was written in Yogi's class: 'The boy stood on the burning bloody deck because everyone else was fucking chicken.'

'You *are* an idiot,' Mutt continued to yell at Fish. 'There's water in your ears from all that swimming.'

'Please don't insult me sir.'

'I'll do what I *want*.' Mutt was shouting. 'Come *here*.'

Fish walked up and stood in front of Mutt, face down.

'Stand *straight* when I'm talking to you.'

Fish looked up, straight into Mutt's eyes.

'Why are you looking at me like that? Think you're very smart?'

'No sir.'

'Don't answer back! Haven't your parents taught you any manners?'

'Please leave my parents out of it, sir.'

That's when, for all of us, Mutt crossed the line.

'Idiot child of idiot parents.'

'Bastard.'

'What? What did you say?' Mutt couldn't believe Fish had said that. We couldn't believe it either.

'Bastard, sir. I said, you bastard.'

Mutt got up on his toes and slapped Fish. Then it was a blur. Fish caught Mutt's hand as he raised it to slap him again, twisted it behind his back and shoved him towards the blackboard, which was actually green, but it seemed so silly to call it greenboard. Mutt's face was on it as Fish held it there, on 1857, MANGAL PANDEY and THE FIRST WAR OF INDEPENDENCE, which Mutt had written on the board with chalk in big capital letters. Porridge and I ran up and dragged Fish back. Mutt turned to look at us, chalk on the right side of his face, because his face had, like a duster, smudged 'Mangal Pandey' and 'First War' on the board. Mutt was purple with anger and we could now see he was also afraid, because he didn't come towards us. We knew Fish could be stubborn, but Mutt had no business freaking out like that, knowing fully students always had to shut up and take all sorts of shit from teachers.

'Get *out*!' he yelled at Fish.

'Sir,' I told Mutt, a favourite student to a once respected teacher. 'If you do anything to Sanjay, we are going to complain against you to the Princi and to our parents.' There was a murmur of agreement from the class behind us.

'Get out, all of you,' Mutt had got his voice back. 'We'll see what happens in the midterms.'

At that, Fish turned back. Then he did something that will stay with me for ever. 'You're a good teacher, sir,' he said. 'Please do what we come to you for.'

Mutt turned away, and looked out of the window, towards the library.

We had our midterms. But Mutt had left by then. We heard he had gone away to some school in the Gulf.

'What the fuck did you do that for?' I asked Fish as we walked to the next class.

'I'm sick of being pushed around, Brandy. I'm not going to take shit any more. Not from Mutt or Mr Verma, or from anyone else. Not even you guys.'

Then he walked off.

I cornered Fish after prep. He had been quiet all day. Word had got around, it seemed, at the speed of light. When Fish walked into the Mess, eyes had turned to him, even those of the teachers. He ate his lunch, mechanically shovelling dal, vegetables and rice into his mouth without a word, head down. He didn't talk to anyone. We lost track of Fish after that for a few hours, but I know he went swimming because when I entered the stadium, back from a run to Madar Hill, which formed the background to the school in so many photos, I saw him walk back to the House, towel rolled under his arm, wearing his colourful flip-flops that he always got from Sing, a new pair every term.

Fish was playing Bob Dylan on his tape recorder. It was 'Sara', and Dylan, whom Fish called Mr Robert Allen Zimmerman—'his real name, man'—whenever he was particularly impressed with him, seemed really nasal tonight, like he was begging for a Vicks vapour stick instead of begging Zenrah, at least that's what Sara sounded like when Mr Zimmerman said it. Sometimes, PT Shoe, Porridge and I would gang up against Fish and chorus 'Zenrah oowoow Zenrah', really pissing him off.

Fish was lying on his back, eyes up at the ceiling. I sat on the bed. Every few minutes, he would reach out, and like a blind man who knew what to do without seeing, press stop-rewind-stop-play to listen to a track he really liked. After we listened to 'Hurricane' for the third time, I reached and pressed the Stop button. Fish didn't move.

'What's wrong?' I asked him.

'Nothing man. I want to forget today.'

'Ya,' I said. 'Bad scene.'

'Ya, totally balls.' Fish didn't say anything for a while. 'Do you think Mutt's going to write to Mr Verma?'

'No, I don't think so. If he does, he'll get into trouble. There are twenty-five witnesses who saw what he did.'

'But they saw me freaking out too, right? But I asked a proper question, right? There was nothing wrong with the question, was there?'

'No man,' I said. 'Don't worry, we'll all take care of you, nobody's going to sneak because it was Mutt's fault. Squash was right. Maybe Mutt's not getting enough sex.'

We laughed, and Fish said, 'Ya, like we're getting a lot of sex.'

Maybe Fish was, I thought, even if he was joking about it. We never asked Fish about it, but he had been seen coming out of the old swimming pool with the Princi's daughter once. She was a swimmer, too, and older than we were. We knew she wouldn't take Fish there to teach him Hindi grammar, but we never asked. You just didn't ask about some things. And maybe, because Fish was nuts, maybe they just held hands and talked about this guy called Bhagwan Rajneesh, who Fish's older sister was totally into and even went to his ashram in Poona. Fish said he was a like a wise man who could connect with the modern world, but from what little we read about Rajneesh in the magazines in the library, he seemed more clever than wise, because he would crack jokes in the ashram, which we called co-educational because men and women lived together, meditated and, we had heard from some seniors, have sex. Smart bugger. He even had tapes, one of which Fish had brought, and in it was a grammar lesson that Yogi would never have the balls to teach. The tape had Rajneesh giving a cat speech to his gora disciples about how the word 'fuck' cleared the throat in the morning, only he called it 'fugg'. Then he taught the transitive verb: 'Jaan fugged Mairy'. And then, the intransitive: 'Mairy was fugged by Jaan.' Just imagine.

'I got another letter from Mr Verma,' said Fish. 'He wants me to stop doing plays and swimming and concentrate on my studies. He wants me to top the Class 10 exams.'

'What will you do?'

'I can't stop swimming, man, I'm the captain. I love swimming. I also told Yogi I'm going to do the play. He really wants me to play Billy Budd, and I like the role. It's a nice play, you know. Anyway, fish-eating Bongo types like you are going to top the exams, so what's the big deal?' He paused. 'Why can't Mr Verma leave me alone? Just because he pays my bloody fees he thinks he owns me...'

Porridge and PT Shoe walked in then.

'Ah,' Porridge said, looking at Fish. 'The Sphinx rises from the ashes.' Porridge was always coming up with this sort of stuff. In March, any ideas he had were the 'Ideas of March', or he would get dramatic before walking in for an exam and say '*Ave Ceasar, morituri te salutant*', like the gladiators in Ancient Rome did just before a fight.

I quickly filled them in about Mr Verma's latest. 'He sounds like *my* father,' said PT Shoe, disgusted. 'You must act like a man, you must ride like a man, must fight like a man—as if I'm a girl or something.'

PT Shoe was being brave, we knew. If his father had heard him talk like this, he would have probably taken a long, curved sword that PT Shoe told us hung on a wall in every room in his house, and run it through PT Shoe, son or not. PT Shoe fingered his moustache which was beginning to show, twirling a few strands around with his thumb and forefinger, as if it was a full-grown caterpillar instead of something that looked like it had been pasted on with glue, like they did for plays. 'So what're you going to do, Fish, really?'

'I'll think of something. I *do* know that I'm not giving up swimming and Yogi's play.'

Rehearsals had begun already. Fish was playing Billy in *Billy Budd,* and Slicko, two years senior, was Claggart, this nasty chap, the master-at-arms, who hated Billy, provoked him at every turn and accused him of all sorts of things, because the crew liked Billy and that made Claggart very jealous, because Claggart was a real shit and the crew hated him. It got so bad that Claggart provoked Billy one day, and gentle Billy hit him in a moment of anger because he was tired of being victimized by him, and killed Claggart. Lokesh, who was called London because he lived in London, had the role of Captain Vere, the master of the ship *HMS Indomitable,* who liked Billy, but was forced to go through with a trial that decided to hang Billy, because Captain Vere was all for justice, even if it broke his heart and he knew Claggart was a bastard.

We thought it was a great play because the dialogues sounded important and everybody would get to wear great sailor-type costumes, and the Main Building, with all its spires and domes and cupolas and windows would make a lovely backdrop for the play, and we thought if people could believe in a play, they could also forget for two hours that the ship was really a building. Yogi must have sensed something about Fish to give him the role of Billy; we thought it suited him nicely, and were quite proud that one of us was playing the role of a guy after whom Herman Melville, the *Moby Dick* chap, had named a book. London, who was school captain, had found the script in London, which Yogi had retyped and then cyclostyled, so everybody in the play would march around importantly holding rolled-up scripts and thinking they were bloody Gregory Peck or something.

Even we. Porridge and I were sailors, and all we had to do was wear T-shirts and pajamas and act asleep, or eat baked beans and sausage from a wooden bowl with a wooden spoon that the carpentry workshop had made for the play, or clamber up a rope ladder that ran up from the bridge that connected the classroom section on the first floor of the Main Building to the curving outer wall of the Assembly Hall, pretending we were climbing up the rigging to lower the sails, and once, when a sailor fell off the mast with a shriek, we would run and get the poor bugger, saying 'Clear the way' and 'Make way' and go off stage and finish the rest of the baked beans and sausage in peace like happy pigs, while Claggart and Billy fought for their lives and the moral of the fucking story.

PT Shoe didn't get a role because he always got nervous speaking in front of people, and he got nervous during the audition, when Yogi made us read from the script or anything we wanted to. PT Shoe had prepared a small speech all by himself for Yogi, which began with the sentence, 'Dear Sir, I wish to fulfil any role that you give me.' But he got really nervous, and kept saying 'filful' instead of 'fulfil'. It was crazy, with PT Shoe knowing he had gone wrong somewhere but not exactly where, so he would begin again and get stuck at 'filful'. We had all laughed, even London, who laughed like he had a billiard ball in his mouth—'haw haw haw'—but Yogi had felt sorry for PT Shoe and said he could be costume manager. We were really thrilled all of us had something to do with *Billy Budd*, and were upset that Mr Verma was giving Fish such a hard time.

'You guys tell me,' Fish said, 'What the hell should I do with Mr Verma?'

Porridge had a king suggestion. 'You can't change your father, bro, it's too late for all that. So just stop writing to him. Just ignore him and write to your sister. He'll get freaked out.'

Fish came alive. 'That's really cool-breeze, Porridge. Thanks man.'

A week ahead of the show in November, around the time the jokes really started to spread about how Morarji Desai, the PM, drank his own piss to stay well, and called it urine therapy, Mr Verma, father to Fish, Bwana to us, came to the school. This was Bwana's first visit since he had dropped Fish off a year after Papa and I had made our journey. When we talked about it later, we had to admit that maybe Porridge's plan had worked too well.

We were away at games. I was practising my heart out at 400 metres, determined to make the team for the Inter Public School meet at Hyderabad, far away in southern India. Shorty, who was taller than all of us and ran 100 metres and had the longest name we had ever known—Maqdum Alauddin Mohammad Murad Salif Asif Ahmed Khan—had a married sister in Hyderabad. Shorty said the food in Hyderabad was fantastic, his sister made super biryani and kebabs, and even if we didn't win a race, the trip was worth it, just for the food. This I could live for, though beating Pansy would be an additional benefit.

Pansy was the pits. He spoke in a drawl that would put John Wayne to sleep, but what really got me was his habit of saying 'yas' instead of a plain 'yes' or 'ya'. On the track, as we got ready to race, Samosa-sir would call out our names, and basically all we had to do was raise our hands, but Pansy would say 'yas' and get us all laughing, and that was a crazy thing to do because we were all warmed up, ready to run and psyched up about winning. I was convinced it was Pansy's ace trick to win a race; he hadn't yet, but he had come very close twice, the shit.

Porridge would be at tennis practice, I knew, caught up with his new Wilson aluminium racket, which we all envied because we knew Jimmy Connors played with a similar racket. Holding Porridge's racket was like touching Jimmy Connors, and even Bull, who lived in Forest Hills in New York and had actually seen Connors play at the US Open, was impressed. I could see PT Shoe at the cricket nets. He was really quite good at fast bowling, and had made the school team that year, so we were quite proud of him. PT Shoe hero-worshipped Andy Roberts and was always asking Fish to play his Bob Marley tapes, so he could get 'the bloody goddamn beat of Calypso, mon'.

The 'mon' bit was correct, we knew, because Bob would say 'mon' quite a lot, but Porridge tried telling PT Shoe once that Bob Marley's music was reggae, not Calypso. PT Shoe had looked so hurt we let it be.

I remembered Andy Roberts because I had seen him play once at the Eden Gardens in an India versus West Indies Test match in Calcutta, in the winter of 1974. He was so fast that he broke Mansur Ali Khan Pataudi's jaw. Papa, who had taken me to the see the match, had muttered one word when that happened: 'Barbarian', and later, grumbled to his friends about how Wesley Hall, some bowler from before I was born, was 'like an animal, but he would never break people's jaws.' But Pataudi, who was the captain and whom everyone called Tiger, came back, jaw wired, and hit Andy Roberts for four consecutive fours. Totally king.

India had won that Test match, and Papa and I were convinced that it was because in the second innings when West Indies were batting and looked ready to win, Papa had placed his packet of State Express cigarettes in a certain way—open, with the foil wrapper pulled out slightly, and two cigarettes from the middle pulled out in a such a way that the bottom end of their filter tips matched the top end of the filter of the other cigarettes. I was sure it had got the captain of the West Indies team, Clive Lloyd, out and after that people around us refused to let Papa touch the packet and offered him their own cigarettes so the magic from Papa's cigarettes wouldn't get jacked. When the match got over, Papa was as much a hero in the clubhouse seats as Pataudi and his men. Vijay-uncle, Papa's friend who was a manager at a tea estate near Darjeeling, actually took Papa's packet of cigarettes, saying he would keep it in the Planter's Club as a memento.

Fish was in the pool, he told us later, doing his laps in the cool water, when Mr Verma marched in. Bhanu Singh, the swimming coach, and among the very few in school who didn't have a nickname, must have asked Mr Verma what he wanted. Or, that's what he must have asked, Fish said, because he couldn't hear it, being at the other end of the pool, where he was taking a break, relaxing as swimmers did, arcing their arms and then dropping below the water to breathe out in a burst of bubbles. But he, and the rest of the swimming team, heard Mr Verma loud and clear.

'I am Mr Verma,' Bwana had said loudly.

'I am Mr Singh, how do you do?' said the coach and held out his hand.

Bwana had ignored it and said, 'I am the father of Sanjay Verma. Where is he?' which Fish said was 'a very rude thing to do, I mean, who does Mr Verma think he is, god? that everyone has to lick his shoes?'

Spotting Fish, Bwana had said 'Sanjay, come *here*, please.' At least he had said, 'please', Fish told us later, but we had gathered it was the only moment of weakness Bwana had displayed that day.

Fish, his ears burning with embarrassment and anger, had got out of the pool and, pretending everything was cool-breeze, walked along, towelling himself dry, to his father. 'How dare you write to your sister and not write to me?' Bwana had demanded, in front of Bhanu Singh and the entire swimming team, before Fish had asked him to please stop and said that if he had something to say, could he please give Fish the chance to change first. They could then go elsewhere to talk.

Bwana had a Chevrolet Impala that he kept at his brother's house in Delhi. He had driven down eight hours to Ajmer in that car. We later wondered at what kind of man Fish had as a father, who would first pressure the hell out of a son and then get angry at a tiny act of rebellion as if his position as head of the family had been threatened, leave his hospital business, take a plane to Delhi from Singapore via Bangkok and Calcutta, and then drive for a day to confront his son. 'It's my destiny,' Fish had said, and it seemed really sad to have a father who gave Fish everything except the one thing he craved from him. We hesitated to call it love, because it seemed an odd thing for a boy to ask of his father, and we wouldn't be caught dead writing 'Love' at the end of a letter to our fathers, but that's what we meant. When I joined Mayo, I'd still write 'Love' at the end, but in less than a year, I figured it was a pansy thing to do, and switched to 'So long,' which was much more grown-up, much more, you know, breeze.

Bwana had sat Fish in the Impala and had driven him to Honeydew, which was the only restaurant in town that didn't have too many flies hanging around, and while he drank coffee and Fish had cold coffee with ice cream, Bwana had buggered Fish.

He had called Fish a 'bloody imbecile' for not listening to him, because Bwana knew best about what was good for Fish, and expected Fish to be grateful because he had not kept Fish in Singapore but sent him to Mayo so he would pick up some Indian culture and grow into a proper man before going ahead and doing what Bwana had planned for him.

'You will first train in a job, then get married, and then join me in the business, as that is a proper thing for a son to do,' Bwana had said. 'Where is swimming going to get you, the Olympics? Can you eat a gold medal?' He had gone further in his anger, asking Fish if he was 'still writing to that Muslim girl in Bombay, how *could* you be friendly with a Muslim girl and disgrace the family?' as if Masuma was something dirty.

Fish had really blown it then, saying he had responsibility to the school as swimming captain, that Masuma was a good friend and 'so what if she's Muslim, her parents don't seem to have any problems with me', and that he really wanted to study economics, and that a teacher—we knew it was Yogi—had said St Stephen's College in Delhi was a good place to study economics. Bwana had fumed, and had blown a fuse when Fish, all confused and angry, had called him 'Mr Verma' to his face by mistake. Bwana had then slapped him in front of all the people in the restaurant, a reverse swing that also knocked Fish's cold coffee and ice cream to the floor.

Fish said he had stood up then, and said what we knew came from his heart, 'I'm sorry that I am not the son you want me to be.'

In a movie or in a book, we knew, this is the time that the son and father looked at each other angrily, then with deep hurt and longing, and then they rushed into each other's arms and hugged for ever. But this father and son had other ideas, and anyway, we were convinced that if ever there was a role for Bwana, it would be as a villain. Bwana had stood up, taken out three or four 100-

rupee notes and flung them on the table. Fish said he wasn't sure whether it was Bwana's way of apologizing to the restaurant management for his behaviour or just an act of arrogance to pay for a bill that could not have been more than thirty rupees. As Fish watched silently, Bwana had delivered his verdict: 'If you do not listen to me, you're not coming back here. You will go to Ambala, and stay with Tau-ji. He will straighten you out, Mr Wonderful.'

With that, he had flung a ten-rupee note across the table towards Fish 'for the tonga', and stalked out. We knew he would go to Jaipur to spend the night at the Rambagh Hotel, which used to be a palace in the olden days, because no place in Ajmer was good enough, or clean enough, for Bwana—well, for a change he was right about something. But the threat of Ambala had cut deep for Fish. He had visited Ambala a few times, to visit his uncle's family, and said it was 'basically an army cantonment with one place that sold bacon and sausage, and a dirty, filthy town'. His uncle had a firm that made microscopes and lab instruments, and we knew from his failed experiments in the bio lab with frogs and rats that working with an uncle who made bio lab things would bring back some nasty memories, besides ensuring Masuma was a goodbye.

'I'd rather fucking die than go there,' Fish said. 'I want to live in Bombay for a few years after I'm through with college. It's a heavy place, better than Sing. Then, I'll go and spend the rest of my life in the Himalaya with Masuma.'

It took Fish an hour to tell us this, with lots of breaks and sighs. Moses had dropped by and sat quietly at Porridge's desk. We let him be. Fish carried on talking and told us things he had never told us before. About when he was eight, and been out in the rain—'in Sing it always fucking rains, so it's hardly a big deal'—and Bwana had taken a whip he had bought in Nairobi and beat Fish with the handle so badly that Fish had missed school for a week. Just before joining Mayo, Fish had fucked up the eleven-times table, or was it twelve, he couldn't remember. That beating then had been with a bison-horn stick, another import from Nairobi. When Fish's older sister and Mrs Bwana couldn't take Fish's screams any more they had covered his body with theirs to make the beating stop. There had been more beatings, for failures in Bwana's eyes, for crimes that we wouldn't get more than a scolding or maybe a slap or two.

Fish said he got beaten even now during hols, and he wondered if it was because Bwana was in the RSS and hated his son's ideas because they were different, like loving a Muslim girl and doing his own thing, while some friends of Bwana's father would visit their big flat in Sing and talk about how the Rashtriya Swayamsevak Sangh was the true saviour of India and they would take care of Pakistan and others like they had taken care of the 'Muslim bastards' during Partition, like being bastards was a Muslim thing.

We were beginning to understand why it had been so easy for the goras to jack this country full of bastards, one move at a time like in chess, which I had stopped playing after I taught Papa the game during a holiday at Gopalpur-on-Sea, just after we had eaten the biggest bloody crabs in the world, and he won in the first game he played with me, grinning like he was bloody Bobby Fischer or something. We finally knew what it must take for a gentle giant like Fish to hold back, what it must have meant for him to defend his parents' honour in front of Mutt, defend even this man who seemed so intent on destroying him.

'Why does he hate me so much?' Fish asked, like some lost little schoolboy. 'He's my father.'

'Maybe he is a bit old-fashioned,' PT Shoe said. We knew he was right and anyway, PT Shoe was the reigning authority on old-fashioned. Anybody who lived in a three-hundred-year-old house knew the true meaning of old-fashioned.

Porridge, as always, had the last word. 'You're fucked, bro.'

Porridge looked a bit jacked, which was strange, because the chap never looked jacked about anything, including that sick porridge at breakfast or with Torquemada and Luther trying to freak each other in his house in Bombay's Navy Nagar. He used to call his flat *INS Buggerall*, like it was a warship, and this was one ship over which Captain Macolm Crasto, hero of 1971, his white uniform full of strips of multicoloured cloth and medals (we saw in a snap Porridge kept in his cupboard under a pile of home clothes), had little control, because Juliet, wife to Malcolm and mother to Porridge, ran this ship, and Miriam, mother to Malcolm and grandmother to Porridge, hated the fact and thought it was nothing more than a silly mutiny of a silly Protestant girl.

Life, Porridge said, was a lot better for Captain Crasto on the missile frigate *INS Mahanadi*, where he could be the hero he was, smoking his pipe in the captain's cabin and eating chicken biryani and caramel custard for lunch, and strutting around the deck yelling 'Ahoy', flashing the ship's light in Morse code to any Paki ship that dared to come close to Indian waters, or maybe it was a gold smuggler's boat that they intercepted on its way to Bombay as they did in Hindi movies. Only that here there was no sound of violin and bongos as they neared the smuggler's boat, just a light flashing m.a.k.e.m.y.d.a.y., as Clint did in *Dirty Harry*.

We knew Porridge was giving some lobs, but we understood the story because it was about Captain Crasto getting away the same way Porridge got away from the bullshit all the months he was in Mayo. *INS Mahanadi* was Captain Crasto's only escape from both his mother and his wife who battled over house keys and cupboard keys and how to worship Jesus Christ, which we thought must freak Jesus a lot, who seemed like quite a breeze chap in the *Jesus Christ Superstar* musical the senior house guys did during centenary Prize Giving, though Judas seemed pretty breeze too, trying to jack Jesus by singing things like 'Too much heaven on your mind'. And Jesus got lashed thirty-nine times under strobe lights while the bass guitar went bing-bing-bang-bing-bang-bang, which seemed like quite a cat disco way of getting lammed, you know, to make it more Travolta and all—trust the goras to think of these details.

Anyway, it all happened a long time ago in a place far away near the Dead Sea, which we thought was a cat name because Arabs and Israelis were always dying not too far from it, and it was nuts because they had even given these leaders of Egypt and Israel, Anwar Sadat and Menachem Begin, whose first name, Fish had told us, was pronounced Mena*kh*em like you had swallowed something and wanted to clear your throat like mad, the bloody Nobel Peace Prize like they gave Mother Teresa one the year after that. And, like the poor in Cal never stopped being poor, these guys never stopped dying, and these masked buggers, like the guys who took Israeli chaps hostage in the Munich Olympics, would hijack planes and blow things up, and I wondered if getting jacked' was the breeze form of 'hijacked' but nobody could tell, not even Fish and Yogi.

It was a mad world, almost as mad as India, and we had talked about how it would be fun to put Grandmother, The Bastards, Old Miriam, Bwana and PT Shoe's dad, and maybe even bloody Kakosa, in one room and let them fight it out for PM of India, and those who drank the most piss, their own, would win.

They would drown in their own piss, I was sure, because nobody would want to give up the battle, but in the end India would be a better place, even though Indira Gandhi wanted to cut men's things off and thought she was god, and the PM after her drank his own piss, and I had always wondered how he drank it, from beakers like we had in the chem lab which the Israelis would call *kh*em lab or from a mug in the loo, or maybe it was cooled in the fridge and served to him in PM-type glasses at breaker, like it was bloody orange juice or something. The papers and mags never said anything about it, and it was like saying someone killed somebody, but not how or why. Or maybe he did it like some magician, waving an empty jug around to an audience, taking care to hold it upside down to show it was empty and then saying 'abracadabragillygillygilly' and, then, all breeze, pouring out some piss into a glass some chick assistant was holding and announce, 'Waterrrr of India' like magicians always did, and offer some to his ministers after taking the first sip. Yuck.

Someday, Porridge and I had decided, we would write our own musical. We had already decided on the name: *Get Lost on the Ganga and All That*, which I had argued about and shortened from Porridge's original suggestion, *Get Lost on the Ganga and All That and All*, saying it was too maka for people and goras to understand. It would be about four friends who were jacked with things so they would run away and from Rishikesh in the hills begin a journey on a small boat called *MV Breeze* right down to the Bay of Bengal past Kanpur and Varanasi and Patna and then take a right before Farakka into the Hooghly. They would sing songs to people on the way about a peace like these hippie chaps did in Woodstock, and screw tonnes of village women, and see India, beautiful like a postcard on one side, only our postcards would also have floating gods and goddesses and half-burnt corpses, dead bodies of children, cows, dogs and all.

The four friends would then try to sink the boat and do some drowning stuff with hands raised in a salute, Porridge-friend navy style with his palm turned in, Fish-friend and PT Shoe-friend army-style with their palms outwards, and Brandy-friend like some air force-type, with palm in centre at a cat angle, because the four friends refused to go back upriver until all the madness stopped, and the madness wouldn't stop.

The last song would have a Spanish touch, Porridge said, and the first line would go 'Adios arseholes, see you in hell and all', and I vaguely thought Papa might like that because it would have a Mantovani touch, and the four friends would dance a little with red rose stems in their mouths and hands in salute. Just as they were about to drown, a boatload of village chicks would come rushing and Zeenie Baby would be standing in front of the boat and then, seeing us drowning, scream 'Nahin, nahin, India needs you, my darlings' and jump into the ocean with a dozen village chicks and save us, The End.

Andrew Llyod Webber would write the songs like he did for *JCS*, and Porridge and I would direct the musical. We would write to Mick Jagger and the Rolling Stones to sing the songs because they were so cat. Porridge and I even had the Stones' tongue-stickers inside our cupboard which Dipi had brought for us from Bangkok. They would surely agree like rock stars had for a concert for Bangladesh because we would write, 'Dear Mick-bhai' because Porridge said that an Indian touch would make our request more genuine and goras sometimes liked loku stuff, 'Could you and others like Keith-bhai and Charlie-bhai please sing the songs of our musical, otherwise we can't get no satisfaction and jump like flash.'

Fish called us idiots when we suggested the idea to him, and even PT Shoe went at it, saying, 'BloodyfoolBrandy.' Some people had no sense of mission.

Porridge was quickly turning the pages of the *National Geographic* the captain had sent, not the way he usually did, stopping to visit America in a leisurely way on his way to Sri Lanka, but like he was on the Concorde, flying across the Atlantic at Mach 2, for a quick haw-haw stop in London before a mad dash to Colombo. Ever since he had got the issue, he was in a daze, it seemed to me, looking at photographs of Los Angeles and the Golden Gate Bridge and all, and especially of some tall chicks with great bodies and tight bums in white togs walking along a place called Rodeo Drive. PT Shoe had looked at it and said, '*See*, I *told* you America had nice chicks,' as if we didn't know, the idiot, because we saw plenty of American chicks in the movies, but PT Shoe could never get his gora chick out of his head. Porridge was slowly getting converted to PT Shoe's religion and I think it started after we leched at Sally and Lucy. After that he was full off it, going on about America along with PT Shoe even if it was after seeing *A Few Dollars More*, which was about America in the olden days when cowboys swaggered around walking bow-legged with all that riding and bathed in small tubs while some curly-haired babe from the saloon would wash the guy with soap and the bugger would sit in a tin tub with his own muck floating about him, the bloody junglee.

'Bastards,' I had told both of them one day, while Fish grinned, 'you'll be filthy all your life if you bathe in a tub.'

'What do *you* know? You've never been abroad,' Porridge shot back. 'I've talked to Bull and he says America is a very breeze place, you can buy nice things and do what you want and you don't have to clean airports like some Indian buggers do in London and all.' They didn't like it at all when I said I wasn't going to arse-lick any gora. PT Shoe had picked up the *National Geographic* and waved it in our face, almost shouting, '*This* is the American Dream, see, it's even *written* here. I *don't* want to be a bloodyfool tourist guide, I want a mansion in Manhattan and to screw gora chicks.' Fish laughed like a maniac because he was the only one among us who had travelled all over the world, even going to London to take flights to Nairobi when he was younger and sometimes going to Hong Kong before heading to Sing. For all his flying about in planes all Fish wanted was to fly free like a bird, but Bwana wouldn't let him, so Fish kept saying it didn't matter where you lived or travelled because what mattered was doing what you wanted to do. I took Fish's side when he said this, but Porridge and PT Shoe had their own ideas.

Porridge was on the bed, lying on his stomach, and he looked away when he saw me looking at him, a bit embarrassed. He didn't say anything and continued to read. There was nobody else in the dorm. I went to the balcony. Christine was there with Charlie-ma'am, talking to Squash about something. She did that sometimes, playing mother, asking if everything was all right.

'Brandy,' Porridge said.' Can I ask you something?'

'Sure bugger,' I said, 'Since when did you ask for permission?'

Porridge stayed silent. I had a drink from the matka, then turned and sat on my bed and started to unlace my PT Shoes. I rolled off the blue stockings, my feet aching from a cross-country run, and started to rub toe jam off with the top of a stocking, first my left foot, beginning with the toe and methodically working my way one toe-gap at a time, then attacking the right foot, big toe first. Finished, I looked up to see Porridge looking at me, all worried, so I held up the stocking, saying, 'Want to smell it? Good stuff.' That got a smile from him.

'Fuck off,' he said. That was more like it. I was getting up to go to the changing room when Porridge said, 'Have you ever smooched a guy?'

I stopped. 'No,' I said, suddenly nervous. 'Why the fuck are you asking? You want to smooch me? I'll bloody kill you.'

'No-no,' he looked shocked. 'No-no, I don't want to smooch you. Bloody Singlet smooched *me*.'

It was my turn to look shocked. Singlet was the quietest guy in class, never said anything. When he played hockey, he was the only back who stayed so far back that he would always let in goals. '*Singlet?*'

'Ya, the bugger piled on to me in hospi when I had gone to get ultraviolet on my arm.'

The story tumbled out. Porridge had twisted his arm playing tennis and had gone to hospi and he was alone, his arm stuck under the ultraviolet, when Singlet had pushed aside the curtains, rushed in, caught his head and shoved his tongue down Porridge's throat, like they did in Western movies, taking care to tilt their heads so their noses wouldn't bang.

'Yuck,' I said.

'Ya, bloody yuck.'

'How did it feel?' I was curious.

'It was horrible, the bastard was sweaty and it was full of his bloody spit.'

'*Yuck,*' I said.

'Ya,' Porridge had his face all screwed up. 'I brushed my teeth three times but I can't get the taste of his saliva out of my mouth.' It was in his head, I knew, and would not go away for a while, but why bother him with detail?

'Singlet's been showing me his cock in class,' he said.

'You should have kicked him in the balls,' I said, getting angry.

'No-no, in Bunter's class he sat behind me and whistled and said to look under the desk, and I thought he was going to pass me a chit or something but the bastard had his cock, hard-on and all, sticking out of his half-pants and the bastard was smiling and all.'

'What was *I* doing?' I asked. 'Why the hell didn't you tell us?'

'I thought he'd stop. And you buggers are always showing off in Sanskrit class with tenses so how would you notice? And Singlet was quiet, you know? And then he piles on. The fucker's following me around or what? I mean, aren't people supposed to say please and all before smooching?'

'So what do you want to do? Next time he says please you're going to smooch him and let him bugger you?'

'*Balls,*' Porridge said, 'I'll bugger *him*.' Then he realized what he had said—I was smiling—and blushed like he was some chick or something. 'No-no-no, Brandy, you know what I mean.'

'Ya,' I said, as I left the dorm. 'I know what you mean.'

I had no idea what he meant. But it would have to stay with me, I knew. Friends talked, and sometimes, you couldn't even tell other friends what they said.

There were no classes for us that day, because everybody involved with the play was given the day off. We hadn't seen Fish since the morning, and we wondered where he had gone. We thought he would be at the Old Swimming Pool, where he usually went on days there was a major thing happening, like a swimming competition, or like the day he knew he would be awarded colours for swimming because the coach had told him and he had dusted out his blazer in preparation. He had done it two days earlier, when we had done the dress rehearsal for *Billy Budd*, and as this was the day of the show, Fish had probably done it again.

We knew he had written a long letter to Masuma a day earlier, coming in late from rehearsals and staying up almost until midnight, writing by the light of his table lamp. He had written it in these long, lined yellow sheets he brought from Sing, and never wrote on the back because he didn't like writing on the impression of the ballpoint pen. I was awake, reading *Mirror Mirror on the Wall*, a really deadly mystery book by Ellery Queen I had borrowed from the library. Sleepy, I had closed the book and kept it under the mattress by the pillow as I usually did with books, and had turned to look at Fish. He was finishing up, precisely folding the sheets and then put them in an envelope, not the white ones but ones with the stamp already on them. He next wrote the address, and I knew what it would be—Miss Masuma Futehally, 182 C Altamount Road, Bombay—because we had memorized it by now, and he licked the yucky brown gum on the flap of the envelope with his tongue and closed the flap. He did all of this slowly, and I watched fascinated, like it was a show. He lifted his head and saw me, then smiled.

'Fish, everything okay?' I had asked.

'Yup,' he said, as he did whenever he was trying to hide something from us. At these times, he would also say 'nope'.

'You don't look too good-ya,' I said. 'Nervous about the play?'

'Nope,' said Fish.

'All okay with Masuma?'

'Ya, Brandy, it's always okay with Masuma, you know that.'

That was true. Masuma was to Fish something we could never be, even us, his closest buddies, maybe because Masuma was a girl, but it was also something more. We weren't jealous of Masuma, because a letter from her always kept Fish happy for days. During that time, Fish's favourite music was Fleetwood Mac. And though we had never seen her, only her photographs—Masuma looked like a plumper version of Samira—we thought we knew her well, because Fish would talk about her.

'G'night man,' I had told him, before crashing, and added a line from a Fleetwood Mac song, 'Don't stop thinking about tomorrow.'

Fish had smiled at that. 'Thanks, Brandy,' he said. 'Thanks for being there, all you guys. I'm glad I met you buggers. It's like destiny, no?'

'Ya, destiny,' I had agreed, though it seemed like too heavy a word to use this late at night. But Fish had finished a letter to Masuma, and we were all tired from rehearsals. 'I can't stop being Billy', Fish had said, 'It's easier to switch on than switch off', like he was bloody Lawrence Olivier. So maybe Fish was in a heavy mood.

'Take care bugger,' I had said, 'We're worried about you, you know?'

'Ya, I know. I'll be okay, breeze,' he had said. 'G'night.'

Fish showed up just before lunch, at the Main Building. Yogi got busy then, and we didn't get a chance to talk to Fish, except to say 'Break a leg, fucker' about an hour before the show, because he had to put on his make-up and go over some last-minute details with Yogi. Some people in the audience had already started seating themselves by then, mostly juniors, and many parents, who had come for the Prize Giving the next day. There would be a second show after Prize Giving dinner, for parents who hadn't seen it, and we heard there would also be people from Sophia (I wondered if Samira would be there), the English department of Government College, and even some senior-school types from St Mary's Convent and St Anselm's, which was a boy's school just down the road from the main gate, and they always raped Mayo in hockey.

Fish was holding the brochure for the play. We had our own and had seen it earlier, greatly excited. It was yellow, and from the top of the brochure hung a rope ending in a noose, and in the middle of the noose was an old-fashioned sailing ship on rough seas, which was supposed to be the *HMS Indomitable*. Nothing on the cover had any capital letters, which we thought was a totally breeze idea but were surprised Yogi had allowed it, and maybe he did it to freak Princi out, who knows? 'billy budd,' it read, to the right of the noose, 'a play in three acts based on the novel by herman melville.' To the left of the noose was written a line by Melville, 'yea and nay, each hath his say, but god he keeps the middle way.' We had decided to sign our names on each other's brochures after the show.

'Break a leg,' I told Fish. 'It's breeze.'

'Thank you, thank you, thank you, ladies and gentlemen,' Fish bowed in front of us in a dramatic way, like we had seen Hamlet do in a movie as he walked into court to bugger his uncle because he had killed his father who made one of the scariest ghosts I had seen, and we had burst into laughter. We had work to do, and shouted our new motto before we split, the line that Claggart taunts Billy Budd with, 'What are you waiting for? Light to dawn? Promotion?' It was a really deadly line, nasty, sarcy and funny all at the same time.

'Arsehole, Porridge,' Fish said before going into the green room passage, between Rat's class and Samosa-sir's. 'Don't drop the stretcher, okay?'

Porridge grinned like a madman, and showed Fish the finger. Friends.

It was the last scene of the play, and the crowd was buzzing. It had looked beautiful at the dress rehearsal and it looked beautiful now. The whole building had been darkened, and a single spotlight shone on the parapet where Billy Budd stood, waiting to die—an innocent, brave sailor, fucked by Claggart, Vere's rulebook, and life. Billy was at the wrong place at the wrong time, a bit like Fish, and maybe that's why Fish was so caught up with the role.

Billy had a rope around his neck. Down below, on the stage that now acted as Captain Vere's cabin, there was a dim light. Captain Vere was at his table, holding his head in his hands, all alone. The sound of a strong wind and the sea came scratchily over the sound system. There was a drum roll which faded into silence. The single spotlight came on and shone on the cupola, and there was Billy Budd, high above, with a spot on his face, a rope around his neck, the area below his knees and a couple of feet above his head in darkness, to hide the end of the rope, which was attached to a metal ring on the ceiling of the cupola.

The audience gasped, and there was at least one loud sob. Tears for Billy. Tears for Fish. It would be over quickly. Billy would stand there, and say one line, his last, and the lights would fade on top and in Captain Vere's cabin to signal the end of the play. We could then go off and finish the rest of the baked beans and sausages in the greenroom.

'God save Captain Vere,' Fish said in his strong clear voice. And then, as the lights began to fade and the applause and roars started, he just leaned forward, and stepped over the ledge. He dropped about two feet, the rope pulled him short and smashed the back of his head against the unpolished marble of the Main Building, and he hung there, swaying gently.

Someone, it sounded like Birdie Ma'am, screamed, 'OHMY*GOD*OHMY*GOD*.' Then it seemed everybody was screaming and running everywhere.

Porridge, PT Shoe and I were in our prize spot from where we could see everything. We sprinted down a level, up the stairs to the bridge and, like madmen, clambered up the rope ladder to the next level, where Billy—Fish—had stood a few minutes before. Bhavani, who had climbed on to the cupola, was trying to bring Fish in by pulling on the rope, which was turning slowly, and we screamed at him to not do that because it would strangle Fish some more. But Bhavani screamed back saying, 'Bastard if I loosen the rope he will drop more and you won't be able to reach him bastard and he might fall to the ground.' He was right.

Porridge leaned out as PT Shoe and I held onto his waist and legs, and after some time, I don't how long, he managed to snag the neck of Billy's long sleeved T-shirt. He pulled at Fish and after a few seconds, I managed to reach out and grab Fish's pajamas. Fish was parallel to the ground by now and I yelled at Bhavani to slacken the rope, and just as he did, we used the momentum to haul Fish in and fell back in a heap, Fish on top of us.

We scrambled out. Fish lay there, his tongue bitten through, eyes bulging, but face somehow without any emotion, like he was still playing Billy Budd and couldn't understand how he got into trouble. Birdie, and I can't recollect how many others, had reached us by then, and Nurse de Silva too, we saw, in her floral printed evening dress but without her high-heeled shoes, which she must have taken off to climb the rope ladder. She pushed us aside and felt for Fish's pulse. Then she put her hand on his chest and pumped it a few times. Then she prised open his mouth with both her hands, which made Fish's tongue go back in, and then Nurse de Silva put her mouth over Fish's and breathed in with these huge sighs, trying to breathe life into Fish. Nothing happened.

Fish's arms were behind him, and Nurse de Silva turned Fish over to his side to get his arms out, we saw Fish had put his hands through a wristband in an eight-loop, so he couldn't free them even if he tried, the bastard.

Nurse de Silva put her head on Fish's chest and her arms around his body, and wailed like it was the end of the world.

Bwana and Mrs Bwana had arrived after four days. After a quick meeting with Princi they went straight to Victoria Hospital, where Fish had been kept in the morgue.

We hadn't been allowed anywhere near the morgue, and any question to Chalu-Charlie was met with a firm 'no'. 'You boys calm down now,' he said. 'Go for games.'

He told us Fish's parents were on their way.

We had heard, in fact the whole House had heard him yelling on the phone to Sing the night Fish had died, having taken special permission from Princi to book a Lightning Call, he had told us later, and because the line was always so bad even between Ajmer and Jaipur, we could only imagine what it must have been like talking to someone in Sing, almost like talking to someone on another planet. Some of us were standing outside the Housemaster's flat, and because only the screen doors were shut, we could hear bits of what Chalu-Charlie said. 'Hallo HALLO, Mr Verma, this is Mr D'Costa, Sanjay's housemaster HOUSEMASTER, there has been a terrible accident ACCIDENT, yes, yes, could you please come as soon as possible? YES, YES, ACCIDENT...Oh Mother Mary, this bloody phone, SHIT...'

Chalu-Charlie was freaking out, but so were we all, in our own way. Porridge had suddenly written a letter to his parents, breaking his vow of not writing more than twice a month. And PT Shoe was inconsolable. Every now and then, he would say, 'Yaar, what did this goddamn bloodyfool Fish do?'

I had gone quiet. I had nothing to say, and didn't feel like doing anything, so I tried to shut my eyes and force myself to sleep, but that bastard Fish kept floating out from the back of my eyes, like it was a movie screen and Fish was in the movies and he was a star; he would smile, and then his dead face with bulging eyes would look at me and smirk: 'Arsehole.'

We let Fish's desk be, but had taken care to dust his books, make his bed and put in our best bit of organizing in as long as any of us could remember, to turn Fish's messy cupboard into such a work of art, our parents would have been proud of it. We had taken down the posters of Parveen Baby and Zeenie Baby, which Porridge rolled up and kept away carefully on top of the cupboard.

Sleep wouldn't come. Porridge had screaming nightmares the first night and he was taken to a small room in hospi in the middle of the night; we heard Doc had given him injections to calm him down and make him sleep without nightmares. As a precaution, PT Shoe and I were also taken to hospi as well and Doc had checked us out, but all we had done was cry and say, 'I don't know' when he asked us what happened, because Fish had trusted us with his thoughts and we couldn't betray that. All we said was that Fish was very unhappy with his home scene.

Doc had been very nice, and Doc Ma'am had come to sit with us for a while, and then Nurse de Silva had come to see us and held us in her arms and rocked us like we were babies and we had all cried some more. Just to be sure, they had kept us in the hospi for the night and given us injections also and we had crashed almost straightaway, waking up after lunch. We found out later that we weren't the only ones who were affected by what happened to Fish; there were about two dozen other boys from other Houses. I saw Punk and Makkhan from 10 B, the others were juniors, and juniors were not worth knowing unless they were cat sports guys or book-wallahs, good at studies.

Chalu-Charlie had come and driven us back to the House on his mobike. Riding three was illegal, but nobody said anything. We could see the Pavilion dressed up for Prize Giving, but Chalu-Charlie told us we didn't have to go if we didn't want to, though we were happy they hadn't cancelled Prize Giving—Fish would have been really upset had they done that.

We heard later that the Prize Giving had gone exactly as planned, and the cheering was louder, like everybody, the students, parents and Old Boys, wanted to forget the play and the insanity of Fish's death. There was no mention of Fish's death, but we were sure there would be soon, because London had dropped by to see us and consoled us with, 'I've asked Princi to say something for Fish at Assembly. You guys take care.'

The only thing that had gone wrong was that Mango had slipped and fallen off the vault during gymnastic exhibition, and cracked his ankle. We also heard rumours that Princi may go because of what had happened to Fish, because parents must have been quite freaked out, thinking their children would now line up to jump off buildings like Fish had. But that sounded crazy because it wasn't Princi's fault, and in 1975 Juicy had drowned in the pool because he had jumped over the wall and gone swimming alone and must have got cramps, but I guess they were looking for someone to blame, to make an example of Princi like he sometimes made an example of the boys.

Porridge was still in the hospi but Chalu-Charlie had made sure the farrash woke us up on time on Monday, thinking that we were drugged with injections, we may not hear the wake-up bell. We had to go back to class, and that was okay with us because it would give us something to do. All of Sunday, we had tried to avoid the guys in the House and the Mess, but they wouldn't let us be, looking at us like we were freaks and asking, 'What happened-ya?' and 'Did Fish really write he was doing this because Princi's daughter wouldn't run away with him?' It was bullshit, but we kept quiet, because we realized that whatever we said wouldn't be believed and the guys would believe whatever they wanted to believe.

Monday morning was a lot better. By then, the attention had shifted from us, to what Princi would say at assembly.

We had walked quickly to hospi and met Porridge just before Assembly. He seemed better, and greeted us with a smile—that bugger was tough—and said he wanted to come to Assembly. Doc didn't have a problem with that so we took Porridge with us, and he seemed really happy that PT Shoe and I had brought along his Jodhpuri, togs and black shoes, and old Ram Pyare, the Jaipur House farrash, had come with us so that he could tie the orange safa of Jaipur House. The guys in the house and the hospi had looked at us as if we were crazy, but we just ignored them and kept quiet. PT Shoe and I had talked about it in the bogs that morning as we brushed our teeth, and I had looked into the mirror and seen the eyes of an old man, maybe as old as Papa.

'Yaar,' PT Shoe said, 'You think the monitors will bugger us if we wear safas to Assembly?'

'Why, bugger?'

'I want to do it, to honour Fish-ya.'

I had looked at him, wondering if we had all finally gone nuts, crazy over Fish, like people outside Mayo, in India, were always bloody going crazy and doing stupid things, but PT Shoe had looked at me as if to say we were no more crazy than any other fucker.

'I want to honour Fish, Brandy. I want to do it like a Rajput. Will you wear the dress-ya?'

'Ya,' I said, deciding two nuts were better than one, and I thought it was PT Shoe's way of doing something for Fish, like an apology, like saying, sorry fucker, but we love you and all, and fuck Bwana and the whole world and who the bloody hell likes losing a brother and all-ya, you know?

We went to old Ram Pyare, who had the keys to the House godown, where all the safas were kept, and had begged him for three safas, one for Porridge, just in case he was better and Doc thought it would be okay for him to be at Assembly, and old Ram Pyare had looked at us for a long time, trying to make up his mind if he should ask us to bugger off or sneak us to Chalu-Charlie, before he nodded his head once and said in Hindi, 'Achchha, it is for Phish-beta, but you give the safa back to me after Assembly or Housemaster sa'ab will get angry.' But I could see he had looked at PT Shoe with respect.

We filed in with the rest of the guys, while they looked at us three wearing Jodhpuris and safas, but even the monitors didn't say anything except look at us like we were crazy but they could do nothing because there was no PD for boys wearing safas and Jodhpuris when they wanted, except for games and I could see Pogo in the last bench giving us a V-sign and mouthing 'peace' and I did the same back to him, and took our seats near the fireplace, near old M.G.H.H.M.S.P.S.B., G.C.S.I., G.C.V.O., K.C.B., L.L.D.D., A.P.C., D.C.L. He looked really king in his blue turban and white tunic, sitting on a black stallion, and seemed to be looking at me today, maybe he was happy to see guys wearing safas.

Princi arrived on the dot at 9.30 and we all shuffled to our feet, and then settled down for the music, some French accordion stuff, and then finished with the ritual of prayers in Sanskrit, Hindi and English. After we finished singing 'Raghupati Raghav Raja Ram', which was Mahatma Gandhi's favourite song, Princi asked us all to sit down.

'We are all disturbed about the tragic passing away of Sanjay Verma, who was an outstanding student and part of our Mayo community,' he said. 'The past two days have been trying ones for Sanjay's family and friends and, indeed, all of us at Mayo, and I must congratulate each one of you for the immense patience and courage you've shown, particularly in ensuring the Prize Giving went off well, and the pride of Mayo, the character that all of you represent, is...intact.'

Princi's favourite phrase was 'alive and kicking' and I thought that's what he was going to say but I guess he must have checked himself in time, because Fish was dead, though he was still alive and kicking in our heads, the bastard.

Then he said, 'The school captain has requested that he be allowed to say a few words. Lavesh, please come.'

London walked up from his customary place under the portrait with less initials, of F.A. Leslie Jones Esq, M.A., C.B.E., I.E.S. who was the Princi from 1917, when World War I was still on, to 1929, a time when Mahatma Gandhi was doing some really cat protests against the British. London looked tired, like he had looked tired at the end of *Billy Budd*, after sentence was passed on Billy.

'I would request you all to please stand up, and pay respect with a minute's silence to Sanjay Verma of Jaipur House.' We shuffled to our feet but it was amazing that nobody, not the squealing Class 6 kids in the front rows to the Class 12 monsters at the back, made any noise. The silence was total. I hadn't heard anything like it before. After some time London started to talk, standing on the steps to the right and slightly below Princi's lectern, the usual place when any boy had to stand when he said something at Assembly.

'Sanjay Verma was an outstanding Mayoite and a brilliant sportsman, and at least I had thought that one day, he would stand where I am standing today, as captain of this school. We will miss him...'

London choked and looked down, and we knew he was trying to hold back his tears, and we knew why, because though Yogi had directed the play, London had actually taken charge and coached Fish right through, as if he had a special feeling for a person he would be forced to sentence to death against his wishes. It was just a play, but it had suddenly become real.

'...we will miss him,' London recovered, 'but we will remember him as he was, as 94, as swimming captain, as Billy Budd, and as Fish.'

Fuck, I thought, London was *such* a good speaker. I was choking up, guys were sniffling around us, PT Shoe was crying silently, and so was Porridge, his hands clutching the top of the bench in front of us so hard, his knuckles white, that I thought he would snap the wood. Princi was looking straight up towards the ceiling, at the beautiful gold-water painting of the sun and the moon, depicting the two greatest houses of Rajputana, the Suryavanshi and the Chandravanshi, his mouth a thin line. Shit, I thought, when I die, I want someone to say something like this about me.

'I will now read you a small piece I wrote sometime ago, that I thought appropriate for this occasion.'

London stopped and pulled out a sheet of paper from the right pocket of his blazer. He opened it, pushed back his spectacles firmly and started to read.

'What about the fulfilment of purpose for which I am here in Mayo? What have I achieved in these years? It is only now when

I am mature enough to have a well-defined purpose in life, that I am able to judge, relative to this purpose, my achievements and my failures.'

London was reading from his own essay in *Mayoor*, 'The Floating Island', which had become legend when London had written it in 1977, and had even had some blue blood sorts writing letters to Princi saying 'pseudos' shouldn't be allowed to write in *Mayoor*. Porridge, Fish and I had joked about it, and Porridge had said, 'Man, I'm surprised they can even spell pseudo', but took care not to say it in front of PT Shoe—just in case he freaked out.

'I am not what I would have liked to be,' London continued. 'Mayo is aiming to prepare me for others. I want to be for myself. But it is growing increasingly difficult for me to prepare myself for myself as my expectations grow greater. A reformed open-hearted Mayo can help me. Till then I shall stand on the beaches, look towards the sea, and wait for a solution to be washed ashore.'

Man, if anyone but the school captain had read that at Assembly, he would be on the first train home. But today was different, I could sense, anyone could say anything and get away with it.

London stopped. He was crying freely, and I think most us were, even the teachers, because we knew, for some reason, we couldn't stop Fish.

We came back after games and saw Bwana and Mrs Bwana in the room, Mrs Bwana sitting on Fish's bed, stroking the pillow like it was Fish lying there under the bedcover. Fish's cupboard was open, Mr Bwana was poking around and that's when we realized the value of PT Shoe's brainwave of removing Fish's filthy gym shoes and sports socks with toe jam from just outside the room, so surprising a trait in a guy like him we used to call him Son of Bracey. Amazingly, the harmless rat snake that sometimes visited the gutter pipe near the balcony of our dorm left Fish's shoes alone, though we thought it qualified as vermin and was therefore wholesome food for a snake.

'So you were his friends,' Bwana snapped, glaring at us.

'Of course they are his friends,' Mrs Bwana stepped in. She had a really kind face, as delicate as Bwana's looked liked a bulldog's; the photographs Fish showed us hadn't lied, I saw. Her eyes were ringed black with grief, but she still managed a smile to make us feel at home in our own room. Then she turned to Bwana and said very formally, in Hindi: 'Aap mujhe in bachcho ke saath kuchh baatein karne dijiye.' Please let me talk for some time with these children.

Bwana, who still seemed angry, glared some more, but didn't argue and went outside. Man, what a king shit Fish's dad was. Why blame Princi?

'Aaplog baithiye,' Mrs Bwana told us. We sat as she asked us. Porridge and PT Shoe were looking down, but I couldn't help looking at her.

'Thank you for looking after Sanjay's things for us.' We kept quiet.

After a pause, she said, 'How was he?'

I started hesitantly, after introducing myself and then PT Shoe and Porridge, with our proper names, which sounded so strange whenever we said it. 'He was okay, ma'am, doing things like he always did.'

Suddenly, I wasn't afraid of talking. Fish's mother had that effect.

'He wanted to make the India senior team in swimming, and try for the Olympics.'

'When are the Olympics?'

'In 1980 ma'am,' said Porridge, 'In Moscow.'

'Achchha,' she paused. 'Did Sanjay say anything?' We knew what she meant, but how could we tell a mother her son killed himself because her husband had tied him in chains?

Porridge and PT Shoe looked at me.

'Ma'am, uh, aunty, Fish...I mean Sanjay'—she smiled at this—'I think Sanjay tried hard to make Mr Verma proud of him...' I couldn't go on.

'Come here, beta,' she said, and I went to her. She hugged me tightly, and asked, 'How are your father and sister?'

I nodded. Fish must have told her about Ma's death during the last hols. She gave me a kiss on my forehead. She held out her arms, and gave a quick hug and kiss to Porridge and PT Shoe. Then she got up.

'I've asked Mr D'Costa to give Sanjay's clothes away to children who need it. If you want any of his things, his tapes or books, please take them. He was your friend; he would have liked you to have them.'

She went to the door, on her way to take Fish's body from Victoria Hospital, and Fish, now surely stinking and rotting even with slabs of ice to cool him, would smell like a cremation ground all the way to Delhi where Bwana would burn his beloved son and I hoped Bwana would trip and fall into the pyre and burn too, the fucker. Nobody would mourn him, and Mrs Bwana would finally be free of him.

She stopped and turned to look at us. It was the only time her composure cracked.

'Even you couldn't keep him back.'

I dragged Moses and Porridge along for a Madar-run. They weren't doing anything. Moses had been excused from games because he had sprained a wrist and Porridge was depressed because Rohu had jacked him 6-0, 6-1 in the quarter-final of the individual tennis competition, and it didn't matter to Porridge that Rohu was really good and had gone on to win the competition. Porridge was keeping away from tennis, his Wilson T2000 racket was in his cupboard, and the bugger hadn't even fondled the damn thing like it was his girlfriend or his cock, as he did whenever he got the chance. Suddenly for him Björn Borg was better than Jimmy Connors and he was talking about switching to a wooden Donnay racket, because that is what Borg played with. He needed an excuse, and that was okay, because, I mean, who the fuck didn't need an excuse once in a while?

It worried me that Moses was moping again because there was some shit news from home, he said, though I think he was really funked he would plug in history and geog in the Class 10 exams, and then Princi might jack him because he was on scholarship. Porridge was still upset over Fish, as we all were, but he was really badly gone and was going nuts once in a while, though what he did to Maindak anybody would have done, even if he hadn't got raped by Rohu in front of what must have been half the school. But Rohu had manners even if he had no sympathy on court, and after the match he had come and talked to Porridge and said, 'Sorry man, and I'm sorry about Fish', as if he knew why Porridge, who played tennis like it was ballet, hadn't been playing his best tennis. Rohu was an okay senior.

Maindak, of course, was nothing of the sort. He had also obviously forgotten that nobody was funked of him any more, not even juniors, after guys in his own batch had turned on him when Pittu, his roomie, poor chap, had come back to the room he shared with Maindak and discovered the bastard going through his cupboard, holding some money in his hand. Pittu had quickly walked out, gone next door to Panda and Pogo, and the three of them had come rushing back before Maindak could run away, and anyway, where could he run, except away from school?

They beat the shit out of him. We all knew what had happened, because we were about to go for dinner when we heard yelling and shouts of 'Nahin, nahin' and 'Please please, I'm sorry-ya' and had run downstairs to see the door to Pittu and Maindak's room shut. After five minutes the door had opened and they had dragged Maindak out, bleeding from his mouth, shirt torn, black eye forming. Pogo had said, 'Motherfucker, you tell Doc you fell off the cycle after hitting the gate,' before dragging him all the way to hospi. Maindak could barely walk. Pittu had gone with Panda, holding Maindak's collar, while Pogo had gone to bash Maindak's bike into the House gates to provide an alibi. They needn't have worried, we were so sick of Maindak we would have signed a letter to the PM saying, 'Dear Prime Minister, could you please cure Maindak with your special medicine, you know what medicine we mean, because we don't know what else will cure him. Thank you, yours faithfully, the boys of Mayo College, Ajmer.'

Maindak had obviously recovered well to taunt Porridge just a week or so later, saying there was now one dish less in the Mess, meaning Fish, and said that at this rate there would soon be one more dish less, meaning Porridge; and Porridge had, without a word, slammed his fist into Maindak's solar plexus and left the bastard there by the side of the museum, which Porridge and I shut before heading to the Mess.

Actually, that wasn't the whole story, and it wasn't how it began. Twice a week Porridge and I would go to the museum because we were part of the Museum Society and had to supervise the museum, and we loved it because it was a really deadly place, and the Visitor's Book had comments like 'Excellent' and 'Best such museum I have ever seen', even from firang visitors, which made us really proud. I particularly liked the Arms Room, which had swords and machine guns captured from POWs and even a Japanese samurai sword from Burma that an Old Boy had donated.

I had come out of there, walking through the Costume Room, the School Records Room, and just as I reached the Stone Room, which had this cat floating stone, a coral, in a tank, I heard Porridge talking loudly, really angry. I ran out and saw Porridge holding Maindak by the collar and shaking him. Both were standing at the top of the stairs, where there was a whole bunch of plaster and bronze casts of people like King George V and Queen Mary, Queen Victoria, General Claude Auchinleck who used to be the boss of the Indian army and had even come for Prize Giving in 1947, and two casts of Venus di Milo and Aphrodite.

Of the two Aphrodite was prettier and leaner. Venus di Milo was plumper and had bigger boobs, and Porridge and I used to feel sorry for her because her face was a sad face, made sadder because she had no arms, and wondered how two goddesses of love could look so different in cultures that were neighbours in a way. Both statues had shiny areas around the nipples and Venus didn't even have nipples, just rounded boobs. I think the shine came from generations of boys who rubbed them on their way up or down. Nobody had actually seen it happen, but there could be no other explanation, Porridge and I would snigger, unless old Lord Mayo with his Michael Caine looks and tassels for balls had got horny one full moon night and had got off his pedestal to pile on to fellow statues, these two lonely chicks from ancient Greece and Rome, while Queen Victoria looked on sternly.

Anyway, Porridge had come out of the Natural History room, on his way over to where I was, when he had seen Maindak standing there, in front of old Venus, frigging. Porridge told me he had said, 'What the fuck are you doing you crazy bastard?' Maindak had turned around and, just then, cum into his hankie, like he couldn't stop himself. Porridge told him then that he would put Maindak's name on a list of people banned from the Musuem, and that's when Maindak had made that comment about Porridge being the next one to kill himself, and Porridge had hit him, good shot. Maindak we couldn't seem to do anything about, that bastard was completely shameless, though his gang had now broken up, Bumble and the Piglets scared they would get jacked like Maindak.

But Porridge and Moses were friends, and for friends I would do anything.

I did the run at least once a week, using the excuse of being in the athletics team to go out of campus. Though Zulfi, the athletics coach, always encouraged us to go on cross-country runs to build stamina, I never did it much until I had come back to school after Ma died. Now I looked forward to the runs, because I felt free and the rush of the wind and the rhythm of the run took away thoughts I didn't like from my head. I had found I was getting less angry, and could even study again. Running had become like a drug, and I had become a Madar-run junkie. It helped me to not think of Ma, Fish and the fact that in four months, we'd be having our exams and I didn't know what the hell I was going to do after that except stay two more years in school. Sometimes it felt good not to think.

It wasn't really a run. What I would do, alone or with anyone else, was to start jogging as I reached the Gulab-Bari gate behind Bikaner and Tonk House, cross the railway line to Jaipur, and cut through the cluster of single-storey whitewashed houses till I came to the base of Madar. The red-earth track would slope up, so I would run up till it was too steep to run, and then begin the climb to the top. It wasn't easy, but it was such fun, scrabbling up through rock and thorn bush and shrubs, sometimes slipping on loose stones but always moving up, first through the part facing Mayo, then turning left to go up through a gully, which would become a waterfall in the monsoon, and then turn right to reach the lower end of the ridge and walk up to the top.

It was so beautiful up there. Out of breath, Moses, Porridge and I sat on a small slab of rock. The sun wasn't as harsh as when we had begun to climb, so we could look around without having to shade our eyes and squint. I always brought some bread for the two kites I saw at this time of day. They would fly above and then swoop lazily to near where I sat. The bread I would keep further away. I wasn't sure if the kites ate that bread, maybe it was the crows or doves or rats or ants, or maybe the wind just blew the bread away, but there was never any trace when I came back with the next lot of supplies.

On our left was the railway line snaking away to Jaipur and Delhi, and I pointed out Madar Station from which a long goods train was just moving out, to Moses who had never been on top of Madar. How he managed that I don't know because all chaps made at least one trip to Madar and to the top of Taragarh, the high hill with a plateau-top to the right of us, and it dominated the skyline of the town to the west the same way Madar loomed over Mayo. School and Ajmer were spread below us, and we could see a lot of the campus: there was the Main Building and the Clock Tower, we could clearly see the Bikaner Pavilion and small figures in white, guys playing cricket, and the left-to-right line of B.T. House, Jodhpur House, Rajasthan House, which we called Raj House, and Ajmer House.

To the left and behind Mayo was a line of brick-red hills with hardly any vegetation on them, and behind that was Bir Lake. It was a nice picnic spot to which whole Houses would go once in a while, and when it had been our turn, ten of us had opted to trek over the hills with Samosa-sir, while another lot of guys had gone cycling with Yogi, and the rest, mostly the youngest and laziest, had taken the bus south towards Nasirabad, and then taken a turn left for Bir.

We had walked under the increasingly hot sun on the track behind Colvin House that rose in sudden turns up the hill, stamped into its side by villagers and goatherds and, as I liked to think, generations of Mayo chaps. Our feet were burning through the stockings and rubber soles of our PT Shoes and sometimes, the mica-like stones in the hills would catch the sun and blind us. I had a canvas cricket cap on, so my head was protected but my feet tried to find some peace in my moving shadow. After crossing the hill we descended on to a valley that was full of vegetables. The path went past a hut, past a big well, and then split into three tracks, and we were a bit lost and even Samosa-sir couldn't recollect if it was the middle track or the one on the right that led to Bir. A grizzled old man was standing near the hut, leaning on a stick, wearing a dirty white shirt and short dhoti. 'Woh neemro,' he had said, pointing with his stick to the track on the right, which went past a big neem tree.

We thanked him and stopped at the well, PT Shoe, Squash and I, and Pat and Vicky too, while Samosa-sir had gone ahead with the other guys, saying 'C'mon boys, don't be such pansies,' like only pansies got tired and thirsty, but PT Shoe had saved the day for us when he said 'Don't worry sir, I speak Rajasthani we won't get lost.' We realized quickly that stopping at the well was a grand idea because there was a young village woman there, filling two aluminium pots with water. We walked towards her and she smiled at us and dropped an iron bucket into the well, which had an earthen ramp on the other side, and a camel was tethered to a rope and we knew what it was. The camel would walk down the ramp and haul a huge pouch of leather full of water and a guy would stand at the lip of the well and tilt the pouch over, letting the water run down a cut in the ramp and then a bunch of channels would carry the water to the fields to irrigate them. 'Carrots,' PT Shoe said, pointing to the fields, a sea of green fronds swaying in the slight breeze.

The woman was beautiful, we saw, with big brown eyes and a mouth like the models in *JS*, full lips and all. She wore a colourful blouse and ghagra, and she had a lovely body, tall and brown, and looked much more breeze than even the Babies. Her tits were high and we could see acres of smooth glistening skin between her blouse and ghagra and when she turned to drop the bucket into the well, we saw her blouse had no back and there she was, herself, from her neck to her waist, and her muscles rippled a bit as she lowered the bucket hand over hand. She had leaned forward and as we had moved to the side to get a better view, we saw her boobs were being pushed out of her blouse. She pulled the small bucket up and Vicky was there instantly, cupping his hands, drinking and trying to look at her at the same time, as she tipped the bucket over and poured the water. Vicky tried to drink without choking because his neck was arched taut like a camel reaching for acacia leaves. PT Shoe drank last because he was from Rajasthan and always played the perfect host. Our bellies were bursting with water because we kept saying 'Thoda aur, please', because we didn't want her to stop, little more please, and we must have drunk three buckets of water between us. After thanking her with folded hands, and she had smiled at that, showing her white teeth, we had taken the track and as soon as we had gone past a bunch of neem and acacia trees we had run to the side of the track and stood side by side and pissed like horses for what seemed like hours. Pat kept saying 'Man did you see her, man, did you see her?' like an idiot, because we had all seen her, acting like he had never seen a babe and all his pondies were bullshit because one village girl even prettier than Zeenie Baby had freaked out his head.

As I swivelled my head to the right, the straggly line of houses that reached up to the base of Taragarh gave way to a saddle, and through that I could see that shine of the Annasagar Lake with these king marble railings and pavilions that Emperor Jehangir, Shah Jahan's dad, had built. Sir Thomas Roe, who first brought a message from Queen Elizabeth I of England, had been received by Jehangir as ambassador to his court in Ajmer, just imagine. Past the lake, another row of hills marched north as far as we could see.

'It's so beautiful-ya,' Moses said.

'Ya,' agreed Porridge.

'Ya,' I said, acting like a proud guide, showing off a wonder of my world.

We sat quietly for a while, just soaking up the scene.

Porridge suddenly turned to Moses. 'Boss, any news of your father?'

'Nothing-ya,' Moses said, as I glared at Porridge. But he ignored me, and I saw Moses didn't mind Porridge's question, and maybe they understood each other in a way that I never would, because Porridge's dad was in the navy, and Moses's had been this king pilot, flying Hunters and MiG-21s, before going missing during the Bangladesh war that India and Pakistan fought. It could so easily have been the other way around—Porridge's dad gone missing or dead if his ship had been attacked, Moses's dad still around, and Moses asking Porridge, 'Boss, any news of your father?'

Moses never talked about it, which we thought was really a brave thing to do, and we didn't treat him differently because he didn't have a dad, so he didn't mind. He was one of the guys. This was a chat between Porridge and Moses, so I just shut up and listened.

'They've got all the POWs, no?' Porridge said.

'Ya, they've been exchanged,' replied Moses. 'But I heard Ammu say that both India and Pakistan had kept some POWs back. Karan-uncle, who used to fly with Abbu and was in the same sortie when Abbu's plane got hit, told her. Karan-uncle swears he saw a parachute, and that's why Ammu still believes Abbu is in Pakistan somewhere.'

'Have you guys asked the government?' Porridge said.

'Ya-ya, but Ammu says they all say they'll do something but

they've done nothing. There has to be some record somewhere. But those buggers don't say anything.' Moses stopped.

Moses was on scholarship, we knew, because he was a war hero's son and the family didn't have much money ever since his dad had gone missing, and his mom didn't earn too much as a schoolteacher. But the guy was so dignified, we admired him. When we were younger we used to cry for our parents sometimes, but Moses never did, maybe because he didn't have a father to cry for, and didn't want to pile pressure on his mom. Papa had liked Moses instantly when he had come to drop me off the first time, and of the other six guys he met, he had specifically asked Moses to come along for lunch with us to the Circuit House where Moses had eaten politely and with perfect manners, not messing up with the chicken curry and roti like I had. The gravy didn't touch Moses's fingers beyond the first finger joint, and he would pick up the pieces of chicken like his fingers were tweezers. Papa approved, because he ate exactly that way with his hand, and had looked at me pointedly, as if saying, 'Learn from this boy.'

'Ammu believes he is in some hospi,' Moses said after a while. The kites had moved on towards the small temple further along the ridge. 'But I think they must have tortured Abbu, maybe killed him. He could even be in a lunatic asylum, gone crazy from the torture.'

Porridge and I were speechless. We had never heard anything like this. It was all crazy anyway because a Muslim war hero from India had been shot down while fighting against Pakistan, a Muslim country, and the 'Pekos', as Ma had called Pakistanis, might have got a bit freaked out, thinking Moses's dad even more of an enemy because he was Muslim. I wasn't too sure about this theory though, because Pakistanis had killed thousands and thousands of their own people, mostly Muslim, in East Pakistan, and all because they wanted more freedom and to do everything in Bengali which is what people in East Pakistan spoke. I had seen a photo book on the war in the library and one photo had got me completely freaked out. It was of a street in Dhaka, the capital of Bangladesh, and the houses, which looked like houses in Cal, had bullet marks on them, and we all knew how they looked because we had seen enough movies and seen the books on World War II in the library. There was the dead body of an old man lying on the street, his white beard curved up and mouth open, and his body looked like it had been cut up and shot to bits. A little girl was passing by on the other side of the road, and she was looking at this body, and maybe he was someone she knew, her grandfather or someone else. Her wide eyes were fixed on the body, and her lips were turned down in horror. I always wanted to know what happened to the girl in the photograph, because if I were there, I might have gone crazy from the horror of it all. How people could fuck each other so badly and then dump all their shit on kids, I had no idea.

'I don't know what Abbu would look like now,' Moses said. 'He would be eight years older, maybe his hair is totally white from the torture. Maybe he's lost his memory and doesn't know who he is any more.'

'No man,' I said, 'Don't talk like that-ya, he's your dad and all.'

'No-ya, that's exactly what I get funked about, Brandy,' Moses was talking faster now, his voice getting excited. 'What if he were to come home and not know us, not know who he was, where he was? What if he's gone crazy, and he drools, like those guys in the movies?'

Moses again became silent, and said after a minute or so, while Porridge and I looked into the sun that had lowered itself to about the roof of the dargah on top of Taragarh, 'Sometimes I think it's better if they don't find Abbu, because it would save everyone the pain.'

He looked at us imploringly, as if what he had said was all right, it was okay for a guy to talk like that about his dad. But how could we say anything, when we couldn't even fully understand what he was saying? We could just *be* there, you know, that's all we could do.

Mayo College
Ajmer
Rajasthan
Pin—305001
10.12.78.

Dear Samira,

I am Barun Ray, and my nickname is Brandy. Do you remember me? I came to Sophia after the movie. I hope you are not angry with me in any way.

I hope you are okay. I am fine. Please don't mind me writing and if you're angry, I am very sorry. If you tell me, I will not write again.

I wanted to write to you before but I could not because I was not able to. That day when I did that stupid thing, there were two more Mayo boys with me. The name of the tall one is Pratap Singh, and we call him PT Shoe. The other boy is Michael Crasto. He is called Porridge because he loves Porridge. Many of us have funny nicknames, and some of us are called by our roll numbers, which become nicknames. If you have been to boarding school you will know this.

You never met my other friend Sanjay, whom we call Fish. The reason I could not write to you before is because there has been a tragedy. Fish killed himself on 24 November, during the annual school play, which usually happens a day before Prize Giving, or on the evening of Prize Giving, after the ceremonies are over and all parents and guests have eaten. He was one of the heroes of the play, called *Billy Budd,* which is taken from a book by Herman Melville, who wrote *Moby Dick,* which I am sure you have heard of. If you have heard of Herman Melville, I am sorry for saying it here.

We are very unhappy, because we are all friends, and feel very sad because we miss Fish very much. I am sure he would have done very well in the Class 10 exams, but he can't do the exams now, the same as he can't swim, and he was the swimming captain of Mayo. One day, he might have become school captain of our batch, and we had plans that we would all be monitors and run Mayo like the Government of India. I am joking.

I have not told my parents about Fish because they would worry. It is nice that none of our parents came for Prize Giving, because they would be very upset and might have wanted to take us away from Mayo. Sometimes I think it would not be a bad thing, because without Fish things are not the same any more. I hope you do not mind my writing this to you, because I need to say this to someone and I do not know whom to say it to. If I tell my father he will get very upset and worry about me and might even take me away from Mayo, because my mother died one year ago and he worries all the time that something will happen to the family. I have a younger sister, and who will look after her if something happens to me, or my father?

I will be going home for the winter holidays on 15 December, to Calcutta by Jayanti Janata Express which goes to Delhi Junction. From Delhi Junction I will take the Kalka Mail to Howrah which is the station for Calcutta. It is a very long journey. I do not know if you want to reply, but if you want to reply, please write to me at the following address:

Barun Ray
C/o, Mr Tarun Ray
3092, Jodhpur Park
Calcutta
West Bengal
Pin – 700068

School reopens on 15 January, and then we will get busy studying for the exams, which are in March. But there is a farewell party for our batch, and I have heard that they plan to make it a Social with Sophia. Will you please come for that? It will be nice.

I think of you a lot, and I think you are the most beautiful girl I have ever seen. And you also have a nice heart, because you did not get me into trouble when I came to Sophia. You are a good lady. Sorry if you are angry with this letter.

Yours sincerely,
Barun Ray (Brandy)
Roll No. 612
Jaipur House

Samira was standing near the reservation charts on Platform No. 1 when I reached the station with the guys who were going to Delhi. As soon as I saw her, my heart felt like it was doing a double somersault with one-and-a-half twists, degree of difficulty 4.5 or something, like Bhanu Singh taught boys to do from the three-metre board. I quickly asked Moses to look after my case and holdall, which the coolies had piled onto a trolley, and walked casually towards Samira, my heart in my mouth and threatening to pop right out onto the platform. If it did, I would keep on walking, I knew, a bit like the headless man in ghost stories, because heart or no heart, head or no head, my feet had ideas of their own, and they walked me, one sure step at a time, towards Samira.

The train was an hour late, I had found out at the inquiry counter at the entrance to the station, so I knew there was time. One of the girls who were with her that day in Sophia was with her. 'Hi,' I said, thinking, thank god I wrote that letter, the envelope marked 'Personal' to the address that simply said Miss Samira Khanna, First Year, Sophia College, Ajmer, Rajasthan, which Porridge had tried so much to not make me post, saying Samira would complain to the police and I would either be expelled or given a month's detention.

It's good I didn't listen to him, because it wasn't like I had tried to bugger some juniors, like Chutney two years ago, and Princi had made him stand in front of the whole school at a special Assembly outside the main building and thundered, 'This sort of behaviour will not be tolerated in Mayo College or for that matter any civilized institution.'

'Brandy, hi,' Samira smiled. It felt great she was using my nickname, and from the way my face was feeling, I knew I was blushing, and from the way my cheeks were aching, I was probably grinning like a bloody fool.

'This is Jasmine.' Jasmine half-smiled and gave a small wave. From her frown I could make out she probably thought Samira to be a bloody fool too. I waved back, not caring.

'So, are you taking a train, or receiving someone?' I asked Samira.

'No-ya,' she said, 'I got your letter.' I just kept looking at her. She was three years older, but that shouldn't matter, I told myself. 'Come, let's go to the refreshments room. Jasmine, come on.'

We went towards the non-veg refreshments room at the end of the platform, past the guys and the trolley, and all the guys except Moses, who winked and gave me a thumbs up, looked at us like we were in a freak show. Brandy with two babes—sorry, ladies—was a dream, only, this was real, we were on Platform No.1, it was crowded as usual, with coolies sitting around smoking beedis, families waiting for trains, a man reclining against his suitcase and taking a nap with his mouth open and small knot of flies hovering around his face, a small boy standing at the edge of the platform, being made to piss on to the tracks by his mother.

We sat at the only empty table, Jasmine insisting the waiter clean up spilt tea and bread crumbs, and then made a face when the waiter did her bidding with a cloth that was black with muck and stank like it had been used to clean up tables from the time the first train came to Ajmer. Samira laughed and sat down, and then looked surprised to see me still standing, but of course I couldn't sit before ladies did. She asked me to sit next to her, and I did, while Jasmine rolled her eyes and looked at the clock, as if she hoped this farce would be over soon and the world could return to normal. Some Mayo guys were hovering around outside the refreshments room, and then two of them couldn't take it any more and walked in. It was Noddy and Sumo, and they made a big show of pretending to look around, then at the rate list on the wall, and I knew the bastards were trying to figure out which chicks I was with, because Moses, bless him, mustn't have said a word when they pressed him for information. Served them right.

Samira ordered 77 cola for all of us, and it was this yuck cola, like watery Coke, which these Janata buggers had started after kicking Coke out in 1977, the same year they jacked Indira Gandhi so this cola was to celebrate their victory, but we thought if we had a PM who drank piss what would these buggers know about cola and all. After the bottles of 77 arrived, brought by an old waiter who said 'Yeh Coke lijiye,' Samira turned to me.

'I'm so sorry to hear about Fish, Brandy. What happened? I mean, I heard what had happened and read a little bit in the papers...tell me, why would a guy do something like that?'

I told her everything. The drink forgotten, I kept talking, telling her about Fish, his anger against his father, how Bwana used to push him and nothing Fish ever did was good for him, and how much he wanted to please his father, make him proud, and bloody hell, Fish had already done more than most boys did, even Class 12 boys, so what kind of shit was Bwana to keep wanting more? I talked about our promise to each other, Fish, Porridge, PT Shoe and me, that we had said we would always be there for each other, no matter what, but Fish had broken that pact when he had decided to go solo and step into thin air.

I hadn't even realized when Samira had reached out, and then she was holding my hands in hers, as I sobbed, angry with myself for letting go in front of the woman I wanted so badly that I thought my undies would burst and my prick would unfurl like one of those paper whistles at New Year parties and hit the table if I moved even an inch, but Fish, the shit, was still in my head and getting in the way. I hadn't even noticed when Samira had dragged her chair closer and held my head and put it on her shoulder, only realizing what had happened when I took a deep breath after a racking sob and inhaled a little sweet and a little sweaty aroma, and it was like the best perfume in the world. I opened my eyes and I could look down the front of her shirt, and there was her cleavage, which I had once called clavicle by mistake, too full of bio, and Fish, PT Shoe and Porridge had never let me forget it. The swell of her breasts was partly covered by her bra, which I could see was white and lacy. I closed my eyes, for some reason feeling comforted, and stopped feeling so horny. We sat like that for ever, till Samira said softly, 'Brandy, have some Coke.'

We all called 77 'Coke', even though the Janata Party buggers had asked Coca-Cola to get lost because suddenly everything had to be swadeshi, like it was with Mahatma Gandhi who wanted to boycott English goods, but none of the guys from the new government, whom Papa called 'a bunch of jokers' looked dignified or acted like Mahatma Gandhi. I took a sip of 77, which was much sweeter than Coke, and looked up and into Samira's eyes. Somehow, I didn't feel ashamed for crying, and Samira's face told me it was all right, she understood. How chicks managed that without saying a word, I had no idea.

'How long will it take you to reach Cal?' Samira asked.

'I'll reach day-after morning.'

'Long journey. Are you carrying any food?'

'Ya,' I said, 'a tandoori chicken from Honeydew.' Moses and I would finish the TC we had bought with some of our journey money even before we reached Kishangarh, forty minutes from Ajmer by train. I had been given sixty rupees journey money because I had to go till Cal, and that meant two dinners, one lunch and two breakers, some chai, bananas, and three sticks of

Rothmans and some emergency money to go home if Papa or Manohar-babu forgot to be at the station. Moses had just fifteen bucks because we'd reach Delhi before dawn. And half a TC cost just twenty bucks so we had enough money between us.

'It's cool-breeze,' I said trying to act grown-up, and Jasmine smirked, the bitch. 'I'll manage. There's always some food somewhere and I have some money. Can I write to you?'

Samira laughed and said of course I could write, and she would be in Sophia through the winter because her parents, who lived in Delhi, would be travelling to see her older brother who lived in Madras and worked in Grindlays Bank, so yes, I could write to her c/o Sophia College, just like I already had.

'Write whenever you want,' she said, as Jasmine gave another of her 'oh god, now what?' expressions. 'Let's go to the platform, your train must be coming.' Then she stopped and peered at my face. 'What's that, a cut?'And I said yes, I cut myself shaving, the blood rushing to my face, thinking, damn, couldn't Papa have given me something better than that stupid Wilkinson blade? I hadn't really needed to shave, but, I mean, you couldn't be in Class 10 and not shave, could you? Jasmine was laughing, and Samira joined in as well, and after a few seconds I began to grin.

Samira reached out and touched my cheeks. I could be with her for ever.

'You take care,' she said, and I wanted to say the same thing but couldn't bring myself to, and instead nodded my head like those crazy glass birds I had seen in shop windows, with long necks and round arses, wearing small hats, that drank this red or blue liquid from a beaker and the physics of it ensured the liquid filled and emptied in turn, so the birds would always bob up and down.

'See you next term?' I asked hopefully. I was grinning like an idiot.

'Ya, see you after your hols. Happy New Year.'

You bet, baby, I thought, like some heavy cat in the movies, and feeling like I owned the fucking planet. Planet Earth, c/o Brandy Ray. I was so happy I even smiled at Jasmine.

I was sitting across the table from Yogi in the house tutor's room. Yogi's specs were halfway down his nose, and a dog-eared book lay upside down on his table. It was called *Fear and Loathing in Las Vegas*, by Hunter S. Thompson, I read upside down. I squinted to make out the sentence under the title: 'A Savage Journey to the Heart of the American Dream'. The room, the same size as the seniors' rooms, was bare except for the table, a chair, a bed that seemed too small for him, the two Head tennis racquets standing by the side of the table, and one freaked-out poster on the wall above his bed, of this skeleton, and it said below, Grateful Dead.

'Missing Fish?'

'Yes sir.'

He smiled. 'Brandy,' Yogi said softly, 'I don't think you should blame yourself for what Fish did.'

'Yes sir,' I said. 'No sir.'

'You've got exams coming up in two months, concentrate on that, okay? Don't blow the exams.'

'Okay sir,' I said. Yogi was always using words like 'blow' and 'avoid', which he said people who went to St Stephen's used a lot. It didn't sound too breeze, in fact, not even cool-breeze, when we tried to say them. We sounded stupid, and maybe we'd have to wait a while to use the words comfortably.

'Have you heard from Fish's parents?' Yogi asked.

'No sir, nothing, but Mrs Bwana sent the three of us a good luck card.' The envelope had Sing stamps on it, and was addressed to me, and the guys were c/o me. 'Dear Barun, Pratap and Michael', she had written, before a rhyme that was printed on the card. It was a silly rhyme, but we thought it was sweet of her to send it.

'Your exams are coming very near,
But please do not fret,
For, with a head like yours,
You'll reach the Top yet!'

And then, she had written, 'Love, Premila Aunty. P.S. I know Sanjay is there in your hearts. I pray for him as I pray for you.'

'That's sweet of her,' Yogi said. Then he waved me away. 'Go on Brandy, get out of here. And no more of this depressing crap, you hear me? You owe it to yourself. Focus.'

Papa had tried to say the same thing during the hols, but I hadn't listened, and refused to study, ignoring him and even Suman, which made them both sulk, and instead read books and saw movies like a madman, trying to force the thoughts of Fish and Samira away. I couldn't wait for school to open and had never wanted to be away from home so badly. Porridge had sent a New Year card saying 'Dear Brandy, Cool-breeze for 1979, arsehole. See you in a few days. Say hi to the Cal chicks. Love, Porridge.'

I badly missed Ma, and maybe I missed her more because I missed Fish as well, and could see that I had grown a little apart from Papa and Suman because while I was away, they'd had to look after each other because Ma wasn't around any more. It was like they had become a small family out of grief, though Moyna-di was around a lot acting all breeze with Papa and I wondered a little about that but, like, *balls*, you know? Something had changed, and I could feel it and felt terrible about it, but I just couldn't bring myself to talk much and ate meals without saying much and without looking much at Papa and Suman.

She and I fought often. Then one day, I think it was the day after Christmas, Papa got really upset because I had refused to go for Christmas lunch to Skyroom, a really cat restaurant on Park Street, breaking a tradition of sorts. Papa had given me a lecture on 'focus'. I had got angry about it, and walked out of the house, taken a minibus to Gariahat and then a tram to the Race Course, walking about aimlessly for an hour or so and smoking a stick of Rothmans, and then popping some Chicklets to mask the smell before coming back home. But it didn't feel like home any more, school did. Suman was staying in our old room, while I had stayed in Grandmother's old room. Toys that hadn't broken were all there, even the two wooden warships Papa had got made, with our names on the bow, my planes and her dolls, and on the shelf I could see my encyclopaedia of planes, the big fat *Illustrated Children's Bible*, the *Mahabharata for Children*, and the row of classics in English and Bengali, Ivanhoe, Nicholas Nickelby, *Pather Panchali* by Bibhutibhushan Bandopadhyay, from which Satyajit Ray had made the movie that had even made Papa cry when we had all gone to see it many years ago in Purna Cinema, *Gitanjali* by Rabindranath Tagore, and so many others. They were all Suman's now, even if I had written my name on them, in English for the books in English and in Bengali for the ones in Bengali. I felt I didn't live there any more, and I had no claims to anything, and the only people I could talk to, my real friends, were all in school.

Soumya, my only remaining friend from South Point School in Cal, had come to visit once, but it was very awkward, and I was relieved when he left after ten minutes saying 'Okaybyegoodluck', and maybe he felt relieved too.

I had stiffened when Papa tried to hug me at the station, and I felt him recoil and he had looked really hurt but not said anything. I had shaken Suman's hand, and managed a grin. She had smiled back, and I could see in her eyes she wasn't sure what her brother had become. Well, at least we agreed on that, because I didn't know what the fuck was happening to me either.

'Thank you sir,' I told Yogi, before turning to leave. 'I'll try. Umm, sir, can I read that book after you're through?'

'Not now,' he smiled, pulling the copy of *Fear and Loathing in Las Vegas* towards him. 'I wouldn't recommend it right now. Maybe next term.'

The Class Party had got out of control.

The exams had ended a week earlier, thank god, and we still had three days to hang around, settling things, mostly trying to figure out which Houses we would move to.

The Class 12 guys had buggered off days ago, their time in Mayo done, class party and farewell over. They had gone to do whatever people do after school, to try for some college, or the Indian Institutes of Technology, maybe to the National Defence Academy, where Peanut Butter, who was called PB for short, this big Sikh guy who loved screaming orders at the National Cadet Corp parades in school, had already got admission. The Class 11 guys were already acting big, because they would be the new Class 12s, princelings for a year, before they went to college and started the climb all over again. And we guys were strutting about, because we'd just given the first major exam of our lives.

Some of us wouldn't be coming back, because our folks were broke, or they thought there was a better school to go to, or our marks in the exams may not be that good. So Mayo, our home for years, for many of us our real homes, would suddenly show us where the door was. That's the way things happened.

We *deserved* a bloody class party.

So it had been decided, and Princi was nice about it. From 7 p.m. to midnight, and one guest allowed per boy, on payment of twenty-five rupees. The guests could stay till 10. Of course, as soon as I had heard I had gone to the Mess and signed a voucher to invite a guest, and had then got permission from Chalu-Charlie to go to town to pick up some rolls of black-and-white film from S.L. Artists on Station Road for the small Yashica Papa had given me when he had visited during the centenary year, saying I wanted to shoot stuff during the party.

After buying the film I had hired a tonga and gone straight to Sophia and handed over an envelope for Samira to the Gurkha, who snatched the envelope and jerked his head, asking me to fuck off without saying a word. I wondered if he ever had to think hard to figure out what he wanted to chop off first, the head or the balls, but I wasn't going to hang around to find out. I quickly folded my hands, did a namaste to him and said 'shukriya' before jumping on the tonga, hoping that would be enough to bribe him to give the letter to Samira instead of tearing it up and feeding it to his pet goat or something.

'Dear Samira,' I had written. 'The Class 10 Party is being held on 10 April. We are allowed to invite one guest, and I would like to invite you. Will you please come? The party begins at 7 o'clock at the Bikaner Pavilion and guests need to leave by 10 o'clock. So long and see you, Brandy.'

I was sure she would come, because she had just dropped by earlier in March during prep leave, six days before the exams started, just like that. Chalu-Charlie had sent a junior to call me to his flat and I went with a 'now what?' I was shocked to see Samira sitting there on the main sofa, drinking orange squash, chatting with Charlie-ma'am and Christine, who finally looked all right after so many months, and was smiling brightly. As a Master's daughter, Christine could attend Mayo—only daughters of Masters could do that in our all-boys school—and though she went to a junior class, she was nice.

I will never forget the time from the previous Holi, when some senior guys from Raj and Ajmer Houses had felt her up while putting colour on her, and she had cried and run away, and other boys who were playing Holi had stopped these guys and asked them to behave and taken Christine back to Chalu-Charlie and Charlie Ma'am. In the evening, Chalu-Charlie had taken Christine out, and they sat on the bench near their flat in the small garden in the middle of the senior rooms, with the rooms in an E-shape around the garden. He had his hand on her shoulder and had sat like that and talked to her almost until dinner. Porridge and I could see them from the dorm balcony and we sat there for a long time looking at them, and I had thought about Papa and Suman sitting and talking like that, especially as Ma was not there and Papa had to be both father and mother to Suman, like sometimes Ma had been both mother and father to us when Papa had gone travelling or had gone away from home after fighting with Ma. Christine didn't go away for day school to St Mary's Convent, as we thought she might do after what happened, but she was a brave girl, and continued to attend Mayo. We always liked her, but I think we respected her a lot after that, but she wouldn't smile much any more and kept away from boys, like she didn't trust them. That I could understand.

Samira was looking very cat in a pair of light blue bell-bot jeans with flares as big as buckets and a half-sleeve T-shirt with blue and white stripes and these small red tomatoes in a row in the white stripes. She was wearing huge platform shoes, which would surely raise her height a couple of inches more over the two inches she already had on me. My throat was dry and I started smiling stupidly, the rare gas tables instantly disappearing from my head. Samira smiled sweetly. I'm not sure, but I think the next to go was V1 over V2 equals under-root of D2 over D1 where D is the density. Graham's Law of Diffusion was running away, the bastard, and at this rate, my chem exams were dead.

'Borun,' Charlie-ma'am said, 'y'all never told us you had a cousin in Sophia. She's *such* a nice girl.' Charlie-ma'am always called me Borun, pronouncing it in the correct Bengali way.

'Yes ma'am,' I said, flushing. 'Sorry ma'am.'

Samira had rescued me then, and told Charlie-ma'am she would bring me back after lunch. I had sprinted back to the dorm to change into togs, telling PT Shoe, who had taken to polishing his PT Shoes at all times of the day, I think out of nervousness for the exams, 'See you later, Samira's here,' and zoomed out before he could break out of his goggle-eyed shock to ask me something.

The tonga was parked under the tamarind tree near Panda and Pogo's old room, I could see the two poppy plants Panda would water every day behind the loo, hoping that someday he could make opium from it, and the red flowers were in full bloom, and I couldn't help wondering who would look after them after Panda was gone. Samira and I had got on to the tonga, sitting side by side. She had taken me to Honeydew.

'My treat, Brandy,' she said. 'For good luck for the exams.' She asked me what I wanted.

'To kiss you, darling,' I wanted to say, but managed to order liver on toast, mushroom on toast and chocolate ice cream soda without making an arse of myself. Samira ordered American Chopsuey and fresh lime soda. I knew it was a mistake because Chinese in Honeydew was horrible. Or maybe I was just spoiled because Papa always took us to good Chinese restaurants, and Ma used to make these lovely dishes from *Mrs Ma's Chinese Cookbook* and this Mrs Ma seemed to really know her recipes because whatever Ma cooked from Mrs Ma's cookbook, from simple fried rice to egg fu yung with crabmeat, and fried fish wrapped in lotus leaves, tasted like it was made in heaven. Suman and I had even started calling Ma 'Mrs Ma', and they both had nice smiles and wore glasses with frames shaped like the eyes of those miniature paintings we had in the school museum. I had thought some day Ma would write a cookbook called *Ma's Magic*, and I was sure lots of people would buy the book and it would be as good as Mrs Ma's book, and I decided I would ask someone in school, maybe Tennis Ball, to write something for the front of Ma's book because he was so good in English and he could write something even more cool-breeze than what was written on the front of Mrs Ma's cookbook: 'Few persons who enjoy real Chinese cooking will fail to understand the old saying in the Far East that Chinese food, a Japanese wife and an American home would make an ideal life for a man.'

I'm sure it was a joke, because it couldn't have been an old saying, I mean America had only turned 200 the year Indira Gandhi landed up in school, and so it was actually a lob, because China and Japan had been around for ages, like India. But I didn't want to upset Samira on what I suddenly realized was my first date, which was so breeze, and if she got cramps after eating chopsuey I knew I would put her on a tonga at the stand just outside Honeydew, next to King Edward Memorial Guest House, and rush her to Victoria Hospital like a gallant knight, going clip-clop clip-clop across Ajmer, screaming at other tongas, carts and mopeds to get out of the fucking way.

'I've got something for you,' Samira had said, after she had asked me how things were at school and how the hols were, and I had blurted out what I had done in the hols, including the shit with Papa and all the stuff about exam prep and the lecture from Yogi. I had asked her if she had a copy of *Fear and Loathing in Las Vegas* and she had said, 'No, and I don't want to read anything about fear and loathing, thank you.'

She slid a small green envelope across the table.

I opened it and pulled out a card, which had lots of flowers on it and inside it was written:

Before you sit for your paper today
Pause, and a little prayer say:
That God will help you all the way.
Best of luck,
Samira
10.3.79.

'Thanks a lot, Samira,' I said, telling myself, bastard, don't start crying you stupid sentimental bastard, and had stopped just in time to make one of those very breeze faces with a tiny smile like Michael Caine, whom I liked because his wife was called Shakira and she was also brown and beautiful, with a long neck and delicate shoulders, her clavicle sticking out like coat hangers—she had looked deadly in *The Man Who Would Be King*. When she had bitten the lip of Sean Connery in the movie, who played the bloody rascal Daniel Dravot, never listening to Michael when Michael reminded him he wasn't god because he accidentally stopped an arrow with his bandolier, I fantasized Shakira was biting my lips. I was in love with her for at least fifteen days. 'Thank you,' I told Samira, looking into her eyes like Michael. 'I appreciate this very much.'

Samira had laughed a little, maybe at my trying to act grown-up, and then reached across and given my arm a squeeze.

'You'll be okay Brandy, just don't do anything stupid, and study hard.'

She then said we could meet after the exams because she would still be there because her first-year exams were only in May.

I had carried the card in the pocket of my shirt through all the exams. My grades had picked up the past term and I was convinced that with Samira by my side, I would get a distinction, even in maths and Hindi, and it would throw Papa's 'focus' shit back at his face.

I was there at the Pavilion at quarter to seven, dragging PT Shoe, Porridge and Moses with me, with Porridge grumbling and saying, 'Why should I bloody go early because you're shitting bricks?' But he came along anyway, smirking. Moses asked him to shut up and Porridge smirked some more, because Moses had suddenly become protective of me. The guys didn't grudge him that because, while Moses would never fill Fish's space, it did feel okay to have a fourth guy back in the gang, you know, and Moses acted like he had found a home.

They had done up the place quite nicely. There was a big sign on the big door facing the pool that said 'Happy Memories and Good Luck to Class 10 of 1979'. In the big room inside the Pavillion was the music system from Raj House; they actually had a Technics turntable that a boy's father had donated, and these big speakers. There was also a small National cassette tape player like the one Fish had, which we now shared in the dorm, and it was plugged into an amplifier and there were cables all over the place which Ram Swarup-ji, the technician, was sorting out. A small case held a stack of LPs borrowed from various Houses and I was sure there would be that silly Boney M album that these Colvin House chaps played all the time, singing 'Ding-ding-ding-ding I'm your Daddy Cool'. Those guys had no taste, and had even refused to play my 'Kiss Alive!' LP, which I had bought from the second-hand record shops on Free School Street, after just two songs on Side 2, after 'Black Diamond', and just when Gene Simmons really starts to go in 'Rock Bottom', screaming 'Ruck Baatawm, Ruck Baatawm', because they found it too loud. Rosy, who had replaced Mutt as Housemaster, had come running to the common room asking if the system was okay, and seeing me there had said, 'Mr Ray, if you wish to play this silly music you should do so in your own House.' I couldn't tell him the reason I had brought record to Colvin House in the first bloody place was because Chalu-Charlie had banned it in Jaipur House—I suspect not so much for the music but because he had seen the pictures of the band on the LP cover, with weird satanic make-up and sticking their tongues out like chameleons, with a couple of half-naked chicks floating around in the green smoke on stage.

Even PT Shoe had asked me politely, 'What the fawk do you get out of this music?' and when I replied, saying I liked the energy and that it freaked people out, he looked at me like I was mad. But I wasn't worried, because Dipi was in charge of the music, and the bugger liked Rolling Stones and Bob James and had promised he would play Fleetwood Mac for Fish. Dipi was a breeze guy about these things, and he was the only guy we knew who could sing rock songs in Thai because his dad lived in Bangkok and the bugger could talk Thai like a machine gun with a cold eating stickjaw.

There were folding chairs and murha along the walls almost to the other end, where the doors were also closed, so the only way we could walk in and out was through the door that faced the cricket ground, bang in the middle of the two lots of steps. The other half of the room had some tables joined together and bed sheets placed on top, where the Mess chaps were already stacking plates and paper napkins. PT Shoe strolled over and asked one of them what the menu was going to be, and came back to tell us grandly, 'Mutton biryani, rumali roti, matar paneer, raita and chocolate ice cream, and orange squash to drink,' when we already knew what it would be because all class parties had the same bloody food. But we knew we wouldn't be drinking bloody orange squash for too long, because Dipi had winked and said, 'Bugger, I've got some Blue Riband', meaning gin, bought on a Sunday from Old Framjee on NH 8. As we found out later, he wasn't the only one carrying booze, and there would also be enough sticks, so many that I thought the cigarette-wallahs in town must have sold out their entire stock of Rothmans, State Express, Benson & Hedges and More Menthol.

The guys had started landing up by 7.15, ready to hog. We were told the food would be served at 8.30. Desperate for Samira, I had dragged the gang to the top of the Pavilion so we could see better and hung around on the boxing ring, now stripped to the wood. Bassy and Dipi were already there, smoking sticks of Benson, and we all took a drag. 'We've got to get drunk today,' Dipi said.

By 7.30, the whole batch was there, and many had their local guardians as guests. I had gone in once to see what was going on. Dipi had ensured the music had started. They were playing some Brotherhood of Man, just to settle the guys down.

Samira walked in right then, and with her were three other girls, and a nun, who must have been the escort. She walked up smartly when she saw me, and introduced her pals. Jasmine I already knew, the others were Puja and Miriam, and there was Sister Agatha, who looked Anglo, and looked really stern. I said to her, 'Good evening ma'am, welcome to Mayo College'.

Porridge, PT Shoe and Moses had miraculously popped up from somewhere and when I looked around, it seemed half the fucking batch was around us, ogling, grinning and saying hi. Samira wore the same clothes she had worn that day at lunch, only now she was wearing a chain of loops, which she wore like a belt. She also hadn't worn kajal around her eyes that day or had her eyelids painted blue, which she did now. I got that feeling again that began at my toes, stopped for a long time at my crotch and then moved up to burst in front of my eyes.

The other girls were dressed alike. All had light-blue jeans with huge bell-bots, with red-and-blue T-shirts and Miriam was wearing a short kurta with batik designs. In comparison, we looked like pansies, wearing uniform grey togs and white shirts when we really should have been dressed like cats.

Sister Agatha looked like a real aunty with them, in her round glasses and white nun's dress down below her knees and shoes that looked like black leather versions of the Dutch clogs Ma had in her showcase, looking at us as if we were really bad guys. She said, 'Well, are you boys going to stand and watch or will you get us something to drink, like Coke or squash.'

The crowd disappeared as quickly it had formed as dozens of boys ran for the table where glasses of cola and squash were lined up. I hadn't moved. Sister Agatha had a smile on her face. I had no idea nuns had a sense of humour. This was getting to be quite breeze.

Sister Agatha and the ladies sat around for a while, drinking their stuff, and some of the teachers started showing up one by one, alone or with their wives—Yogi, Chalu-Charlie, Samosa-sir, Lucy, who taught science and even Princi, who stayed for ten minutes, sat chivalrously next to Sister Agatha, who was sitting with the Sophia chicks by her side, chit-chatted and left, saying 'You boys enjoy yourself, but no hanky-panky or going on late.'

As soon as Princi left Dipi dumped Brotherhood of Man, and put the Rolling Stones LP on cue, bang on Jumping Jack Flash. As soon as I heard the signature 'Boo-bawn' on the bass I almost ran to Samira and said, 'May I please have this dance?'

She grinned and took my arm and got up. Dipi went straight for Sister Agatha and bowed low and said 'Ma'am please' and amazingly, she got up too. We started dancing hesitantly as the guys stood around watching us. But Dipi went crazy, whirling, jumping, squatting, so crazily that Sister Agatha started to laugh and clap, moving with light steps in these little hops, twirling around, and then the other girls came on their own and suddenly six or seven boys were dancing with them. I was beginning to relax and started trying out some moves with a lot of hand-flinging and head-shaking. Samira was laughing and started to copy me. Man!

We went on like that for a while, Sister Agatha sitting down after a couple of numbers, and Dipi again bowed low and escorted her back. How the bugger had the balls and style to do that, I had no idea. Maybe it was the gin, but I think he just loved to dance. And Sister Agatha was pretty cool-breeze too, and didn't look odd at all dancing like that. When Dipi led Sister Agatha away, everybody clapped and whistled like mad, and Samosa-sir even walked up to her and said 'You dance very well ma'am. I would be honoured if you agreed to dance with me after a while.' She nodded, and I thought, man, all sorts of guys were being different guys tonight.

Samira suddenly looked at me, and kept looking for a while, then bit her lip and said softly, as if she had made up her mind about something, 'Let's go out.'

As I got up, I saw Jasmine giving her one of those looks, but she ignored her and walked, and I walked with her.

'I want to talk to you about something,' she said. 'Is there somewhere we can go where there's no crowd?'

I looked around. There were guys all over the Pavilion. I could see some glows in the darkness near the boxing rink. Guys were smoking sticks.

'The gym' I told her. 'Nobody'll be in the gym.'

I led the way and she walked quickly—behind the cricket screen, past the curved wooden catcher and the long-jump pit and down the slope into the gym. Nobody was there. We sat on a mat next to the vaulting horse, which was put away against the wall the gym shared with the pool.

'What did you want to talk about?' I asked her, a little breathless.

She didn't say anything, and we sat like that for maybe five minutes. I asked her again. She didn't say anything, but suddenly turned and grabbed my head and planted her mouth on mine. I almost choked and tried to pull away till I realized what was happening, that I was smooching a girl. Samira had pulled back to look at me and saw me grinning. I loved it, and thought Porridge must smooch girls for a change. She smiled and dragged my head back. This time she put her tongue in and moved it around the roof of my mouth. It was feeling really tickly, but that went away quickly. My head was buzzing and I knew I had a hard-on that felt like it was as big as the pyramids.

We went on like that for a while, as Samira taught me how to kiss, gooey spit and all but it was so beautiful.

She stopped after some time and put my hand on her T-shirt and I realized with a shock I could feel her boobs, really her boobs, there was no bra because she must have removed it some time while I was busy going mad smooching her. She put my hand under her shirt and then reached down to hold my crotch while we kissed. Something told me that I should be doing something more than just touching her boobs, which felt like satin, and dribbling spit into her mouth, so I leaned low, lifted her T-shirt and started to kiss her boobs, and she pushed my head in so hard I thought I would die. I fumbled for her jeans. Samira moved back against the wall, took the chain belt off and opened the top button of her jeans and pulled down the zip and took my hand and put it inside. I didn't know what I was doing but I knew somehow I had to be slow and gentle and then my finger slipped past the panties and the pubic hair and touched her. 'Silky!' I screamed in my head, and I thought I was going to burst in my undies right then. Pondies had never told the real story and in the photos people hardly kissed and seemed only to screw each other madly in every possible way. And now this was the real thing, like a recipe from Mrs Ma's cookbook.

'Kaun hai udhar?' someone shouted. Fuck, I thought, it's the chowkidar.

'Brandy, stop, just sit quietly,' Samira said, breathing heavily, and we arranged our clothes and sat. The chowkidar walked on. We still sat quietly. All I wanted to do was hug Samira; I hugged my knees instead.

'I'm sorry Brandy,' Samira said after a while. 'I shouldn't have done that.'

'Don't be silly,' I replied, breeze like Michael and all. 'It was nice.'

'You're okay,' she said, and ruffled my hair, and I melted again and thought I had taken all my clothes off and so had Samira, but it was only in my head.

'Let's go back,' she said after a while, and we held hands as we walked back to the Pavilion. She stopped me behind the cricket screen, and kissed me once on the lips. 'You take care,' she said.

I don't know what made me do it, but the good luck charm Neelu, my cousin, had given me once, a small elephant carved on a small disc of sandalwood that I wore with a black string around my neck, I took it off and gave it to Samira, putting it in her hand, and then not letting go. 'You too,' I said.

'Brandy,' she said. 'I won't be coming back. My father's getting posted to the States, and I will be going there to study.' She had mentioned her father worked for the government. I listened to her numbly. 'You take care,' she said once again, before gently taking her hand out of my grip, and then turned and walked back to the Pavilion.

I stood there for I don't know how long. I knew I didn't want to go back inside, because I couldn't face Samira. I slowly went up the steps instead, to the glows that seemed many more now. I looked at my watch. 9.30. I had spent the last two hours in heaven and hell.

'Brandy, fucker, come and sit, bugger,' Dipi said. He was gone, I knew. 'Try a stick.'

Squash was with him, and I could make out the shapes of Bulldog and the Piglets, also smoking.

'Ya bugger,' said Squash. He was slurring. 'The teachers and guests have fucking gone. Now it's breeze.' There must have been twenty or twenty-five guys on the roof, all smoking and drinking.

'Old Monk, fucker?' Squash asked, and passed a short, fat bottle before I could hit him, suddenly angry at all the cursing. I took a long swig and choked, and the guys laughed. 'Relax,' it was Squash again. 'It's breeze.'

And suddenly, it was. I realized that Squash and I would cancel each other out back home with Papa and Moyna-di, because if Squash ever told Moyna-di I was drinking I could fuck him too, but maybe he was just stoned and having a good time and being Moyna-di's cousin and all didn't matter. I took another gulp, tearing up my tongue and throat with the neat booze—it was so strong and felt like I was swallowing fire, and took huge puffs from the stick Dipi handed me. It had a big gold band between the white tube and the filter, so it must have been a Rothmans International. My ears were ringing.

Something was happening out on the cricket pitch. Fuck, some guys were actually playing cricket. I couldn't see any stumps though, and then something glinted as some guy lit a stick out there. Bottles, the arseholes had planted booze bottles in place of the stumps and were playing pretend cricket. Someone must have taken a tape recorder out there because I could hear Boney M. The Colvin House buggers even had Boney M on cassette, bloody despos. But, I thought, all dizzy, it's our class party, we can do what the fuck we want. We're big boys now.

Porridge was standing in front of me. 'Brandy, you mad bastard, come on, time to go to the House. You haven't even eaten, you bloody fool.'

'I'm not going,' I told him, and swallowed some more rum.

'Three cheers for Class 10, Fish and all fucked up things. Hip, hip, hooray,' I shouted, and took another gulp, standing up. The burning had stopped, and it was feeling good though I was swaying, and I just started to dance, to no music at all. Some guys had gathered around and were clapping, and yelling 'Cheers' and 'Hip hip hooray' and 'Brandy fucker' and whistling like it was a circus or something and I was the clown, but fuck it.

'Balls you are not coming,' Porridge said, and grabbed my shoulder, as PT Shoe and Moses landed up from somewhere and walked me away and slowly helped me down the narrow back stairs of the Pavilion. We trudged back to Jaipur House in the moonlight, and that one kilometre seemed like one hundred.

'I was worried when Samira came back, and left soon with the other chicks and Sister Agatha,' Porridge was angry. 'What the fuck happened? What's wrong with you?'

'Samira, man,' I managed. 'She's going away. Everybody fucking goes away just when we really become friends. Ma's dead. Fish went away, Samira's done it, and you buggers will also do it. I'm sure of it.' I was crying. 'Fucking bastards all of you.'

The guys didn't say anything. They just took me home.

Porridge, PT Shoe and I were at the station. I had the Jayanti Janata Express to catch at 7 p.m. to Delhi, and then another train to Calcutta. Porridge was being driven to Jaipur airport in a Mercury Travels car to take a plane to Bombay, so he and PT Shoe still had a day together. And PT Shoe would leave only after the two of us had. As usual, he was being the perfect host. 'I'm from Rajasthan, no, bugger?' he said, as if we didn't know. 'So I'll go home after you guys bugger off.'

He was getting really sentimental, we could tell, because he wouldn't be coming back. PT Shoe's father wanted to take him out of Mayo and put him in a military school in Chittorgarh, so PT Shoe would toughen up in the way his father wanted, but we suspected the real reason was he was shit scared for PT Shoe because of Fish but could never say it because people like PT Shoe's dad never showed weakness. The school was near the fort PT Shoe's hero Rana Pratap had wanted so badly to recapture, but had died before he could, in the care of his Bhil tribal friends, who stood by him when the best warriors in Rajputana wouldn't, and I read in a storybook that Rana Pratap had died a sad man, looking out at the grand fort of Chittorgarh, where the ghosts were as alive as in Mayo. It didn't take too much imagination to stand on the grand ramparts, like I had done on a school trip many years earlier, close my eyes, and hear the guards challenge an intruder, 'Katthe jaochho?'—where are you going? I could even hear the sound of battle and the women sing before they jumped into their own funeral pyre because their men were dead in battle and they didn't want to lose their honour to invaders.

We didn't want to ask PT Shoe about whether going to a military school would help to do what we knew he was probably going to end up as—a rich guy with a big moustache who was a bloody tourist guide, or maybe not—and years later maybe I would open a *National Geographic* and see a snap of PT Shoe standing in a big drawing room with Farah, his hand raised in a peace sign, and the caption would say, 'Mr Singh, the Indian prince, and his lovely bride in their Manhattan mansion; Mr Singh says all his dreams are now in American.'

We finished the chai, and then ordered another, joking and laughing about some of the Class 12 buggers. Candy Singh was a nice guy but he was a mad bugger, and two weeks before the Class 12 exams had shoved his hand in a beehive just behind Pat and Vicky's room, so he wouldn't be able to give his exams and his folks would have some reason to let him live. The bugger had been stung all over, the bees for some reason preferring his face. He was fucked, but got okay in a week and was forced to give the papers. He'd plug for sure. 'Too much bravery in your Rajput heads to think, man,' I pulled PT Shoe's leg.

But he was up to it, and said, 'Too much fish in your Bongo heads to think, bugger,' and reminded us of Tubby, this Class 11 Bongo guy from Ajmer House, who had picked up a hockey stick and with a big shout of 'Joi Ma Kali', slammed it on his forearm, cracking the bone. Only he was a righty and in a reflex action he cracked his left arm, so he had to give the bloody exams. We were laughing really loudly, starting off again when Porridge said, 'Fucker, east meets west,' and ignored the stares of people on the platform.

I was clutching the House photograph, which I had wrapped in brown paper and was hanging on to because I didn't want it crushed in my suitcase because the only place it was safe was at the bottom, and the aluminum strip along the lining had come loose and I was afraid it would rip into the photograph, but there was enough space for *Fear and Loathing in Las Vegas*, which I had got from Yogi as a going-away present, and all of Fish's Dylan and Fleetwood Mac tapes. Porridge had written something weird at the back of the House photograph, which I thought was quite idiotically Porridge: 'To Brandy, May your days be nice and sunny. Hope your wife is fat and funny.' PT Shoe's message was a surprise, written in formal, perfect English. 'To dear Brandy, with whom I spent some of the best years of my life. Pratap Singh of Paladhi.'

In the picture, Porridge, PT Shoe and I were grinning madly, and it wasn't because of Mr Artist and his silly onetwothreeriddyshtiddyshmiiiiile, but we wanted to put the year back together, so that in 1979 we would always be smiling, and nobody who ever saw it would know any different. Only we would know there was no Fish this year, and there would never be a message from him anyway because he'd always said he didn't believe in writing silly messages at the back of photographs because it was a 'childish thing to do', like he was the oldest man in the world or something. But the fucker was in my head, so he could leave whatever message he wanted whenever he wanted and for as long as he wanted, and I knew he would, the bastard, because Fish never let go once he got his hook in.

It was time for me to get on the train. Moses was already in the compartment because he hated goodbyes, and anyway, he wanted to let us be, one last time. Punk, Bassy and some of the other guys were further along the platform, finishing up their farewells with their gangs. I could see Dipi, who would be going to Cal with me, and I don't think he was coming back, like some of the other guys in other Houses, because he had confessed to Chalu-Charlie that he had smoked and drank at the class party. Someone had sneaked on him, and it was good we never found out because whoever the sneak was, he would never come back to Mayo, and we'd make sure of that. Dipi had reassured me earlier, when all Class 10 boys from Jaipur House were made to line up outside Chalu-Charlie's flat and sent in for questioning one by one, because Princi was really angry with all the shit lying around the cricket field. Dipi had said, 'Don't worry Brandy, I won't tell Chalu-Charlie what happened.'

I had made up my mind I'd call him the day after we reached Cal. I would need a friend like him because I wouldn't want to be home much, with Papa and all, looking at Ma's photograph and wondering what had gone wrong and trying to figure out whether guys who read pol science and geog in Class 11 ever got to become pilots, or would I end up like Kissing-da, in love with an idea and go missing and all.

Maybe Dipi would have an idea. We could go for some 'A' movies at Globe Theatre on Lindsay Street and talk breeze stuff like would Pakistan and India would bugger each other again now that some Peko army-types had hanged Zulfikar Bhutto, the guy who became their PM after India had buggered Pakistan in the Bangladesh war, because now dictators had taken over Pakistan again and they had some chip on their shoulders, which was a breeze expression though I wondered how they could have the place for it, because they wore uniforms with big fat shoulder boards and medals all over, like the chaps who played bad songs during marriages, like Jai Bharat Band or something. Maybe Dipi and I would talk about mullah-types taking over the whole world the same way this Khomeini had jacked the Shah of Iran in Jan, asking him to bugger off, and this was the same Shah for whom Indira's dad, old Jawaharlal, I had read somewhere, had opened up the Taj Mahal so the chap could do honeymoon stuff with his wife in a fancy graveyard, just imagine.

The world was changing, and the only way to deal with it was by drinking beer and hogging mutton kebab rolls at Badshah Restaurant after a movie. Badshah was a place where people who didn't want to be seen by people they knew went, sitting in the first-floor booze section while families and unbooze-wallahs hung around downstairs. We liked Badshah, and I had gone there with Dipi the previous summer hols for a Coke and rolls after watching Jacqueline Bisset in *The Deep* and we knew we would dive to the bottom of the fucking Mariana Trench for her if she smiled at us wearing her wet T-shirt and said 'Coffee, Tea or Me?'

We pretended to be very breeze, like we were going away every day, and were actually making a pretty good show of it despite all the awkwardness.

'PT Shoe, write okay?' I said. 'I hope you get your gora chick.'

He was crying. Maybe I was too—I could see Porridge was.

'Man, take care,' Porridge told me. 'See you in July. Don't be too hard on those Cal babes.'

I couldn't help smiling. Friends are so, so king. The train started to move.

'What are you waiting for?' we screamed as one. 'Light to dawn? Fucking promotion?'

I hugged the guys quickly and jumped on to the train. I stood at the door, waving at the shape of Porridge and PT Shoe through a haze tears until the train curved and took them away from me.

Acknowledgements

I first discussed a three-line idea for this book with David Davidar several years ago. His encouragement was unstinting when I finally got around to writing it in 2004; and publishing it the following year. As *Tin Fish* now travels from Penguin to HarperCollins, I would like to acknowledge again the editorship of Ravi Singh at Penguin India, and his associate at the time, Poulomi Chatterjee.

This was never meant to be—and it is not—a book about Mayo College, Ajmer, but a story of a particular time and place in India's coming of age. My thanks to the Class of 1981—we journey as well as we can—and to my friend Dipi, who chose to leave this world early, and now journeys in our minds.

To my editor at HarperCollins India, Karthika V.K., for her belief in the continuing appeal of *Tin Fish*—and the story of Brandy Ray. The sequel, *The Avenue of Kings*, was published by HarperCollins in late 2010. The reception is heart-warming.

And so, my deepest gratitude to readers everywhere, because without them there can be no writer.

S.C.

October 2011

THE
AVENUE OF KINGS
Sudeep Chakravarti

There is No Curfew for Kites

A Sikh boy is set aflame in the chaotic aftermath of Indira Gandhi's assassination; a house party rages in Calcutta while the country mourns the fading dream of Rajiv Gandhi; a young Muslim boy contemplates answering the call of militant fundamentalism in the wake of the demolition of the Babri Masjid. But somewhere in the debris of recent history lies a resolute hope.

Through this journeys Brandy Ray, wanderer, cynic, journalist—and incurable romantic. As 'New India' delights and disappoints in turn, Brandy grapples with his own life—his deeply passionate and tumultuous relationship with the lovely yet slipping-away Suya, his conflicts with his father, the joy of travels with friends and the trauma of them losing their way.

In these three edgy, touching novellas—*The Avenue of Kings, The Cradle of Innocents* and *The Well of Three Wishes*—that form interlinked narratives, Sudeep Chakravarti takes the reader on a rollercoaster ride, a journey of aspiration, longing, betrayal... and the sheer joy of being alive. Imbued with wry wit and keen insight, *The Avenue of Kings,* the long-awaited sequel to *Tin Fish,* is a brilliant portrait of a country dealing with change.

Praise for *The Avenue of Kings*

'Sudeep Chakravarti yokes together, with quiet but intense passion, stories of a country in the throes of a political, social and cultural ferment... [He] makes perfectly intelligent use of his multiple skills as storyteller, political commentator and journalist [to produce] a string of narratives both edgy and sensitive'

– *India Today*

'...juxtaposes the angst of a young, upper middle-class India against a nation in turmoil...Chakravarti provides some memorable descriptions...evokes the sounds and smells of an early morning in Old Delhi beautifully'

– *Business Standard*

'In language that is brutal, acrid and visceral, Chakravarti gives us a series of characters, encounters and confrontations that together form a portrait of the pivotal moments in the 1980s and early 1990s in India...a bold, impassioned work that seeks to remind us of the past and doesn't shy away from asking the elusive, difficult questions that are as relevant today'

– *HT Mint*

'The storylines are as absorbing as India's defining decades... There is an edgy rawness that uplifts the book'

– *Mail Today*

'(The) sense memory of Delhi ... is what is best about *The Avenue of Kings*...true to life, and truly moving'

– *Timeout*

'*The Avenue of Kings* is the kind of book that shakes you from a dream...the three novellas are uncompromising, not frightened, unapologetic, and disturbing. It leaves you with a sense of disquiet and optimism at the end of it all. I for one am looking forward to reading more of Brandy's adventures'

– CNN-IBN Live

'With a restless, bohemian hero, assassinations and suicides in the background, sarcastic tone and abrasive usage of language, the author cleverly succeeds in making his point amidst the turbulence spread across the book...Chakravarti's *The Avenue of Kings* shakes one out of stupor...a riveting take on the real India...an unforgettable read'

– Zee News

'*The Avenue of Kings* is emotionally honest... The books is about "belief", and what is "me" and "you"... (The) tone is irreverent and politically wrong. It takes guts to be so past caring what readers think about you'

– *Asian Age*

Tin Fish

Sudeep Chakravarti is the author of *Red Sun: Travels in Naxalite Country* (2008), a work of narrative non-fiction about India's ongoing Maoist rebellion that was shortlisted for the Vodafone Crossword Non-fiction Award 2008; and three novels, *Once Upon a Time in Aparanta* (2008), a dark satire set in the self-proclaimed paradise of Goa, and *The Avenue of Kings* (2010), the sequel to his bestselling first novel *Tin Fish* (2005).

Praise for *Tin Fish*

'Reminiscent of Salinger'

– *Outlook*

'Chakravarti's India is the real India'

– *India Today*

'Riveting ... a fresh and unpretentious take'

– *The Statesman*

'[Chakravarti's] telling is straight, frank and honest. It makes no apologies.'

– *Tehelka*

'[A] story which will stay with you a long, long time'

– *The Hindu*

'This fine coming-of-age novel is set in the mid-1970s ... This is slice of life at its most engaging: the narrative moves unselfconsciously from one episode to the next, without stopping to get preachy along the way ... Highly recommended if you're from that generation, but even more so if you don't know a world without cellphones and cable TV'

– *Business Standard*

'It took me three nights to read this book. That's not because I can't wade through 236 pages in a single night but because I wanted to delay the gratification and spread it out ... Chakravarti has captured a slice of life. And in a way that is not only evocative, reminiscing, sentimental in a black humour kind of way, but literary, insightful, sensitive in a very touchable manner'

– *Indian Express*

'I think it's excellent. It's the first book I've read since *English August* that captures accurately a certain kind of Indian's adolescent experience of India. The British do it quite well, books like *Lucky Jim* come to mind, but for some reason [Indian writers] haven't managed to write interestingly about the public school experience'

– David Davidar, author and publisher

'*Tin Fish* brings to life the magic of living ... Sudeep Chakravarti does not try to make the book just another boarding school romp where every problem is solved over a midnight feast. That, and his skill at teen-speak, make the book a truly "cat" read'

– *The Week*

'*Tin Fish* is funny and it is sad. It makes you giggle with its boyish, and sometimes wry, humour. It takes you through the lows with pretty much the same intensity. Feelings run deep here, even as there is a conscious effort to camouflage emotions – a typical boy-doing-the-big-man act ... When you reach the end, the book disappoints, but only because you wish it hadn't finished yet. There is so much more to know about Brandy and his chums. You are left wondering if life treated them kind and if they lived out their dreams and friendship. Sudeep rewinds your childhood and makes you relive its uninterrupted joys and its turbulence. His manner is lucid and he is a natural storyteller'

– *Tribune*